PRAISE FOR *BROOKLYN MOTTO*

"*Brooklyn Motto* is a stylish, propulsive mystery that beautifully captures late 90s New York City in the convulsions of enormous social and economic change. Alex R. Johnson combines novelistic texture with cinematic pace to great effect, and narrator Nico Kelly is the perfect guide to this world full of danger, corruption, and also hope."
—**Sam Lipsyte, author of** *No One Left to Come Looking for You*

"*Brooklyn Motto* is my favorite kind of hardboiled thriller — smart, funny, fast-paced, and wonderfully cinematic. I didn't want it to end… The characters are beautifully drawn, the details are spot-on, and the central mystery that fuels his stunning, richly-layered debut is as good as New York noir gets. Johnson brings the city's dangerous and gloriously seedy, pre-gentrification era to vivid, glorious life — the late nights, last calls, and loneliness you can only feel in a city you share with seven million others. I loved this book ... and now I'm waiting for the movie."
—**Chris Nashawaty, author of** *The Future Was Now: Madmen, Mavericks, and the Epic Sci-Fi Summer of 1982*

"With *Brooklyn Motto* Alex R. Johnson manages to check all the boxes when it comes to concocting a contemporary detective story, weaving a taut and thrilling tale peppered with legitimately funny moments. If you've ever wondered what kind of books Elmore Leonard would write if he logged some miles on the downtown NYC music scene circa 1998, this is the book for you!"
—**Tom Scharpling, comedian, podcaster and author of** *It Never Ends*

"*Brooklyn Motto* is both a love letter to its namesake borough and a microcosm of the American Dream sold short. Nico can pull up a barstool alongside the great PI's of the genre, but they might need to spot him a round. I really dug this."
—**Craig Clevenger, author of** *The Contortionist's Handbook*

"*Brooklyn Motto* is Raymond Chandler by way of Lou Reed: street-smart, razor-sharp, humming with menace. Johnson doesn't just capture the city on edge; he drags you down its avenues, one gut-punch line at a time."
—**Alex Abramovich, author of** *Bullies: A Friendship*

D1521760

"[*Brooklyn Motto*] is an inventive hard-boiled mash-up starring a reluctant GenX PI who accidentally finds himself in way over his head. His backstory and future relies on a complicated extended family and their immigrant Brooklyn culture. A love letter to NYC & detective fiction."
—John Doe (X), musician, actor and author of *Under the Big Black Sun: A Personal History of L.A. Punk*

"Alex R. Johnson's playful, witty, brooding, and heartfelt *Brooklyn Motto* is everything readers of classic private detective fiction could want — but placed in the nothing-like-classic East Village and Brooklyn of 1998. Either Johnson has a photographic memory for places and moods, or he's done remarkable research in bringing that time and those places to life. Brimming with distinctive characters, clever language, and crisp observations, the book is a thoroughly engaging and deeply satisfying read. I tore through it and had a lot of fun."
—Evan Handler, actor, author of *Time On Fire: A Comedy of Terrors*

"A thriller that remains clear throughout. Politically bold, a surprisingly tender story. A young PI, half Philip Marlowe and half Holden Caulfield... fights corrupt landlords and cops while drinking in the hippest bars of 90s Brooklyn, and all under the shadow of the worst Mr. Big anyone could imagine: Rudy Giuliani."
—Todd McEwen, author of *Arithmetic, Fisher's Hornpipe, Who Sleeps with Katz?* and *McX*

"Alex R. Johnson's *Brooklyn Motto* is written beautifully, disturbingly, and hilariously, which is to say perfectly. And as a lover of both New York City and crime (both the committing and solving of), it felt like a sting operation to me in the best of ways."
—Dave Hill, comedian and author of *Tasteful Nudes* and *Dave Hill Doesn't Live Here Anymore*

"An impressive work. A rich, almost palpable sense of the city from a unique perspective. (Alex R. Johnson) brings it alive. Wonderfully drawn characters. A great read. More please."
—Kim Henkel, filmmaker and screenwriter of *The Texas Chainsaw Massacre* and *Last Night at the Alamo*

"A wonderful, sharp and snazzy read that puts the big screws to detective fiction conventions. The real star here, though, is the NYC of 1998, a forgotten, pre-digital New York of payphones, dollar vans, sidewalk eccentrics, East Village dives and shabby one-bedroom walkups that were still affordable."
—Jim Knipfel, author of *Slackjaw,* and *The Buzzing*

"*Brooklyn Motto* is a top-shelf cocktail infused with the ghostly flavors of a vanishing New York. One part Raymond Chandler, one part Pavement, and one part Blow-Out, Alex R. Johnson serves up the tastiest 90's neo-noir this side of 14th Street."
—Rahne Alexander, musician and author of *Heretic to Housewife*

"*Brooklyn Motto* reminds me of the best of Elmore Leonard and Walter Mosley, a murder mystery that keeps peeling back the layers of New York City until the reader, and the novel's hero Nico, can see the city's dark beating heart. Nico Kelly's world-weary, big-hearted voice is unforgettable. Alex R. Johnson's debut made this former New Yorker miss my city very much."
—Leland Cheuk, author of *No Good Very Bad Asian*

"Alex R. Johnson's beautiful *Brooklyn Motto* paints a vivid picture the 1990s NYC I knew and loved. It made me feel like I was at Dojo eating a soy burger dinner - IYKYK. AND it's funny! AND it's an action-packed mystery!"
—Chris Crofton, comedian, musician and author of *The Advice King Anthology*

"(Alex R. Johnson's) vivid portrayal of late 90s Manhattan provides an authentic backdrop complete with mixtapes, pagers, payphones, and Y2K fears. With its unique cast of complex characters and engaging storyline, Brooklyn Motto is a fresh take on the detective genre."
—Fred Beshid, author of *Free Nancy Esting*

"Thoroughly entertaining and just odd enough to keep us guessing. I could smell the boroughs of New York in every sentence. Loved the book, highly recommend it! A real page turner."
—Jesse Dayton, musician and author of *Beaumonster: A Memoir*

BROOKLYN MOTTO
Alex R. Johnson

Copyright © 2024 by Alex R. Johnson

Book Cover and graphic title page by Caspar Newbolt.

First edition 2025

ISBN 979-8-2185-2401-2

ISBN 979-8-2185-2402-9 (ebook)

BRKLYN

A NOVEL BY ALEX R. JOHNSON

MOTTO

For Annie and Charlie

NYC

1998

CHAPTER ONE

1998

MY DAD TAUGHT ME to notice things, remember things.

Well, that's not really true. I mean, he didn't teach me *literally*. It's more a habit developed as a result of his casual parenting. His watching me when he had other plans—and he always had other plans—usually meant me tagging along wherever he was going. "It'll be fun." And while it was fun for him, it was numbingly boring for me. At least until I started entertaining myself by watching people, eavesdropping, noticing behaviors, listening to conversations. It was easy—after the initial hellos, everyone generally ignored me. I would be the invisible kid sitting on the one uncomfortable black wooden chair available at a gallery opening; or the quiet one, sitting cross-legged on a dirty penny-tile floor in an East Village hallway; or the mopey one with his head pressed against an arched floor-to-ceiling window in a SoHo walk-up—the type of place where the host would let you into the building by dropping keys in a balled-up sock or lower them to the street tied to thirty feet of string.

My dad's circle was mostly art and music types, and cultural references were as mandatory as they were involuntary. An image that reminds you of a movie. A smell that reminds you of a song. Shit like that. I had no chance to contribute with art, and I took a bunch of big whiffs with music, but talking about film was where I could fight above my weight.

The common language of New York City always seemed to be film. It still is.

Hanging with him wasn't every day, though. This was weekends. And not every one. Maybe once a month, twice if I was lucky—but generally once. He'd postpone, cancel, forget. Mostly, I was in Nassau County with my mom and Paul the Dentist (*yawn*). Riding bikes. Playing soccer. Going to movies as much as possible so I could chime in with something, anything cultural the next time I got to visit my dad. But that habit of pocketing moments, of noticing things—it stayed with me beyond the basic movie reference.

So I notice when the curtains move at the row house next to where I'm parked. And I notice when the larger-than-average man opens his front door and walks toward the beat-up Chevy Nova parked right in front of me. And I especially notice—after he starts it up and puts it in reverse—that he's shining his white reverse lights on my face so he can get a good look at me, adjusting the mirror to stare and suss out the situation. He must have seen me clicking my Pentax earlier at his neighbor's house across the street. His eyes narrow, and I can see that brain inside him is processing some soon-to-happen future that involves me in a way that I'm positive I'd prefer it not.

He turns off his car, exits and heads back to his house, where I know one of two things is happening: either he's calling the cops, or he's grabbing a baseball ba— *Oh, yup, it's a baseball bat.* Must have had it right by the door. My camera takes a bounce as I drop it onto the passenger seat and start up my rental as fast as I can, pulling out too quickly and scraping his car's left bumper on the way.

I should have left when I saw him at the curtains. This is the Bronx. The Bronx always goes for the baseball bat.

—

I manage to rub out the scratches on my bumper before returning the rental car and head home to dump my gear before going out to meet Pete. He works in film production, mostly commercials, and between us our schedules make for difficult meeting times. We'll hang together every month or so, taking turns at picking the place. Last month, we met at the Howard Johnson's in Times Square. I picked it—I guess ironically, but we stayed, and he didn't complain. That's the rule. You have to go where the other says, and you can't complain about it. Which explains why I'm now at a strip club in Queens.

I don't get the non-solo outing to a strip club. Does communal arousal build bonds I'm unaware of? Strip clubs are supposed to be places of quiet, isolated desperation. Go alone, do something you regret and then reassess your life. Tomorrow is a new day. A rising phoenix from the asses. That sort of thing.

Since Pete picked the place, I can't complain verbally about it, but I gotta say, man—it smells. Mold. Bleach. Dirty taps. Stains. Good lord, the stains. Place might as well be called Legionnaires' Disease.

"Yeah, I'm a filmmaker. Indie stuff mostly. You wouldn't really … I dunno. You've probably never heard of anything I've done."

Done? He makes coffee and drives vans.

Shit. They're both looking at me. Did I say that out loud? I think I said that out loud. *Play it like you meant to say it.* Nod. Smile. *Barfly*-esque shake of a beer bottle in their general direction.

There ya go. All seems forgiven. I light a cigarette to continue the con and begin to plan my escape under cover of smoke, but before I know it, Pete leans in.

"Hey," he says. "I'm leaving. You good?"

"You're leaving? Like … with her?"

"Yeah."

"Isn't she working?"

"She's about to end her shift."

"And I'm gonna stay here?"

"I mean, you don't have to. You can do whatever you want."

There's no rule about leaving, just the one about no complaining, so I have no real play here. But I do make a note to add that to the rules: the person that picks the place cannot leave early. That's rude.

"Awesome. You go. Have fun. Have a great night." I nod as they split. Again with the nodding.

I get annoyed when people lie about their job. Enhancing it. Embellishing it. It bothers the hell out of me. Just deal with how you've chosen to spend your waking hours. Don't lie. Don't exaggerate. We all hate our jobs. We're all miserable. Admit it and move on. I especially hate it when the lie helps the liar get laid.

"Can I bum a cigarette?"

I turn toward the disinterested stripper to my left. She's got a bit of an alterna-chick vibe. Or a drug problem. Maybe both.

"What? Yeah. Sure. Take it. Take whatever." I slide the pack over to her.

"I saw that yellow pack from across the bar and bolted over here. Don't see that brand much in this place."

"Yeah, organic carcinogens really make all the difference."

"Don't get clumsy sarcasm much here, either. Does your friend really work in the movies?"

"No. I mean, he works in the business, but no. He doesn't write. I mean, he says he will. He always talks about writing. But he never writes. He's a PA—a production assistant. That's it."

"What do you do?"

I should say something here. The honesty thing I was just yapping about? I haven't really tried it yet. But I'm gonna. Right now. Here goes.

"I take pictures."

Eye roll.

"Not those kinds of pictures. I take pictures of ... how do I say this? Okay. You know when somebody has an accident on the job and they hurt themselves? And insurance kicks in, or they start getting disability?"

"No."

"All right, well, it happens. In my case, we're talking about city jobs. MTA. Sanitation department. Cops. Firemen. And a lot of times, it's fraud. Like, they faked the injury, or they made it seem worse than it was to collect the insurance money."

"Okay."

"So, the city hires me, and I follow these people, and I take pictures of them. I try to get evidence of them doing something that their injury should really be preventing them from doing."

"Like what?"

"Lifting something heavy. Going dancing. Stuff like that."

"Huh. So, you're like a snitch."

"Well, no. I mean ... they're committing insurance fraud, so I'm collecting evidence. I'm not snitching."

She takes a deep, disinterested breath.

"Seems like snitching." She exhales and puts her head down on the bar.

Inside I know whatever I was hoping was gonna happen here isn't gonna happen. But who knows? I don't know anything about her. Don't know her life. Her fucking complications. How she got here. She's tired. Working hard, dancing for assholes. And she's tired, so she put her head down on the bar. She's cute, though. Probably a grad student. Too smart for this place, I bet.

And she's right. It is snitching. And I'm a shit for doing it.

"I'll blow you for fifty."

The small wince of a smile on my face. There's that rock-bottom feeling I was looking for.

"Yeah, I don't have fifty."

"What do you have?"

"I got twenty bucks, and that has to get me through the night, so ..."

She sits up and takes another deep breath. "You shoulda told me you were broke."

"I didn't, uh ... I didn't know what this was about here. I thought we were having a conversation."

"Yeah. Real scintillating stuff." She readjusts herself in the barstool. "Listen, I'm gonna take your cigarettes, all right? And don't make a big deal about it, or I'll get the bouncer to break your fingers. He owes me."

I involuntarily give my digits a flex and decide I like them better unbroken.

I'm not gonna protest.

"Do what you gotta do." I only really ever smoke at places like this. Or sometimes if a girl I like smokes. Or if I'm drunk. Or if a cigarette is offered to me. I guess I sort of smoke.

She swipes the pack as she gets up and takes a cursory glance across the room for her next mark. I feel like I should say good-bye, but feeling like saying good-bye mostly means you don't, so I just smile and give her a nod.

Fuck, what is it with me and the nods tonight?

CHAPTER TWO

I TAKE THE N to Twenty-Third Street and get out early to walk the rest of the way home. I like to do that. Air out the clothes. Walk off the booze. Get some fresh oxygen in the lungs. *Cue the trash truck dripping some freshly squeezed and extra chunky onto Third Avenue as it growls past.*

By Fourteenth Street I'm mostly sober and already thinking about how things are gonna be different. At Ninth Street I hang a left and head toward the Alphabets, toward home. But maybe ... ?

I look at my pager—almost 2:00 a.m. Bars are open for another two hours. Pinball would be good. Medieval Madness and a pint. Then bed. Get that fresh start I was talking about. I dig my hands deep into my dad's old pea-coat pockets and head toward 7B.

It's trash night, but really, it's always trash night in New York. Black trash bags bursting with takeout are piled three high and three wide down the sidewalk. They twitch as the rats inside them fight over leftover lo mein and chicken wings.

My dad would tell the same damn joke every time we walked past piles of garbage like this: "Oh, yay! It's the day the city delivers the trash."

I smile, remembering the thousands of times he told it, and then stop smiling when I remember the hundreds of times I've seen him fucked up and stumbling down this very block. As nostalgia goes, that memory was one for, one against.

I shake my head to forget and walk through the pair of too-close-to-each-other doors into 7B and get immediately carded by the same steroid-swollen asshole bouncer who cards me every other fucking day. I tuck the driver's license back into the black binder clip I use as my wallet and push through the crowd to the bar.

I know better than to order a Guinness here, but it's late, and I'm doing that whole fresh-start thing tomorrow, and Guinness always treats me right, so ... I order one and then watch as the bartender pours it too goddamn fast and hands it right back to me like the fucking monster that he is. I could get mad, but when the bad thing you thought was gonna happen happens, whose fault is it, really?

I drop a ten on the bar and ask for four back—two of them in quarters—and take a sip. One of these days I'm calling a Guinness rep on these clowns.

It's that second wave of prime time at 7B. Not quite desperation yet—folks haven't given in to going home alone. There's still that hope of pairing with someone else. Things won't turn sad for a little bit. We're still in that sweet spot between buzzed and sauced, emotionally and alcoholically speaking.

I'm trying to get a read on how many are waiting for the next turn on Medieval, but a ruddy Wall Street head keeps blocking the view. He's strayed from his cabal of buddies that loudly occupy the tiny table next to the jukebox. A bunch of sweaty, overstarched Brooks Brothers suits giddy with motherfucking excitement about hanging out on Avenue B. There's always some of them around at this hour. Overconfident, coked up and horny for hipsters. These are the guys that go from flirting at the beginning of a sentence to assault by the end.

"But you're not even giving me a chance! That's not fair. Don't you want to be fair to me? That's not very nice. Don't I deserve you being nice?"

"I don't even fucking know you, man. And I'm waiting for someone, all right? I am not alone, and I'm not fucking looking for you." She's angry. And cute. Cute and angry.

"Well, I guess I'll just wait here with you and help you pass the time, then. I'll leave when this friend actually shows up."

I normally don't get setups like this and never from assholes like him, so I step in, giving her a nudge on the shoulder. "Have you been here this whole fucking time? I was standing right here waiting for you! I started to think you split."

She turns, looks at me quick and gives a shake of her head before going back to her drink.

Maybe she didn't get what I was trying to do. I lean into it. "Sorry I'm late."

An exhale. She turns again and looks at me wide eyed and then overly dramatically mouths: "*I don't need your help, creep-o.*" She really holds on to the *o* in *creep-o*, an emphasis that honestly seems unnecessary.

"This idiot bothering you?" Brooks Brothers snorts.

Okay. My flirting disguised as chivalry has taken an unfortunate turn here, and from the grin on her face, it looks like this woman is well aware of the power she now wields. If she says yes, this shaved ape is going to grab me by the collar and toss me around like a Samsonite. If she says no, I'll be fine, but it will be far less entertaining for her.

Her head bounces and her nose wrinkles as she ponders her options. *Am I bored enough that I want to watch this clown get trounced?*

"He's my friend," she says.

"That's bullshit," Brooks Brothers says. "You don't know this guy."

"I do. I was just fucking with him is all."

I reach over and give Brooks Brothers an overly patronizing slap on the shoulder and pause as I wonder if shoulders are supposed to be that terrifyingly muscly. "Thanks for keeping her company."

He ignores me. "If you know him, what's his name?"

Oh, shit.

She gives me a long look over, trying to see what sticks. "This is, uh ... George? Yeah. Sure. Why not? George. Georgie Porgie."

Ouch.

"You just made that up," Brooks Brothers says.

I smile. "No, it's true. George is ... evidently my name." It's not, though. It's Nico.

Brooks Brothers looks pissed. He knows the game is fixed, but he can't figure out which of us is hiding the card. Confused, he returns to his natural state.

"Fucking faggot. Fucking dyke. You can have each other." He turns and sits with his brethren, repeatedly mumbling about downtown queers and how this place sucks. A moment later they leave in a chorus of chair scrapes and are probably going to beat up the first non-normal-looking person they see in Tompkins Square Park, and for that, I apologize to whomever ends up on the receiving end.

"George?" I say.

"I dunno. You look like a George. What's your real name?"

"Nico. Short for Nicholas."

"You ever go by Nicky?"

Not if I have a say in it. It's Nico as in Nicholas, not Nicky as in whatever the hell that's short for. I hold the *las* for a long time, giving it the Spanish pronunciation that my mom insisted on when I was a kid. "Let them know," she would say. I tell her I'm named after a great-grandfather in Ecuador that I've never met. She tells me her name is Maggie, after an old college friend of her mother's that *she's* never met and then buys us another round before we move to an open booth at the end of one of the horseshoe legs of the bar.

It's the same booth Paul Newman flirted with Charlotte Rampling in when they got sauced in *The Verdict*. The same booth where Al Pacino met his new bagman in *Serpico* and the one next to the booth where Jodie Foster shows Todd Graff the lone surviving penguin John Turturro stole from the Bronx Zoo in *Five Corners*.

I love that 7B has been in so many movies. It makes it feel more comfortable to me, if that makes sense. Like, I knew the place before I even started drinking here.

Pavement goes into Neutral Milk Hotel and then back into the same goddamn Pavement song as we talk. From the side-glances in between bits of conversation, it's clear that the actual friend Maggie's waiting for is one of the bartenders.

"You waiting for the sort of Randy Johnson–looking one or the Keanu-looking one?"

For a brief second, she gets embarrassed, and then a sparkle of pride hits her face. "Please. Keanu, of course."

Evidently, she's hooked up with him a few times before, but so have most of the women still lingering in orbit at 3:30 a.m. We've now hit the sour hour, the sad times. When you see yourself at the bottom of the glass and realize how bad tomorrow is gonna suck, so you might as well get really ripped.

I start losing interest in Maggie as a coping mechanism for having no shot with her, and I dig into sarcasm. She counters with the same, and pretty soon it feels like actual flirting. She asks about my work, and I keep with the self-depreciating honesty, but she actually lights up about it.

"So, to do stuff like that, do you need a license or something?"

"Yeah."

"What kind?"

"Private investigator."

"Holy shit. You're like a PI? Like, for real?"

"Yeah, but I never investigate anything. I just take pictures."

"But you could? You could, like, go find the Maltese Falcon and shit?"

"I suppose. Yeah."

"Can I see it? Your license?"

I pretend to be reluctant about pulling it out, but I'm eager to do it. She seems genuinely excited.

"It just looks like a driver's license," she says.

I start telling her that's because it's a just a state license, and all state licenses basically look the same, but I see my words fade into the background as she begins to fixate on the Keanu bartender as he flirts with a girl who looks a few months shy of voting age but, to be honest, only a few years younger than Maggie.

"Let's go somewhere else," she says into her glass.

"Somewhere else? It's almost four."

"Brownie's. Let's go to Brownie's."

I push back in the booth and take a long look at her and exhale.

Crap.

"Sure. Okay. Let's go to Brownie's."

CHAPTER THREE

I WAKE UP THE next day on the couch at about 1:30 p.m., fully clothed and hugging an empty Gatorade bottle to my chest. Odds are the stickiness all over me means it wasn't entirely empty when I passed out, but at least I had enough sense to attempt to hydrate before it all went dark.

Sitting up, I cough myself more awake and try to remember what happened after 7B. *Right ...*

Brownie's.

There are two establishments called Brownies in New York City, and strangely, they're about two blocks from each other. One's a music club on Avenue A. That's Brownies—*the non-possessive one*. Generally, the worst thing that can happen to you there is that you faint from heat exhaustion because they've oversold Elliott Smith and crammed about 350 people into a venue that's only ever supposed to hold 150. Or maybe the person you came with goes home with somebody else. Both of those scenarios are very plausible bad things that could happen at that particular Brownies. But they're more like inconveniences. Not *bad* bad things.

The other Brownie's—*the possessive one*— is about three blocks north of Tompkins Square Park, just off A. There are many, many legitimately bad things that can happen at this one. We'll start with the obvious.

This Brownie's is an after-hours coke bar full of people doing coke. It's also owned by a pimp named Brownie, hence the possessive form. Now, maybe the least bad thing that could happen here is you start talking to some stranger about "Band on the Run" by Wings, and then the next thing you know it's 11 a.m., your jaw is sore and you're somehow in Yonkers on that dude's couch *still talking about Wings*. On a scale of one to five (with a one being annoying and a five being horrifying), that's a one. A two would be if that same exact thing happened, but the Yonkers dude ended up on *your* couch at 11 a.m. and you had to figure out a way to get him to leave. A three would be a fight breaking out, even though fights never last long there. The bouncer would beat the shit out of both parties and toss them out the back door by the second blow, but the entire scene would fuck up the night's mood. Four and five are both reserved for medical incidents. If it's happening to someone else, it's a four. If it's happening to you, it's a five.

So, wait. What happened?

We got there a little after 4:00 a.m. Maggie got a table while I navigated the very dark darkness and got us some drinks. By the time I sat down, she was already cutting a line of coke. She offered some to me, and I gave my usual, all-smiles, hands-up "I'm good."

She wiped the edge of a credit card and licked whatever dust was saved off her finger and then leaned into the line. I took a sip of my drink and looked away. I don't like watching people use. It's a moment I don't want to be a part of. It feels like watching a dog take a shit in the park. Just look away and give the beast its privacy.

A tingle started in my lips, and I remembered they lined the glasses with coke there. I gave the lip of my glass a wipe down with a cocktail napkin and took a fresh sip.

I prepared to receive the usual shit about me not using, but she didn't throw it at me right away. She sat back in her chair, sipping her booze and licking her teeth as she tried to figure it out.

"You drink. You smoke. You don't do coke," she said. "Do you smoke weed?"

"Sometimes."

"But no coke."

"Nope."

She's about to ask why.

"Why?"

And this was where I usually said, "Because I just don't like it," but this time I didn't. Maybe it was connected to that honesty I'd been trying out all night, or maybe it was just on a whim, but I told her the truth. "My dad was an addict. Coke. Heroin. Anything, really."

"Was?"

"Was."

She tightened up a little. Involuntarily wiped her nose and sniffed, hoping there was no stray dusting of coke left there, before she offered her condolences. "Sorry. I wouldn't have invited you here if I had known." It was an awkward situation I'd been in before. I've tried a bunch of responses to the "I'm sorry your dad OD'd" sentence, but everything always feels hollow. Nothing really makes them—or you—feel any better, so you move on.

We had another round, and that's where things got blurry. Booze after midnight can linger into your morning. Booze after 4:00 a.m. can erase your entire next day. We did more basic learning about each other. Both of us went to SUNY Purchase—her for the whole stint, me for two years. I didn't tell her I dropped out to take care of my dying dad. Why bring the room down, twice?

She studied acting, had done some short films but nothing "real" yet. I had just decided to become an English major with a film studies minor when my dad's neighbor called to let me know he'd found my dad collapsed in the vestibule of his apartment building, skin jaundiced, with barely the hint of a heartbeat. He was shutting down. I came home to help take care of him, to try and help him hit the right path, et cetera. He didn't last long.

I walked him to and from his first two dialysis sessions. By the third, he insisted on walking himself. He wanted to listen to music and stretch his legs. He was in a good mood, and he actually looked healthy for the first time in ages. He was talking about writing a new song, something that had crawled into his head after I came home. Some anti-folk "Cat's in the Cradle" bullshit. Whatever it was, it was the first time he had talked about writing in years, and it was good to hear, so I let him do his thing. But instead of heading to dialysis, he went to Avenue C, scored, found a quiet doorway of a basement apartment to shoot up in, OD'd and died.

So, yeah. I didn't bring any of that stuff up. I just said I dropped out.

I was about to say, "I could do another if you wanna do another" when Maggie locked eyes with someone at the bar. I followed her sight line and winced as my eyes landed on Keanu. Fucking Keanu. He gave a nod for her to come join him and that was it. I can't compete with the confidence of a tiny head nod like that.

"I think I'm gonna split. It was fun. Thanks." She stood and headed for the bar, all smiles, giving him a flirty arm punch when she got there. Keanu played along with it, rubbing his arm, playing hurt. That same arm effortlessly went around her shoulder and guided her to the door. Then they were gone.

Annoyed that I was annoyed, I went to the bar and ordered one more. I needed to give those two a head start anyway. There was probably a lot of stumbling and kissing, kissing and stumbling happening on the street right then. I didn't need to see that. I could imagine that just fine, thank you very much. I don't need an actual ocular experience. I finished my drink and went to the bathroom to take a piss before leaving.

I swayed drunkenly as I read the graffiti on the wall and gave a squint as some of it caught my eye. Angularly scratched into the black paint just above the condensation-dappled chrome on top of the urinal, it read: "After all that, you went home alone."

Indeed.

A blurry bodega stop for Gatorade was sometime after that. Shortly thereafter, the darkness. And here I am, back in my apartment. Hungover. Unlaid. Poorly hydrated and late for work.

CHAPTER FOUR

I HEAD TO THE second bathroom, which I use as a darkroom, and grab the photos I need for my meeting. And yes, I have a second bathroom. I inherited this apartment from my dad after he died. Actually, before he died. During one of his flirtations with sobriety, he switched it from his name to my name. He was worried he'd sell it off, like everything else he ever owned. It was the last reminder that he had ever been a success at anything, and he didn't want that gone. Guitars and amps could dance to and from the pawnshop, but the apartment stayed.

My dad was a musician, one of the regulars at SideWalk Cafe. He was popular, but open-mic popular. Stale popcorn and flat beer, pass-around-a-bucket popular. He did have some celebrity musician fans who would show up from time to time. That kind of chum in the water eventually brought out some A&R reps, which led to his signing and to a label and a very poorly marketed LP release in 1990. The label had a big showcase night for him during the College Music Journal Festival one year—it sort of replicated the kind of open-mic night my dad was king of at SideWalk, but nobody showed up. Pimply-faced college radio DJs don't come to CMJ to experience an Avenue A open mic. They come to see death metal bands play synagogues and lo-fi garage bands play in the belly of a rusted-out tugboat. Shit like that.

Dad told me he knew right then and there that it was over. The way the label's tone changed from before the showcase to after. He knew they were going to cut their losses and move on. He did manage to hit the top one hundred of college radio a few times, but as my dad said to most things, "Who the fuck cares about that?" It bums me out. I feel like with a little actual marketing, he could have gone higher.

But none of that ended up mattering, all because of that One-Named Indie Darling. He knew my dad from back in the day and always said my dad taught him the basics of songwriting. When he first moved to New York and crashed on my dad's couch, they'd smoke and drink and listen to Washington Squares cassettes. Without my dad he would never have evolved. He felt like he owed him, so when he got big, he did a big thing and covered one of my dad's tunes. To his credit, he totally made it his own. My dad's hooks were still there, and the lyrics were there, of course, but the rest was so different. At first my dad hated it, but as it got popular, it grew on him. And when the checks started coming in, he really started liking it. And when they put it on the soundtrack for that movie and a few really big checks started coming in? Shit, then he loved it.

Somewhere in those salad days, he reached a balance. He had money. He was writing new songs. He was excited about the future. He bought the apartment. He even paid back my mom some of what he owed her—at least financially. The emotional debt was too massive, too overwhelming.

But it was just a pause. That moment of zero gravity at the top of the track before the roller coaster starts pulling you backward into the loop. The shift was sudden. At some party, on some night, at some apartment, he went back to coke. He went back to heroin. And then the great sell-off began. Guitars. His TV. I went over there once, and his couch was gone.

After he died, we found out he even sold the publishing rights to the big song to the manager of the One-Named Indie Darling. Pretty soon the only thing left was the apartment I'm standing in, and that was only because in that one fleeting moment of sobriety, he put it in my name.

I stuff the photos in an envelope and head for the F train. I was supposed to be in Brooklyn an hour ago.

—

I get out at Atlantic Avenue and head toward Third Avenue. I'm deeply late, but it isn't just my hangover that's to blame. I'm also F-train late. That's not the same as 7-train late and definitely nowhere near G-train late, but it's plenty late, and goddamn it if I'm not going to use it as an excuse. I figure Finch has already relocated for afternoon happy hour, so I skip his office and head straight for the Doray.

If any establishment could be the physical embodiment of darkness, it is the Doray Tavern. Painted black both inside and out, it's a convenient hole to hide in with very affordably priced beer. It's the type of place that closes at 4:00 a.m., opens at 8:00 a.m. and has regulars waiting outside by 7:00 a.m. It's a bar with multiple histories, but these days it's gone as stagnant and stale as the beer it serves. I open the door, and the light spilling in from outside cuts through the velvet dark, leading me to Finch. He's deep at the end of the bar, a *Daily News* laid out in front of him as a tabloid tablecloth. He's gently rolling a hard-boiled egg over Mike Lupica's face as I approach him.

"Hey, Esquire," I say, and drop the envelope of photos next to him on the bar. The sound of it slapping down makes him spasm, and that sudden movement rolls his egg off the bar top and onto the stained cement floor behind it.

"Goddamn it. I lost my egg." He turns toward me without looking at me. "You made me lose my damn egg, Nico. That's half my lunch." He immediately starts rolling what I assume is the other half and then begins to gently peel away cracked shells as they loosen.

"Why don't you let me get you some real food? A slice, a sandwich ... something?"

"No. I don't want real food. Eggs are all I can take nowadays. My fucking gut." He rubs his belly as he leans back and then grabs the envelope. "This the MTA job?"

"Yeah. There's not much. He took the trash out, but he dragged it. Didn't carry it. He might actually be hurt. I dunno. Seems like it's for real."

Mikey, the white-haired, sixtysomething bartender, is leaning back against the register, his arms folded, his eyes staring unfocused out the filthy window toward Atlantic Avenue. I immediately imagine the intense self-reflection happening inside his head. Waves of failure and bad choices. He looks so lost. He shoulda finished school. He shoulda started school. He shoulda never walked in here. "What are you thinking about, Mikey?" I shout to him.

"Honestly? About all the fucking Arabs moving into my neighborhood." He looks over to me. "You want something?"

"Uh, yeah, I'll take a Bud." *So much for self-reflection.*

The bottle he pulls out from the ice-water-filled coffin behind the bar forms a small puddle in front of me after he puts it down. I reset the slippery beer label that slides against the glass of the bottle, point toward Finch and mumble, "It's on him." Finch is nose deep in the photos, and either he doesn't notice as Mikey takes the singles off his pile, or he doesn't care. I'm going with the former.

Finch isn't happy with what I brought him. "This is all garbage. There's nothing here."

"I told you. I think it's a legit claim."

Mikey leans back into his reflective pose again, this time closer to us. "You know I gotta walk four fucking blocks to get a goddamn six-pack now?"

Wait. Is he talking to me? I look up. "What's that?"

"On account of the Arabs. They took over the bodega on my corner. Got rid of booze. Got rid of smokes. Says it's against their religion. Now I gotta walk an extra four blocks just to get a sixer. It's fucking criminal."

"I don't think they 'took it over,' Mikey. They bought it, right? If *you* bought it, you could do whatever you wanted to it. So can they."

"Yeah, but it's my bodega. My spot. That's gotta matter for something, right? I was there first."

I take a swig and give a shrug as I think, *I'd like this conversation to end very quickly, thank you very much.*

He doesn't like my indifference and gives me a good, hard squint. "You know, I've been wondering for a while now … What are you, anyways?"

There are certain questions that tell you more about the person asking them than the answer tells you about the person asked. Does that make sense? I think that makes sense.

I lower my bottle. "What am I?"

Finch puts down the photos. "Nico's a spic. Or a half a spic, at least. What are you again? Peruvian or some shit?"

"Ecuadorian. At least my mother is. So, yeah, half."

Mikey leans forward enough to get a look at me. "Shit. I always pegged you for a Jew. Maybe half a Jew."

Jesus. I liked this bar better when I had to imagine what this guy was thinking. I sip my beer and turn toward Finch. I'm ready to get my assignment and get out. "What's next?"

"You gotta buy a video camera, or I can't hire you anymore."

"Wait, what?"

"The city's lawyers want video. Photos can be misinterpreted, misrepresented. Video is more definitive. You gotta get a camera, or you gotta get a new gig. Your choice."

"Fuck. Okay. I'll look into it."

"Also, I'm not covering your car expenses anymore. Other guys have cars. You don't. That's not my fault. That's your fault. That's your lacking. That's not my lacking. I cover mileage. I cover gas. I don't cover car rental."

"How the hell do I stake someone out without a car? Hide in the trash?"

"I don't fucking care, Nico. I'm just not paying for it. Buy a car. Get a car service. I don't give a shit." He rubs his stomach. "My fucking gut."

"Car rental is a legitimate expense, Finch."

"Cry me a fucking river."

Asshole. "So, do you have a gig, or what?"

"No gigs till you get a video camera. You get a video camera, you gimme a call. Then you get another gig."

I know what's actually going on. Finch's anxiety is linked directly to his gut. If he's ill, he's anxious. And if he's anxious, he owes someone. And if he owes someone, he's probably overbilling the city, and me asking him to pay me actual money for things like a rental car—something I'm sure he's *already* billing the city for—that cuts into his ability to make some extra scratch.

I down what's left of my beer and turn toward the pinhole of light that leads to Atlantic Avenue.

This sucked.

—

At home, I call up Pete for some advice. I figure even his limited film production experience will mean he knows something about video cameras. "Just go to the Wiz, charge it and then return it at the end of the month."

"Yeah, but I need it longer than a month."

"I know. You return it. Then you go to another Wiz and buy a new one. And then you do it all again. They have a crazy return policy—you can return anything for a full refund within thirty days. Most folks shooting docs on video nowadays, that's how they do it."

That was kind of genius.

I thank him, go to the Wiz, buy a camera and head home. One fucking box checked. The other box? The car box? That's going to be more difficult.

CHAPTER FIVE

T HERE ARE TIMES WHEN you find yourself crammed into a subway car, one hand holding the overhead grab handle, the other
holding your Discman, headphones on, music playing and your eyes in
an unfocused dead stare straight ahead. You rock back and forth from
the movement of the car, occasionally brushing the person next to you,
causing you to mumble an inaudible "Excuse me" or maybe just raise
your hand slightly as a sign of an apology for crossing over into their air
space. Somewhere in there, you realize you've been staring at an NYPD
police-recruitment ad for the past two minutes and you surprise yourself
by thinking, *Maybe?*

That's where I am. Under the East River on the L heading to Bedford.
The ad says the cut-off age to become a cop is still thirty-five. No need to
rush into anything. Six years left to ponder.

I squeeze through a pair of *abuelas* with their metal rolling carts full of
churros, exit the car and let out a "Fuck" once I realize I'm at the wrong
end of the train. The doors close behind me, and the Canarsie-bound L
begins to ramp up to speed as it heads for Lorimer/Metropolitan. I try
to hold my breath as I make the long platform walk through the aerosol
wake of urine, rot and rats the movement of the train has activated, but
I can't last long. *Hold. Gasp. Hold. Gasp.* I'm probably sucking in more
than if I was just breathing normally. I'm an idiot.

Up top, it's drizzling but not enough for me justify buying a five-dollar black umbrella. Not even a three-dollar one. I pull up the collar on my dad's old black pea coat and squeeze the Discman into the left pocket as I make my way through the twilight on Bedford Avenue. If it starts raining any harder, this fucking coat is going to weigh fifty pounds by the time I get to Cookie's place.

I should have bought that umbrella.

A dollar van slows down next to me and gives a tap on the horn. I wave it off, but it lingers. Another couple of honks and then I hear "Ni-*co*!" under the Digable Planets spilling out of my headphones. I turn and give a squint. I have no idea who that is. "Nico, get your *medio-gringo* ass in here. You're soaking."

Holy shit. It's Frankie Balls.

Frankie Balls isn't named Frankie, and his dad wasn't named Balls, but that's what everyone calls him. I met him on the subway coming back from an all-ages hardcore matinee in 1985. I had seen him at the show—it was kind of impossible not to—and then was surprised to see him on my train and then incredibly surprised to see him get off at my stop. We got a slice and talked about the scene—I was a casual visitor, skimming the surface and peeking in the door but never really walking through. He was the real deal. Straight edge, with giant Xs on his Frankenstein's monster-sized fists and an ever-changing wardrobe of homemade black-marker band shirts. He lived for the matinees. I went out of curiosity. Something to get me out of the apartment on Saturdays. He went to be his true self. A Dominican kid who loved hardcore.

After my mom split from my dad, we moved in with her younger sister Cookie in her Williamsburg two-bedroom apartment for about a year. It was tight, and not in a slang-for-awesome kind of way. It was fucking small. My mom and I in one tiny room and her sister in the other. Anything I could do to get out of that apartment, I did; so whenever Frankie invited me to shows, I went. And while the music never took with me, it was fun to visit the scene. People at the CB's matinees may have looked odd to some, but they were generally accepting and forgiving. They just wanted to have fun and to belong somewhere. So when a poseur like me wanted to lean against a side wall and pretend to know the words being sung, they didn't give a fuck. They were too busy smiling and screaming.

That was the vibe of the Saturday matinees at CB's. But that was not the vibe of Sundays at City Gardens. I only once made the hike out to Trenton for a City Gardens Sunday matinee with Frankie, but that was enough. I quickly learned that the Jersey scene was not as open armed and joyous as the CB's shows. It wasn't just the pain-in-the-ass train to Trenton and back. It was the club. The whole place had another energy, a sticky darkness that kept you on edge. That's when I learned Frankie had two nicknames—he was Frankie Balls in any of the five boroughs, but out in New Jersey they called him Hunter/Killer.

After the first few folks kept calling him "Hunter," I started to think that maybe I had finally learned his real first name. Then a few nods with "Hey, Killer" turned into most folks simply nodding, looking at him and saying, "Hunter/Killer" and giving a point in his direction.

"I'm sorry, Frankie. Are they ... are they calling you Hunter/Killer?"

"Yeah."

"Why?"

"It's what they call me."

"But why?

"It's what I do out here."

"Hunt and kill?"

"Yeah."

"What the hell are you hunting and killing?"

He cracked one fist of giant banana fingers into another and smiled at me. "Nazi skinhead fucks."

That's when I found out the very thing I loved about the CB's shows—their being (generally) accepting and positive—that was the one thing Frankie didn't like. There were never any Nazis around to beat down—not consistently, anyway. They mostly knew enough to keep their distance. As a Dominican skinhead, Frankie saw it as his duty to beat down racist Nazi fucks.

I'd always assumed he was good at fighting; I just didn't know how much he loved it until City Gardens. The smile on his face when he connected his knuckles solidly with a jawbone was strangely just a little bit smaller than the smile on his face as his own jaw was getting clocked.

"Well, if you have to crack somebody's skull, you might as well crack a Nazi's." He literally said that in court to the judge that sent him to juvie. The judge calmly reminded him that in truth, nobody *has* to crack anybody's skull, which Frankie pondered and reluctantly agreed with.

Luckily, Frankie got a serious beatdown in the fight as well. If it had been more one sided, they might have tried him as an adult, but a Dominican Frankie Balls versus three white Jersey skinheads made it hard to say he wasn't acting in *some* self-defense. The swastikas on their jackets didn't help their cause any. He knocked out two (one of them hit his Nazi head on the cement, thusly cracking his Nazi skull and causing a bit of brain damage—that was what ultimately sent Frankie to juvie), and the third hit Frankie with a pipe on his back just as the cops arrived. That helped—the cops seeing the pipe connect.

I watched it all the from a side wall of the club, hiding in the shadows. Not that I could've helped at all. I'm pretty useless in a fight. I did what I could in court, though, saying two of the skinheads had called us "spics" and spit at us. They did spit at us, but not till Frankie spat at them. And they did call us "spics," but not till Frankie called them "Nazi fucks." Which, you know, they were.

Frankie only had to go to juvie for four months, but those four months were when my mom hooked up with Paul the Dentist, which resulted in her packing me and her up and heading us out to Long Island to live in orthodontal bliss. I never got to say good-bye to Frankie. I heard about him through Cookie from time to time, and I'm guessing he heard about me the same way.

"Holy shit. Frankie Balls." I open the van door and lift myself into the passenger-side front seat. The sticky sweetness of the half-a-dozen air fresheners hanging from the mirror fill my nose and mouth until Frankie pulls me in for a giant hug. His heavy cologne beats that sweetness back into submission quickly. I can still feel the burn in my nose after he leans backward.

"Motherfucking Nico the *medio-gringo*. How the fuck are you?"

Medio-gringo. Frankie gave me that nickname. Most of the Dominican kids would call me gringo, but Frankie would always stop them. "*Basta*. The kid is only half. He's *medio-gringo*." It was like "No, he's cool." And it helped.

"I'm good. What about you? You're driving a dollar van, now?"

"You better fucking believe it. 'Cept I don't just drive. I own. I got five. I keep the Bedford-Manhattan-Wythe route for myself 'cause it's home and I like to catch up with motherfuckers like you." An idea comes to him. "Oh, shit ..." He smiles wide and pops a faded cassette into his tape deck and immediately starts punching his fist in the air as "Victim in Pain" by Agnostic Front kicks in. He's grinning and nodding, trying to get me into it, and for a moment it's fucking 1985 all over again, me self-consciously leaning against a wall, him in the pit waving to me, trying to get me to join.

"*Carajo, Frankie. ¡Baja esa basura!*" Evidently, the music isn't winning over his usual passengers, especially the *abuelita* behind us. Frankie lowers it as he does his Muttley impression, heavy with that Hanna-Barbera wheezing laugh. This fucker loves Muttley.

"What are you doing on this side of the river?" he asks.

"I'm going to see Cookie."

"Family visit. I love to see it. *Love. To. See. It.* All right, settle in, then. We'll hit Northern on my next return loop."

"Shit. She's working? I thought she worked mornings."

"She's been driving nights lately. Pressed for cash, like we do, like we do ..."

I ride with Frankie as he trolls slowly down Bedford, up Manhattan and then back again. All the while folks give a wave, and he pulls over and lets them in for a three-to-ten block ride. He has a bodega-deli-sized old scratched-up mayonnaise tub hanging on the back of the driver's seat. Folks drop in a dollar or two based on how far they're headed. They're unlicensed operations, dollar vans, but the city and the Taxi and Limousine Commission look the other way in the outer boroughs. They don't get the yellow cabs like the Upper East does. These places need the dollar vans to fill in the gaps.

It's good to catch up with Frankie. He knows everyone and everything happening in that neighborhood. The Pope of the Northside. He fills me in on the happenings of folks I knew and folks I didn't know that he thinks I should. As he pulls up to Cookie's work, he gives me his card, and I give him my pager number, and we make tentative plans to get a drink. I didn't see any Xs on his hands, so I hope his straight edge has dulled and his drinks have hardened.

—

I can see Cookie working on a crossword through the glass of Northern Car Service's storefront window. She's ten years younger than my mom and only eight years older than me. If we ever actually hung out, you might think we were brother and sister. But we never hang out. She looks up as I walk in and immediately puts the newspaper and pen down on her lap. It takes her half a moment to recognize me and another half a moment for that small smile of recognition to fade into worry.

"Oh, shit," she says. "Who died?"

—

Cookie and my mom weren't ever super close, and that meant neither were Cookie and I. The strain of us all living together in her place only heightened the differences between the sisters. And my mom abandoning Brooklyn for the suburbs always felt like selling out to Cookie.

"How's your Spanish?"

I exhale my response through a too-hot bite of pizza. "*Comme ci comme ça.*"

She leans back in her chair, but somehow it feels like she's leaning forward. Cookie's barely over five feet, but she can carry herself tall when she feels like it's necessary. "Is that supposed to be funny?"

"*Sí, Tía. Claro que sí.*"

"'*Claro que sí.*' That's all you ever fucking say. You studying? Listening to tapes?"

"I got some CDs I was going to listen to. I just haven't found the time. I will. I promise."

"You better." She takes a bite of her slice and then gives a nod to an old-timer with a limp walking toward the bar. We're sitting in the tiny pizzeria portion of the Charleston bar on Bedford. I offered to get her a beer, but she said she was driving tonight and that was a no go. "So, what's up? What's with the trip under the river?"

Old-school, die-hard Brooklyn constantly talks about crossing the river like it's some sort of epic fucking journey with multiple quests and challenges. Like there's a wizard with a staff at the shoreline and you have to answer five questions to pass. When I lived with Cookie, whenever I went into Manhattan to hang, she'd always say, "Why do you need to go into the city?" *The city*. As if we weren't already in the same fucking city. To Cookie, Manhattan is for doctor's appointments and tax payments, and neither is a good thing. The idea that anyone would head there willingly is nuts to her.

"I need a favor."

I lay it out—my job, my financial predicament, and my specific need for a car. Maybe on nights she isn't driving, I could borrow hers?

"No fucking way."

"No way?"

"No. It's how I earn my living. It's my office. Would you let me take your office and drive it around, most likely uninsured, all over the goddamn city?"

"I don't have an office. And if I did, it wouldn't have wheels."

"So, I should give you mine?"

"No, I just ... I need a favor. You're family. I thought you could do me a favor."

"A favor? What you need is a car. Go get your own. Sell that apartment your father left you, rent like the rest of us and then buy a goddamn car."

"I'm not selling my dad's apartment."

"Well, that's fucking loco, babycakes. If you sold it, you could buy a car, plug the rest away into savings, and your problems would be solved. But no, instead, you seem to think it makes more sense to come and ask others to sacrifice for you. Does that seem right? Does that seem fair?"

"Cookie, the apartment is the last thing I have that's his."

"That ratty fucking jacket you're wearing was his, no?"

"Yeah, but—"

"Then don't tell me you don't have anything else of his. I'm sure you got all sorts of his junk in that apartment. Whatever he didn't pawn." She's starting to piss me off, and I let my face tell her. I can see her make the adjustment and downshift. "*Mijito*, you know I had issues with your dad. I didn't like the man. I didn't like how he ignored his responsibilities. And I don't mean to speak ill of the dead, but it's tough all around, you know?" She takes a deep breath and then reaches over and covers my hand with hers. "Sell the apartment."

I pull my hand out from under hers. "I'm not selling it."

"Well, my car's not available, even for charity. I need to pull doubles for the foreseeable future, so it's not even an option."

She takes another bite of her pizza, and as she chews, I can see an idea begin to form in her head. Her chewing first slows then speeds up as the concept becomes more congealed. "Now, if you wanted to hire me? That'd be another story."

"Hire you?"

"Yeah. By the hour, by the night. I'm sure we could work something out."

"So, just to be clear—you're not proposing I rent the car from you or anything. You're saying that I hire you as a driver?"

"You got it."

"I don't know if I can afford that."

"You can afford it." She's smiling now.

"It has to be less than I would pay to rent a car; otherwise, there's no point to it."

"I understand business, *mijito*. I'll keep the rates competitive. And I won't charge you for the Spanish lessons, either." She stands. "We done? I gotta start driving."

—

I call Finch from a pay phone on Bedford and leave a message before I head back below ground. I want him to know I've checked both boxes and am ready to work. The longer I'm out of his loop, the harder it's going to be to get back in.

CHAPTER SIX

"**H**EY, GEORGE!"

I hear it, but I don't hear it.

"Georgie!"

Something clocks me in the back of my head as I walk down Avenue A, and I turn to see Maggie sitting on a wobbly wooden stool outside Accidental Records. In a city with a thousand tiny storefronts selling used CDs, you need a hook. Accidental's is that it's open twenty-four hours a day, every damn day of the year. It's called Accidental because the owner opened it with settlement money he got from getting hit by a cab or a bus or something. The good stuff is safe inside. The bad stuff is outside in fifty and seventy-five-cent bins. Maggie appears to be guarding the garbage.

"Hey," I say. "You work here?"

"Yeah. One of the many pebbles I drop into my bucket. Can I have my pen back?"

I pick it up off the ground and hand it to her. "I didn't really expect to see you again so soon."

"It's a small town."

"It's not really."

"Except, it sort of is."

"You do know that my name isn't George, right?"

"I mean, I know it's not, but isn't it, though?"

She tells me she's working till about midnight; I tell her I'm heading to International Bar on First Avenue to meet a friend and that she should swing by. She says she might, but something in the way she says "might" lets me know she won't. It's clear that I'm a plan B, C or D for Maggie, and let's be fucking honest—she has no goddamn idea what my real name is.

I carry that feeling straight through my second Red Stripe and into the finger I am currently pointing into the air to let the bartender at International know, that *yes, I will have a third*. My friend Tommy finally pushes through the door just as the bartender lightens the pile of bills in front of me. I met Tommy about seven years ago when we were both temping our way through the first few years of our twenties. That era of lying about Excel proficiency, stealing office toilet paper and typing much slower than our résumés promised. At some point, I got paired up with Finch, and my path started to congeal. Tommy took some night classes in programming and is now working twenty-four seven to prevent the great Y2K computer disaster, which he's repeatedly assured me is *definitely going to happen*. It doesn't matter how many fucking decimals he moves in the code; he swears there is simply not enough time to keep the world from going tits up.

He slaps me on the back as he sits down. "You buy any gold yet?" He's spent most of the money he earned preventing the Technological End-Time on things that help him prepare for it. He has storage lockers in both Queens and Brooklyn filled with toiletries, water, canned food and iodine pills (and, I'm now guessing, precious metals?) and is on the verge of buying a motorcycle. "I'll need to be able to maneuver around all the nonfunctioning vehicles."

Somewhere in his rambling about how the post-2000 barter system is going to work, my feeling of being *just drunk enough* begins to overlap with *general annoyance*, and I'm getting dangerously close to telling him to shut up. I take a deep swig as Tommy's new-economy babble circles my head. Misanthropic drunk two nights in a row is going to hurt. I make a note to take tomorrow off.

There was a time when Tommy was as good an ally as any to sit, drink and stare at others with, but those days seem to have passed. He moved here from the middle-class suburbs of Saint Louis and is lingering longer than most in that pupa state lots of out-of-town transplants go through. The Y2K gig might have given him some recent professional confidence, but he still carries around that heavy defensiveness about style and personality that so many do in their first few years here. As he drinks, his uncomfortableness will begin to manifest itself in a series of Tourette's-like motions—a twitch of a finger; a jerk of a shoulder; obsessive, repeated side-glances at others who he just assumes are side glancing at him. When the drunken self-conscious tells arrive, an angry dumping on our current location will follow. It's not his fault. It's the building. It's the bartender. It's the jukebox.

"Who the hell puts jazz on a jukebox on a Friday night?" *Here it comes.* "I'm sick of this place. Let's go to Max Fish."

Max Fish. Most people seem to love it. I don't. Too fucking bright, too fucking self-aware, too fucking Max Fish.

But I'm too drunk to say no. I don't want to be alone, but I don't want to be with Tommy, and Max Fish is as good a place as any to shake him and find someone else.

The rest of the night goes the way nights like this can go, and by 4:00 a.m. I am one half of a sloppy couple making out on Ludlow Street before sliding away into the dark. It's that drunken kind of face eating that leaves your eyes dry and your mouth pasty, all while your brain is screaming at you to take back the saliva you're so chaotically handing over. That moisture is the thin, slimy line between you and a pounding headache.

Three hours later and it's that headache that's making me try to figure out the best way to climb out of this loft bed without waking up Susie. We've hooked up a half a dozen times before, never during daylight hours. But if it's late enough, and we're drunk enough (and both in the same bar), we always feel ourselves being pulled toward each other.

I push myself backward, trying not to pull the covers off her as I slide over the edge, telling myself that my toes will hit the ladder eventually, but it never comes. How the fuck did we get up here? I hang, naked, holding the wooden lip of the bed until my feet find her dresser below and stabilize.

As I stumble my way through the tiny studio apartment to the bathroom, my shins zero in on every goddamn table, every goddamn edge, and then I stop short when I hear the unmistakable sound of an upturned bong spilling onto a carpet that I can only imagine has had this bong spilled onto it many times before. I find the bong, right it and move on, trying not to step in the puddle, but the cold, stink-funk squish beneath my toes tells me that I've failed at that as well.

In the bathroom I close the door and turn on the light but not before my bong-water-wet feet crunch and cake themselves with loose kitty litter, kicked out onto the bathroom tile by a cat I have no memory of ever seeing anywhere in the apartment. I turn on the faucet to cover the sounds of opening Susie's medicine cabinet but there's nothing resembling pain reliever to be found. Just a plethora of Demeter bottles filled with scents like "Dirt" and "Earl Grey Tea." I bend over to wipe the kitty litter off my bare feet, and the shift in blood flow punishes me as my pulse somehow begins to crush my brain with each thump. I need to get out of here. I need some fucking Advil.

I mostly dress, and I'm carrying my shoes, thinking about leaving a note, when my sock-covered feet press into the bong water, the dry cotton soaking it up hungrily. Even my socks are dehydrated. I scribble down my number paired with the sad one-word question "dinner?" on a ConEd envelope, slide it under a Coney Island magnet on her fridge and then finally escape out the door and into her building's prewar hallway. I slouch toward the fireball of daylight that I'm assuming is the vestibule.

On the stoop a jogger steps around me as I sit, trying to pull my shoe over my wet sock, and I wonder what a 7:00 a.m. workout feels like. The jogger looked good. Sweaty but good. I'm sweaty too, but yeah. Not good. I stand and die about fifty times on the short walk to the corner bodega and then wince as I dry swallow a fifty-cent pack of Advil seconds after buying it. I buy another pack for later and head outside. I need to get my bearings. Third Street and Second Avenue. Perfect. Barring any stops to puke in a trash can, I should be in my bed in ten to twelve minutes.

I need to start mixing water in between the booze. Pace myself. Something.

Goddamn this fucking sunlight. 7:00 a.m. is a bastard.

—

I spent the rest of daylight sleeping and eventually woke up after the sun went down. At some point I called up Rosario's for a pizza. They've been in the neighborhood for over thirty years, and I swear to God the owner has memorized the faces and addresses of all his repeat customers.

"Rosario's."

"Yeah, can I get a large cheese pie?"

"Name?"

"Nico."

"Glasses Nico or No-Glasses Nico?"

"No-Glasses Nico."

"All right. Gimme twenty."

Boom. That's it. The pie is now on its way to me, No-Glasses Nico. Somewhere within Rosario's delivery area, Glasses Nico is sitting in his apartment, doing whatever a Nico with glasses does in the privacy of his home, but me, I'm hungover on the couch and pretty fucking excited about eating as much pizza as I can cram into myself.

I eat half the pie and watch *Barney Miller* reruns on WPIX until about 2:00 a.m. I flip through the film listings in the *Voice* and plot out a plan for the next few days. Somewhere in there I fall asleep. Sunday will be better. Sunday will be new.

CHAPTER SEVEN

COOKIE MUMBLES TO HERSELF, her face deep in the fold of the *Daily News*, its back page featuring a boldly positive headline about the Jets being in first place. *Ridiculous.* Everyone knows when the Jets are in first place, they're not really in first place. They're in motion. Waiting to find their true level. A paper boat floating on the surface of the water, waiting for the liquid to permeate the porous fibers and pull it down to the depths. Eventually the sucker always sinks. It just takes time.

It's about 9:00 p.m., and I'm in the back seat of Cookie's Town Car, video camera up, waiting for the mark to do something he's not supposed to do. We're in Bay Ridge. Finch paged me earlier and gave me the choice—NYC cop in Bay Ridge or an MTA bus driver in Yonkers. I normally avoid cop gigs, but I didn't think Cookie would agree to a Yonkers haul, especially my first time asking, so Bay Ridge it is.

"What did you do today?" She folds the paper and dumps it on the passenger seat. She's bored already. I can tell.

"Nothing much. Saw some movies."

"Like at home? Like you rented a bunch of videos, what?"

We're only forty-five minutes into this thing, and I'm already regretting it. "No, I went to a movie theater. Saw one movie. When it was over,

I walked to another theater and saw another one. Then I walked back to the first theater and saw the third."

She turns to look me in the eye. "You got free time like this every day?"

"When I'm not working, sure."

"Must be nice." *Oh, man.* The fucking attitude squeezed into those three little words. She moves right along with the distant-asshole-relative-at-Christmas line of questioning. "Who'd you go with?"

"Nobody."

"Nobody?" She turns to look me in the eyes again. I'm blowing minds here.

"I like to see movies by myself."

"You *like* to see movies by yourself?"

"Yes."

"Why? Who likes to go to the movies by themselves?"

"Me, Cookie. I do."

"But then who do you talk about it with after?"

"Nobody." That's one of the main reasons I like it.

"So, I'm guessing you're not dating anybody, then."

"Cookie. Please. Could you just? I need to stay focused here."

"Stay focused? Nothing's happening."

"But if it does, I need to tape it."

Annoyed, she picks up the paper again and gives it another headline-only read, exhaling as she flips from page to page to page. I know I told her I go to the movies alone, but that's not exactly true. Sometimes there's the guy with the Zabar's bag filled with newspapers. Then there's the crossword lady with the mechanical pencil. Sometimes there's the Greek-fisherman's-hat guy and his giant bag of sunflower seeds. He's there a lot. If I'm lucky, that cute, sorta mean (but I dunno, maybe it's more of a company policy on how to treat customers?) barista from Porto Rico Importing might be there.

My favorite is when I see multiple films at multiple theaters in one day, and the same folks are also making that pilgrimage with me from film to film. I have no idea if they ever notice me—I generally don't have anything recognizable on me besides a *New York Press* and bad posture—but seeing them feels like belonging to something. Like, it's social but you don't have to talk to each other. Do you know what I mean? Does that make sense? I think it makes sense.

"So, who's this guy we're squatting on?" Cookie asks.

"A cop. Had some sort of accident on the job. Supposedly fucked up his back."

"Wait … wait. We're staking out a cop? Are you serious? Did you maybe think to give me a heads-up about that? I'm not actively looking to get on any cop's shit list. I gotta drive in this city."

"He's just a cop, Cookie. Not fucking Columbo. He's not going to notice us. And anyways, what we're doing is completely legal, so he can't hassle us."

"I got news for you, Einstein. Cops don't need a reason to hassle citizens."

I am well aware, but it doesn't seem like something to admit to Cookie. The last cop gig I had ended with a golf club to my rental car's taillight. But that guy was a detective. They notice things. This guy isn't a detective. At least, I don't think he is. Honestly, Finch didn't give me much info on him besides the address. *Goddamn it. I bet he's a fucking detective.*

"How the hell do you even get a gig like this? It's a weird goddamn way to make a living, you know?"

I give her the Cliff's Notes version of the story: How I started temping for Finch in his office, then mostly helping Wally Tinderman, Finch's longtime PI. I didn't need a license as long as I worked under Wally. But Wally split after a few years to work with the DA's office, and if I was going to keep working with Finch, I needed to step up and make it official. Wally pretty much rabbied me through the process of getting a license. After that, I became Finch's main guy.

"Does your mom know what you do?"

My head bobbles from side to side as I process my answer. "She knows I work for a lawyer." Not a lie but not really the truth.

"She'd absolutely crack if she knew what we were doing right now."

I give a wide-eyed, silent nod of agreement to the back of her head and then pull up the camera as the mark steps out onto the brick porch of his row house. He taps a pack of smokes, sliding a cigarette up enough for him to mouth it, and then lights it. It's all so goddamn smooth and efficient, I'm guessing it happens at least forty times a day. After a drag, he zips up his olive-green bomber jacket and skips down the stairs, walking toward a beat-up Camaro.

"Fucking cops. They always look like cops even when they're not trying."

"Hey, uh … I'm also recording audio here, Cookie. So, speak with that in mind, eh?"

"*Carajo, mijo.* You shoulda told me that before."

I watch through the blue-tinted eyepiece as the mark starts his Camaro and pulls out. "Can you follow him?"

The Town Car starts with a deep, slow cough. "*Finalemente.* Some action." Cookie blesses herself, adjusts her mirror, click, click, clicks the transmission into D, and we're out.

—

"What do I do when he stops?" Cookie asks.

We're heading north on Fifth Avenue with Sunset Park coming up ahead.

"If we're right on top of him, I could hop out like you dropped me off? Something like that?"

Her posture straightens as his brake lights go red. "Oh! Oh! Oh!" She's chirping now. "Look at that. I predetermined it." The Camaro pulls up to a hydrant in front of a takeout spot called the No. 1 Chinese Restaurant. I know about seven No. 1s. I know of no No. 2s. The mark puts on his hazards, hops out, jogs to the apartment building next to the restaurant and leans against the peeling wood door as he pushes a buzzer. Zooming in, I can see the usual apartment buttons—three brass nipples for each floor—but the mark presses another. A plastic rectangle with white fibrous medical tape above it. I get the camera tight on it and try to hold it still, which I quickly learn I'm not very good at. Maybe someone with the city can freeze-frame and translate the Asian characters scratched into the white tape.

I miss the simple click of my Pentax.

The door buzzes open, and the mark pushes through.

"Your boy's going to get his pole greased." She says it in between teeth sucks.

"What's that?" I mean, I'm pretty sure I know what Cookie's talking about, but a little clarity would be nice.

"That's a massage place, like a whorehouse. Koreans, mostly, some Colombians, too. This part of Sunset Park is lousy with them. I mean, I know you said he hurt his back and all, but that's not a recovery-from-injury type of place. That's a cash-only, happy-ending, don't-tell-your-wife type place."

"How do you know?"

"I've been driving Brooklyn for fifteen years, babycakes. I have eyes. I have ears." She tightens up. "Shit. He's back." The mark exits the building and heads for his car. "He's a bit quick on the draw, eh?"

"That would be record-setting quickness, Cookie. He was barely in there. Maybe he was doing something else."

"Yeah, maybe. Maybe not. We following, or what?"

"Por favor."

We tail him, and within another ten blocks, the cycle repeats two more times. Hazards. Sketchy buzzer. Him inside for two minutes, then him out and back cruising down Fifth Avenue.

We hit Park Slope and push through it, eventually taking a left onto Atlantic and heading down toward the Brooklyn-Queens Expressway. I squint through the dusty glass of the Doray as we pass by and look for Finch. He's in there somewhere. A slouched shadow, rubbing his gut, hunched over a Jameson and ginger and a pile of ones.

"Am I getting on the BQE?" Cookie asks.

"If he is, you are."

"Okay, babycakes, but a heads-up—I'm not leaving Brooklyn."

"Fair enough."

It doesn't look like it's gonna come to that. The mark's Camaro pulls off a few exits later, at Metropolitan Avenue, and we keep up a sleepy tail behind him as he slides through the asphalt quiet of Williamsburg. At Lorimer he makes a U-turn and double-parks in front of the Sons of Verona Social Club. Cookie gives us a clear view, parking us right across the street. We're only about eight blocks from her apartment.

"Members Only" is hand painted with care on the door to the club. Welcoming looking lettering with a fuck-you message.

"What is this place?" I ask.

"It's a social club. One of those goombah private clubs for old Italian folks to drink and play dominoes. Except this one also runs numbers. The biggest on the Northside." The mark gives a nod to the pair of septuagenarians sitting in folding chairs outside the club and then pushes through the door. Cookie gives a squint toward the pair. "I think I know one of the guys at the door." She clicks the car into drive and curves across the double yellow of Metropolitan, pulling in front of the mark's Camaro. After she notches it into park, she leans toward the passenger side window and gives a tight whistle with her fingers. "Hey! Vinnie!"

The smaller of the two ancients looks over and then rocks back and forth for a moment, trying to create some momentum to help him break free of the gravitational pull of the chair. Once up, he shuffles his way toward the Town Car, his worn gray slippers making slow slaps on the sidewalk as he does. At the car, he leans in. "Cooks, my love. How you doing?"

"I'm good, Vinnie. I'm good."

"You playing the numbers this week?"

"Yeah, put me down for my usual set." Cookie pulls a twenty out of her bra and extends it toward Vinnie who immediately holds up his hands in a chivalrous rejection.

"Oh, please. No. I'll send the kid by tomorrow. He'll collect."

"Thanks, Vinnie. Listen ..." Cookie leans closer to him. "Is it me, or did a cop just walk in there?"

Vinnie turns and spits on the pavement and then leans back in for privacy. "The weekly shakedown. Vice gotta get their cut, you know?"

"Ah, right, right, right. And so it goes, and so it goes ..."

"Around and around and around." He leans back and tries to straighten the angle of his body, never quite reaching vertical. "Take care of yourself, Cooks." He gives the top of the Town Car a slap and shuffles back to his chair as the mark exits the club and heads toward his Camaro.

"Looks like your boy's dirty, babycakes."

"Looks that way." The Camaro pulls around us and heads back toward the BQE. "You got the legs to tail him for a little while longer?"

"Sure, baby. Consider me intrigued."

—

He hit two more spots, then went back to Bay Ridge, where he disappeared with a six-pack into his Archie Bunker castle. We're parked and waiting outside. I'm going to give him till midnight and then call it. Cookie's killing time dozing in the front, while I'm staring at his house with the camera in my lap trying to figure out what the play is on this.

What the fuck am I going to do with this footage? All I fucking need is some group of crooked cops pissed off and tracking me down. I dunno. If I erase it or ignore it, I'll piss off Finch. But he wants this level of agita even less than I do. If I just tell him and let him deal with it, he'll probably bury it. He's a logical motherfucker with enough chaos on his plate already, right? Finch won't want this kind of headache. The more I think on it, the clearer it gets. There's no goddamn reason I have to take on this decision when I have management ready and waiting to absorb the burden and then bury it.

That calms me. I take a deep breath and sigh it out. I'll take it to Finch. He'll bury it. And then we'll forget that any of this ever happened.

I feel my pupils shrink as a pair of high beams crests the road ahead and then cuts out moments before their car rolls to a stop in front of the mark's house. Cookie's face winces as she wakes up. "What's going on?" She gives her eyes a rub and sees the car. "Oh, great. More cops."

More cops? How the fuck can she tell?

"Shitty Crown Vic. Tinted windows. The color of the bumper doesn't match the paint job. Clump of antennas on the trunk. Those are some undercover assholes. Also, they dress like *that*." The driver gets out, Rangers jersey hanging baggy on an overpumped frame. The passenger is smaller and more weaselly, Kangol hat on top, baggy jeans sagging below. Cookie guffaws. "Those idiots think they look like citizens." She settles back in and closes her eyes.

I know I said I'm gonna forget about all this, and I know that I really *should* forget about this, but something inside me says to record it, so I do. I watch through the eyepiece, the blue glow shining a little brighter on my face than I'd like as the mark opens his front door. The two costumed undercovers push him back in and shut the door behind him. Nobody looks happy about anything, including me.

CHAPTER EIGHT

I STAY UP MOST of the night sitting on the couch, NY1 flickering on my eyes as I wait for them to cover what happened. Some story. Some report. Something. In between staring down the prerecorded thirty-minute news broadcast they loop between 1:00 a.m. and 4:00 a.m., I rewatch the video again and again and again. I connected the camera to the TV and am using it like a VCR—I now know what that third yellow cable on those RCA cable bundles is for, so there's my growth for the day. Two minutes after Rangers Jersey and Kangol Hat pushed into the mark's house, you can see it—two quick flashes in the front window and then one more. The strobe of something creates a solid rectangle of light around a pulled shade—you can only see it in a few frames for each time, but it's there. And with headphones on and the audio cranked, you can hear them. The pops. Short and tight. *Pop, pop*—pause—then a final one: *pop*. And then Cookie saying, "Oh fuck." Three minutes later, the undercovers exit out the front, skipping down the goddamn stairs without one fucking worry weighing them down.

We waited for them to pull out, and then we split the opposite way, rolling slow and stopping carefully at every light, using each blinker, crossing every goddamn *t*. Cookie wanted me to erase the tape then and there, but I couldn't. I dunno. I gotta tell Finch something, and if I have no tape, it just makes it worse.

Somewhere around 5:00 a.m. I fall asleep on the couch, chin on my chest, hands intertwined on my lap, like an uncle nodding out on Thanksgiving. The sleep is warm and calm, and I don't want to come out of it. But I can hear NY1 news anchor Pat Kiernan's voice sliding in. "Murder-suicide ... Officer Palmer killed his wife and then himself ... was on leave ..." At some point I stop breathing and I wake with a gasp, staring at the same Archie Bunker castle we were parked at last night on the TV. This time yellow police tape is marking the borders of the property, warning folks to stay back. I wish we had stayed back.

Wait. Murder-suicide? They killed the wife, too?

Fuck me.

—

It feels safer to use a pay phone, so I walk to the ones on A across from Tompkins Square Park and start calling Finch around 9:00 a.m. There's no chance of him picking up, but I need to feel like I'm doing something. I get his machine at the office, so I start calling the Doray. After my second call, Mikey the bartender basically tells me to fuck off and call back at three. Finch never gets there before three.

I know that, asshole, but shit is weird right now.

I head to Odessa for some breakfast, but all I'm doing is downing cup after cup of coffee as I repeatedly double-check my pager. It's out on the table next to the creamer. I pick it up, check it, put it down, spin it and then repeat the dance. Underneath the table I can feel my right knee bouncing up and down like a fucking jackhammer. Is this how I handle stress? *Jesus Christ.* I need to learn how to keep things cooler than this.

I grab a butter-stained *Daily News* from an empty table next to me and start flipping through it, hoping to clear my head, but really, I know what I'm doing. I'm looking for stories. Something about the cop and his wife. Anything. But there's nothing. It must have happened too late for them to cover it. Who found the bodies? A neighbor? A cop? A kid? *Fuck.* I hope there were no kids. My pager buzzes against the tabletop, and I snatch it up immediately to read the numbers. It's just Cookie. She's gonna want answers, and I got nothing yet, but—fuck me—I also have nothing else to do, so I drop a five on the table and head back outside to call her from the pay phones.

I fill her in, but the conversation is really just two nervous people being nervous to each other on the phone, resulting in not much being said. She thinks we should keep our distance from each other till I figure shit out, which very much feels like me being out on my own, but I know what she's doing. It's what I've been doing calling Finch over and over. She needs to feel as if she's doing *something*, as if she's controlling some aspect of this very out-of-control feeling we're both swirling in. I get it. I tell her I'll let her know what the next move is after I get in touch with Finch.

—

I get to the Doray around 1:30 p.m. and remind myself not to get too drunk while I wait for Finch to show. I know he probably won't get here till 3:00 p.m., but I have nothing to do but worry, so why not do it in a dark bar. It feels safer. I had spent the rest of the morning driving myself insane trying to figure out how to make a VHS tape copy of the video from the Hi8 tape in the camera. It took a call to Pete for guidance, but I was finally able to figure it out.

By my second beer, my head starts to float, and I realize I haven't eaten anything since dinner last night. I flag Mikey down and buy a few twenty-five-cent packs of Wise chips from him and try not to choke from the dust that flies off them when they hit the bar top. Mikey sees that I'm annoyed at something, and I swear to God, he looks primed to ram the bags down my fucking throat if I say anything, so I take the hint and nod politely. I see Finch shuffling down Atlantic Avenue outside, so I scoop up my cash, cram the chips in my pocket and head out to meet him, Mikey's eyes on me the entire time.

On the sidewalk I tell Finch I'll only talk in the office. He mumbles something about it being a goddamn mess, but I'm already guiding his bony, curved spine back down Atlantic and away from the Doray. I can see him lick his lips thinking about that Jameson and ginger he was so close to getting.

Fuck you, Finch. You got me into this. Now you have to get me out. Happy hour can wait.

—

"Jesus Christ, are you living here?" I can see the cot sticking out from behind a row of filing cabinets. And Finch was right. The place is a fucking mess.

"Back off, Nico. Seriously. Anyways, it's only temporary." He collapses into his pillow covered desk chair, and for a minute, I'm positive it's gonna flip him backward and send him flying out the window and onto Atlantic Avenue, but somehow it holds. He leans forward and starts to unroll a fresh pack of Rolaids. "Let me see this goddamn tape."

I eject the porn out of the TV/VCR combo that sits on top of the short filing cabinet next to his desk, and I don't even feel the urge to make a joke about it. Shit is dark, man. No time for wit. I move past it, put in the tape, press Play and talk him through the cash stops the mark makes and tell him about the conversation with the old-timer at the Sons of Verona. Then back to Bay Ridge. Rangers Jersey and Kangol Hat. Pop, pop, pause, pop. "Oh fuck." And them skipping lightheartedly down the stoop.

Finch keeps staring at the black TV screen after I stop the tape, pondering everything he just saw. "Play it again."

I do and we watch it all, but Finch's face looks none the wiser because of it. I want to see an "aha," you know? Some fucking epiphany moment that leads to some astute and calm words that will resolve everything. Instead, he pops two more Rolaids and speaks through them as he chews. "This is a very fucked-up situation."

I'm not quite getting why he's not immediately saying let's erase it and forget we were ever there, so I offer that up as a choice.

He says it would be foolish. "There's paperwork. We were contracted. The city hired us to be there."

"Do you think somebody knew that was going to happen? That they wanted us to see it?"

"No, that's— No. But as *farkakta* as city agencies are, eventually that address and that name are going to pop up in somebody's file, and it's going to say you were there on that night, at that time, blah, blah, blah."

"Me?"

"No, not literally *you*. I mean us. The firm." He takes a deep breath. "But if they asked me, sure, I'd say it was you."

"Thanks, pal."

He gives a sarcastic nod of "you're welcome" and turns toward the window facing Atlantic, mumbling a series of never-ending "fucks" under his breath. Finally, he turns around.

"I think we have to come clean with it," he says. "Give it to someone."

"Who?"

"I know someone who was a part of the Mollen Commission. I think that's the safest place to start."

"What's the Mollen Commission?"

"Big anti-NYPD corruption thing under Dinkins that Giuliani turned into a symbolic circle jerk once he took office. After he came in, he created his own committee 'cause he didn't like the first one's report and then ended up ignoring everything both committees recommended. That guy loves his fucking cops." He gets lost for a moment, then resets. "Giving it to someone that was part of the Mollen Commission feels safer than going to a cop, even Internal Affairs. IAB is hard to trust. Those fuckers will burn you and turn on you to get what they need ..." He takes another moment to reassure himself. "Yeah, we'll go to this guy. To my guy. That way we can create some distance between us and the tape, but it'll cover our asses. When they ask us, we can say we officially submitted it to someone. If we sit on it, it's worse. Much worse."

"I gotta say, Finch, I was sorta hoping you'd say, 'Let's erase it and move on with our lives.' "

"Yeah. I was sorta hoping you had the brains to do that before you brought it in to me, but here we fucking are."

—

I know I should call Cookie and give her an update, but I just can't deal. What do I say? We're going to an unnamed friend of Finch with the tape? Trying to create some distance between us and it, whatever the hell that means? The more I think about it, the more I spiral, so I need to stop thinking, or I need to forget. Put my brain onto something else, something trivial. Obsessing over a little steel ball while getting lit generally brings a smile, so pinball and beer it'll have to be.

I head to 7B right from Finch's and make it before the happy-hour rush. It's always sleepy between three and five, so they typically load the pinball machines and the jukebox with free credits to keep folks hanging out till the crowds roll in. I pick fifteen songs. I order a pint. I play pinball. Wash, rinse, repeat. By evening rush, I'm buzzing, the bartender is sick of my songs and I'm only occasionally thinking about the tape.

Goddamn it. Now I'm thinking about the tape again.

I give a nod to the bartender to set me up with another—the sort of Randy Johnson–looking one, not that Keanu-looking motherfucker; he doesn't get my tips anymore—and then I see Susie walk in. Ninety minutes later and we're arm in arm heading west on Seventh Street toward her place, and who should walk past us but Maggie, *her* arm in some other guy's arm as they head toward 7B. As we pass it's like one of those Coen brothers shots where two cars drive past each other, and the drivers are looking *right* at each other, and they keep cutting between shots of the two as they pass. It feels like that, except it's Maggie and me, and she's giving me this sarcastic "nice job" look about Susie, like she's outa my league or something, which I'm well aware of, but there's knowing and there's telling, and I prefer the former—ideally packaged as an internal dialogue that I can ignore or beat down with booze.

The next morning, I wake up to Susie's loft bed shaking and see her small hand doing the shaking. She's down below and dressed for work. I get it. This is the heave-ho.

"I gotta go?" I ask.

"You gotta go."

I slide off and dress as fast as I can, Susie watching me, keys in her hand.

"You look nice." She does. I've never seen her in work type clothes, just in attracting-people-in-bars-type clothes. She looks good in both, but I'm realizing I kinda like the getting-shit-done look more.

"Oh. Thanks." The voice is different. This is work Susie, not night-time Susie. This one seems easier to piss off. I give a nod and grab my pea coat, deciding to put it on as I make my quick exit.

Outside, it's cheek kisses and awkward waves. She walks this way, and I walk that way, which is honestly the wrong way; I just went that way because she went the way I wanted to go. Walking up Second, I see

B&H Dairy up ahead and try to remember if I ate anything yesterday. I didn't. Maybe some popcorn in between pints and those chips from the Doray, but that's it. At B&H, I squeeze in and slide onto a counter stool, order some French toast and coffee, giving the necessary smiles as the guy behind the counter calls milk "cow juice" and silverware "tools," just like he always does. Down below, I feel a buzzing in my right front pocket.

It's Finch. The food comes and I start to shove the French toast in my mouth when my pager buzzes again, but this time Finch's number has a "911" at the end. I shove a few more bites in, pay my tab and head out to Second Avenue, making a beeline for the first pay phone I see, digging change out of my pocket as I do. I give the receiver a wipe on my pea coat and call him, but the phone just rings and rings and rings. At the tenth ring, I hang up and then—*buzz*. The pager. Again. I pull it out of my pocket—Finch's number and three "911s" in a row. I call again. Nothing. No answer, no answering machine even picking up. *What the fuck?* Then I think ... *What if he can't answer the phone? What if he had that fucking stroke that's been chasing him for years, and he's lying on the ground or something? He hasn't looked good for a while. I mean, honestly, I don't think he's ever looked good, but lately? Not so good.* I sprint to the Astor Place subway stop and push through the crowds heading to their jobs, their classes, their appointments. At the platform, I squeeze through a murder of NYU kids, a sea of bright eyes ready to start their day, just as the doors close and then grab a pole as the train lurches forward.

CHAPTER NINE

I DON'T KNOW HOW long I've been staring at Finch. One minute? Five minutes? Ten? I dunno. He's hunched over his desk, hands sprawled out on either side, one of them holding a .38. Even with the gun in his hand, I assumed he was passed out, assumed he was sleeping, assumed anything besides this. Then I saw the splatter on his TV. The chunky white and red smeared across the dead black glass.

This made no sense.

He looks like he's been dead for at least a few hours. The blood on the TV seems a bit dried, the brain a bit crusty, but really, I have no fucking idea. I snap out of my frozen panic and then turn, taking a fast step toward the door, and stop. *What am I doing? Running? Where the fuck am I going? What am I running from? Think. Calm down and think. He paged you. 911. He wanted to talk to you. But then he didn't pick up. Why didn't he pick up?*

Because he was already dead.

He didn't kill himself. There's no way he killed himself.

Yeah, and he also didn't page you. Somebody else did. Somebody did both.

Fuck. Fuck, fuck, fuck.

Okay, okay ... but why? Why did they page me? Why the 911?

They wanted you here. Wanted you to see this. Wanted you to see ... Shit. *The tape. Where's the tape?*

I grab a pencil and use it to press Eject on the VCR, but there's nothing there. I look around, but the closest thing to the tape I find is the worn, empty oversized box for the porno I took out before I showed the surveillance copy to Finch.

Fuck.

Fuck, fuck, fuck and fuck again.

I need help. I need advice.

Wally Tinderman. Call Wally. It swirls in my head like a siren.

So I do. I call Wally.

—

When I worked under Wally, he was constantly spouting advice. It was as if he knew early on that he was leaving, and he was always prepping for me to step up, to take over. I never thought I would, never thought I was ready to commit to something like a career. Not yet, anyways. That seemed like a post-thirty-year-old-type thing. Getting a PI license seemed like such a specific life choice, and I wasn't ready for life choices. For commitments. But I did it. It was a door that opened in front of me, a door I stared at for a long, long time. And truth be told, it's a door that Wally eventually had to push me through. I wouldn't be here if he didn't give me that shove.

And of all the advice he ever gave me, from how to tail a mark, to what to say if you got made, to where to piss in the city during a stakeout, there is one key bit of advice screaming in my head right now: "Do not ever willingly talk to the police without counsel present." Never. Not once. Doesn't matter if you're guilty or innocent, doesn't matter if you're a witness or a victim. Don't ever do it.

But I'm doing it. And I can hear Wally's voice in my head telling me not to. Honestly, I wish I could hear Wally's actual voice here in Finch's office, but he said it would take a while for him to get here.

He told me not to wait to call the cops, so I called them, hoping he'd show up before they did, but now I'm staring at two uniforms and wondering, How do you *not* talk to the cops when you're the one that called in the body?

The answer is you don't. You talk. I'm not getting into anything about the tape, or the mark and his wife, or Rangers Jersey and Kangol Hat and their efficient trigger fingers, either. I tell them Finch paged me, what our relationship is and that this is definitely not a suicide. These two don't press. They're twenty-in-and-out types. They're not here to make a case; they're here to make a pension and take it to Aqueduct Racetrack. Or maybe just the OTB. Anyways, afterward they sit me down in the hallway and tell me to wait, so I wait.

It doesn't take long after that for Wally to show. I can hear his dramatic exhale at the bottom of the stairs. It's the kind of exhale you make when you're back someplace you don't want to be, about to climb stairs you don't want to climb, about to see things you don't want to see. He walks up at a sleepy pace and stops to rest at least once. When he gets to the landing below me, I can see why.

"Yeah, I know. I got fat." He starts taking deliberate steps up the last flight toward me with his left hand repeatedly pulling on the handrail, doing what it can against gravity. It's a little shocking. He's not quite Orson-Welles-in-*Touch-of-Evil* fat, but he's getting there.

"It's not like you were ever skinny, Wally."

"We can't all be thirty years old with a thirty-inch waist."

"Thirty-two-inch waist. And I'm twenty-nine."

He stops at the step just before me and ponders my correction. "That's somehow worse." After a beat, he smiles and brings me in for a quick, one-slap-on-the-back hug and then holds me out at arm's length. "Not for nothing, but it's not my fault."

"What isn't?"

"It's this goddamn prednisone they got me on for my arthritis. Made me blow up like a fucking whale."

"Oh, well ... you wear it well, so there's that." It's true. Wally's always seemed big, now he is big.

"Yeah, tell that to my fucking knees." He gives a sad smile as his mind goes somewhere else. "Where's the old man?" He always called Finch the old man, even though he and Finch were both in their late fifties.

Were.

I give a nod toward the office. "I don't think they'll let you in till Homicide gets here."

"You stay. I'll go take a look, et cetera, et cetera, et cetera."

I sit back down as he shuffles past me, fully expecting him to get turned around, but I see him flash an ID and mumble something about the mayor's office, and just like that he's in.

I'm staring down the closed door, thinking how bizarre it is that I'm not allowed in that space anymore without permission, wondering what the hell kind of ID Wally flashed to that uniform to get him to open the door as quickly and as wide as Wally needed to get his body through, when the smoke hits my nose. Looking down to the next landing, I see the cigarette and the short man sucking it. His shaved-bald head is down, his eyes on the stairs hitting each one like he's in the middle of a workout, the tip of the smoke glowing orange as he climbs. He's got a notebook in his hand, and I figure he's a tabloid scribbler, until the head rises, and I see the NYPD shield hanging around his neck.

He walks a few steps past me, stops and offers me a smoke. "You want one?" He's Korean, somewhere in his forties, and the Queens accent hangs on him like syrup. "Full disclosure, it's menthol. I know some folks got hang-ups about actual flavor, so I'm giving you the heads-up."

"Uh, no. No, thanks."

"Got a question for you." He speaks to me as if we already know each other. I nod, waiting, anticipating something Finch related. "When is a drag not a drag?" He tilts his head and smiles, getting ready to answer his own question. "When it's a Kool." He slows on the *oo* of *Kool*, stretching it out, and I get a flash memory of an old commercial for *Smokey Robinson's Greatest Hits*. The one where the skinny white dude is getting in the car, retelling how his dad would tell him to "Turn that music down!" and he'd respond, "But Dad, it's Smokeeeeey," stretching out the *eee* like he was the Fonz. The musical tone of it reminds me of how this guy stretches out Kool, but I don't say anything about it.

"I gave them that," he says. "The slogan. Sent them a letter and every-thing. Best goddamn slogan for the best goddamn smokes in the world, but they ignored it. Stuck with 'Come up to Kool,' whatever the hell that means. I guess it's better than 'Alive with pleasure,' am I right?"

He brings his smoke back to his lips and takes two long drags that turn the entire cigarette to ash in seconds, like some zoot-suit-wearing cartoon wolf up to no good. He stubs the butt on the handrail, tucks the filter in his right suit pocket and begins to take a few sliding steps backward, looking at me the entire time. "You the employee that called this in?"

"Yeah."

"Lemme take a look, then I'm gonna come chat, okay?" There's a melody to how he says it, how he moves his arms.

"Yeah."

He gives me a nod and turns on his heel with a dancer's pivot. He seems goddamn giddy to be here, or maybe he just really loves his job. Either way, I need to figure out how deep into the truth I'm willing to wade, and if his happiness is linked to his skill, the wrong choices could make things sticky fast.

I stare at the frosted glass on the door intently after it closes behind him, willing it to open, begging it to go wide and let Wally out before Woodside's Fred Astaire comes back at me with his pivots and his questions.

Normally, I don't believe in that shit, but goddamn it if it doesn't work.

—

Wally and I head to one of those tiny coffee shops for factory workers off Atlantic Avenue. The type that opens at 5:00 a.m. and closes at 2:00 p.m. The room's narrow and I feel bad for him as he uses his right hand to hold in his gut so it doesn't drag against the backs of the blue collars eating their lunch. We settle at the far end, and Wally leans in close while eying the nearest customer. The message is clear: do not listen to this conversation. He gets the picture, downs the cold puddle of coffee in his cup and heads back to his hourly. Satisfied, Wally realigns his focus to me. "Tell me everything."

I bring him up to speed. From the mark right up to the graceful detective.

"Yeah, that's Zach Hong. He's good. Smart. Don't try anything fancy with him; don't blur the truth. Just cut it clean."

I give a nod and slide my cup two inches toward the server, and she quickly tops it off. When she motions toward Wally, he covers his cup like she's offering him poison, and from the look on her face, there's a good chance she is. He adjusts himself on the stool and finishes his thoughts with me. "Listen ... *I* worked for the Mollen Commission. After I left Finch, I went from the DA's office to the Mollen Commission. But he didn't call me. He didn't page me. Nothing."

"Maybe he knows someone else who was on the commission?"

Wally takes a thick, wet breath before continuing. "Finch has a better chance of knowing two people being investigated by the Mollen Commission than he does of knowing two people working for it. No, he must have meant me, but ... yeah. He didn't reach out. Not a peep. I wish he had. I wish he had."

I have no reason to think Wally's lying, but everything about the past twenty-four hours has me thinking I need to circle my wagons and hit Reset on who I trust. Everything has to be earned at this point.

"Who'd he call, then?"

Wally drops three bucks on the counter and does his best to stand up. "The wrong guy."

—

I head back to Finch's and see Detective Hong smoking outside while he talks to a female uniform. She's smiling as he holds his left hand in the air, palm out, and his right hand on his stomach as he throws down a few merengue moves. "You should come with me sometime."

"Eh, I can't dance like that," she says. "Not without a few drinks in me."

"So, we bring a flask to class. We keep the lubrication portable." He sees me, gives a wink to the uniform, and then waves for me to come over. "Let's walk and talk."

We start down Atlantic toward the river. After a few steps, he opens his notebook and reads a scribble. "So, Nicholas Kelly." He looks up at me. "Folks call you Nick, Nicholas, Nicky ... ?"

"Nico."

"Nico. Got it. I totally whiffed that one, huh?" He asks for forgiveness with his smile. It's a look he's a little too good at, a look I can tell a lot of people have seen, both socially and professionally. "So, tell me, Nico. What do you got against me?"

"Um, nothing?"

"So, why complicate things? Why mess up this perfectly good suicide?"

"That perfectly good suicide was my boss. My friend."

Friend? Really? I dunno if Finch was my friend, but when you have a chance to make a cop feel bad, you take it.

"I'm sorry, I'm sorry. It's just ... it looks very cut and dry to me." He stops walking. "Tell me why it's not."

"Before I do, I just ... Did Wally tell you anything?" A negative head-shake and a drag on a shrinking Kool from Detective Hong. "Well, this thing ... it involves a couple of cops doing some very bad things to another cop. Another cop and his wife. And I need to know that what I tell you stays with you and that things are gonna be okay for me and my associate."

His entire face changes. He flicks the butt of his smoke to the curb, and the dancing charmer disappears. "If you're referring to what happened a couple of days ago in Bay Ridge, and you're telling me that's actually a cop-shoot-cop type of scenario, you better fucking start talking, and now."

CHAPTER TEN

"**I**'M GUESSING YOUR PLACE doesn't always look like this."

My apartment has been tossed. Drawers open, couch cushions on the floor. The place is a fucking mess. "No."

I filled in Detective Hong back in Brooklyn, and when he couldn't find any sign of the tape in Finch's office, he offered to give me a lift to my place so I could give him the original. I look over toward the TV and its sad, dangling RCA cables with nothing to connect to.

"Fuck," I say.

"What?"

"The video camera is gone. I had it connected to the TV."

"Where's the tape?"

"It was in the camera." I notice that they also took the copy of *Ran* that I rented from Kim's Video a few days ago. I've rented and rerented that film three times and have yet to see it. I guess they must have assumed I also recorded something onto that? Another copy, maybe? *Crap.* That's like eighty bucks on top of everything else.

Hong rubs the stubble on the back of his head and exhales. He looks at me and gives a long stare. "When were you here last?"

It takes me a minute to remember. I'm about to say this morning, but then I realize I haven't actually been here since I left to drink coffee at

Odessa yesterday morning. The morning after the night I followed the mark.

Jesus, time feels fucked up right now.

"Yesterday morning," I say.

"You weren't here last night?"

"No."

"Girlfriend?"

"Girl, yes. Friend, maybe."

"Is that more you or her?"

"It's probably mutual."

"It's *probably* mutual? Don't you talk? Nobody talks anymore."

"Can we get back to the tape?"

"I'm going to need her info to confirm your whereabouts. And then I need you to guide me through the times of your boss's pages and when and where you made the calls from this a.m."

"You're checking to see if I'm lying?"

"Ah, yeah, ya think?"

"Do you actually think I could kill Finch?"

"First off, I'm still leaning toward suicide until evidence points in another direction. Secondly, I don't know you at all, so I don't really know what you're capable of. But I know that you have a very complicated story that needs corroborating. And no offense, but you telling me something? That's just you telling me something. That's all it is. Once I get to check my boxes, it has more weight. So, how about you give me what I need so I can check my boxes, okay?"

I give him all the info: Susie, the pay phone outside of B&H, what I ordered, how much I ate, what time I think I jumped on the train at Astor Place. After he writes it all down, he starts rubbing the back of his head again, the shaved stubble giving off an audible sandpaper scruff.

"Yeah, yeah ... Okay, okay." He gives a few quiet nods as a plan seems to congeal. "I'm gonna leave. Gonna go do my job. You're gonna call this in like a regular break-in, all right? Don't offer up anything about your dead boss or me unless they ask you a question so direct that you can't squirm out of it. Don't lie. But don't go out of your way to tell the truth."

"Is that smart?"

"It's both dumb and smart, but it's what you're gonna do."

"What about Rangers Jersey and Kangol Hat? Shouldn't Internal Affairs or whatever get involved?"

"Not without the tape. Maybe later after some questions get answered and some boxes get checked."

"That's probably why they took it. So no one would believe me."

"*If* they took it, yeah, that's probably one of the reasons. The other is they probably don't like any evidence of them killing a cop and his wife on tape, but I'm sure your veracity and honor is foremost in their thoughts." He turns to split and then pivots back toward me with that same goddamn grace he showed in the hallway outside Finch's. "Listen, if you got any weed in here, anything worse, anything you don't want the cops to find, get rid of it before you call it in, all right?" I give a nod, and he takes another look around at the destruction. "You got anywhere else you can stay? Someplace safe? If there's even a chance that this is going down the way you think it is, I don't like that they know where you live."

Shit. I didn't even think about that.

—

It's two days later, and I'm back in Williamsburg, sitting at Kellogg's Diner with Cookie. She's let me stay on her couch for the past two nights, but it's obviously time for me to find some other accommodations. Frankie Balls seems to have an option, so we're drinking bad coffee while we wait on him. She's made it repeatedly clear that she has no intention of sticking her neck out with mine about the existence of the tape. Even if she did talk to the cops, I don't think it would make a difference. Her word plus my word really just adds up to words. Nobody is going to care without that tape showing up; Hong's made that plain. Taking all that into account, I get why Cookie wants me out of her place—right now there's nothing besides her voice on the tape to connect her to all this, and there's no reason for us to be close enough that someone makes that connect.

Wait. That's not entirely true.

"You used my name. You called me Cookie."

I try to downplay it. "Yeah, but no one is going to be able to ID you from that. It's not on your license. It's not even your real name."

"But it's what I'm known by. Anybody looking for a Williamsburg-based car service driver who answers to Cookie is gonna eventually find me."

Shit. It's true. It wouldn't take much snooping. Maybe half a day of calling around. "You should warn your dispatchers to give you a heads-up if folks come calling."

"Yeah, I'm not an idiot. I did that already. I'm more worried about Rangers Jersey sliding a twenty to another driver who's jealous of my fares. That's gonna be how I get flipped."

"I didn't realize livery driving was that cutthroat."

"Don't be so goddamn patronizing, Nico. If I wanted to feel like shit about my life, I'd call your mother."

That makes two of us. "Sorry."

Frankie arrives and leans on the table, spilling our coffees as he slides in next to Cookie. He's ready with some napkins the moment it happens and immediately starts to dab up the caffeinated water as he smiles. It's like this is the predictable side effect of him sitting down at *any* table and he's always got the goddamn napkins on hand. He gets one look at Cookie's face, one look at mine, and takes an immediate read of the room.

"Enough with the pissy frowns, guys. C'mon." We both stay silent, but he's not having it. "So, you don't like living together. You get on each other's nerves. So what?" An exhale from Cookie. "You've both been on your own for too long, you know that? You forgot what living with family is like."

Cookie takes a sip of what's left of her coffee. "There's other stuff going on, Frankie."

"Yeah, I'm aware, Cooks. Even more reason to suck it up and have each other's back, right?"

Some shoulder movement from both of us and the beginnings of hesitant nods as the slow unraveling of our stubbornness begins.

"*Right?*" Frankie repeats.

"Right," we both say, eager to move on.

We get into it quickly, this meeting to discuss "the business"—that's what we've started using as code for Finch and the tape; Frankie started it and it sounded both ridiculous and perfect at the same time. Cookie and I kept trying to call it something different, but Frankie would step in and calmly and gruffly reaffirm that, no, it was to be called "the business" and nothing else. He seemed to enjoy saying it, so we just let it happen. It's good to keep Frankie and his fists happy and on your side of a battle. Disagreeing on semantics doesn't seem like a good enough reason to risk losing that, so "the business" it is.

"So, old business first." I see Cookie give a small eye roll as Frankie says it. "The good news is, I found Rangers Jersey and Kangol Hat."

I lean forward. "You did? Where?"

"That's folded into the flip side—the bad news." He lets that sit for a minute and then continues. "They're at the Seven Five."

A long exhale from Cookie, a dour face from Frankie and total confusion from me. "And that's bad?"

Cookie is staring down at the table. "It's the opposite of good, so yeah. It's bad."

"I don't understand. What does it matter what precinct they're from?" I lower my voice to a whisper for the next part. "I mean, they killed two people. Three if we count Finch. Did we expect them to be saints? No."

I can see Frankie ponder his response for a moment before he answers. "It's about the culture of the place, right? At some other precinct, they're two bad apples. At the Seven Five, they're two of—I dunno—a shit ton of bad apples. A fucking truckload of bad apples."

"So?" I say.

Cookie takes over. "So, corrupt protects corrupt. Rot protects rot. With them at the Seven Five, they've got dozens of dirty brothers in blue who'll have their backs. We start sniffing around, we ask the wrong person, things can get bad for us, and quick."

"Okay, okay. I get it. How'd you find them?"

Frankie very vaguely says he has some acquaintances who are cops who have a knowledge of both sides of the badge. "I'd prefer to not get into exactly what that means."

Cookie and I both look at him with a little comic disbelief. "I think it's pretty clear what that means," I say.

"Yeah, that's super obvious, Frankie," Cookie says.

Frankie looks disappointed, and I'm guessing that somewhere in his head he makes a note to be vaguer next time. Honestly, he's liking the intrigue of this situation a little too much. To him there's a game element to it all, and that's disconcerting to me.

He shakes off our comments and picks up where he left off, telling us that Rangers Jersey and Kangol Hat are an infamous pair with a predictable and repetitive wardrobe. Once Frankie found out they were in the Seven Five, he decided to stop asking questions and stop pushing buttons until we talked. He never got their actual names, but he knows they're at that precinct. As Cookie said, snooping there will make things hot, and quickly. But knowing they're in the Seven Five should be enough for Wally to get started, to start squeezing some stones.

But first there's the matter of this new crash pad Frankie has lined up for me. He smiles wide and rubs his hands together. "You're gonna fucking love this."

—

We're taking the J train as it clicks and clacks over the Williamsburg Bridge because Frankie refuses to drive his vans into Manhattan. He says it's mostly for safety—"Gotta protect my fleet and all"—but he also says he doesn't want even the possibility of another dollar van service thinking he's moving in on their territory. After a pause he tells me a story. Three years ago, a Bushwick crew tried to move in on his Williamsburg routes. He gives me a wink as he says, "Being unregulated is both good and bad, you know?" The good? No official organization or city agency to complain to when your tires are slashed and your driver's fingers are broken. "Just to be clear, that's me doing that to them, not them to me."

"Yeah, Frankie, I figured." *Jesus.* "What's the bad?"

He thinks for a long moment. "I guess the bad is if you're them and not me. The bad is if you underestimate me. So, for me it's good and good. And for them it's bad and bad." He continues, explaining how the bruising and breaking went both ways for a while between the crews, but

Frankie decided to end it with a timed strike. A heavy beatdown on each of their drivers and each of their vans, all at exactly the same time.

He finishes the story as we head underground and eventually our train pulls into Delancey. As we both exit the car, I realize that somewhere after juvie—shit, maybe *in* juvie, I don't know, but somewhere along the way, Frankie Balls and Hunter/Killer fused. Yeah, Frankie is still Frankie, but there's some serious darkness under the surface now. Frankie became an adult; he developed, got stronger; and he never lost awareness of his own natural ability to inflict harm, to create mayhem. And the joy he gets out of inflicting it seems doubled now.

As we climb the stairs from the subway up to Essex Street, I look at him and realize that this adult Frankie has probably gone far beyond the occasional ethical beatdown of racists and their unfortunate skulls. This Frankie no longer seems to need a righteous stance to justify his violent acts. It's his innate ability to dominate that now provides justification for the action. If you have the power, use it. Frankie has it and he does. The trick on my end is to keep him from wielding it on me.

—

"I love that smell!" Frankie's doing his best Frank Booth as he snorts deep breath after deep breath through his nose. We're on Essex, just south of Grand, walking past Guss' Pickles. It closed hours ago, but the entire block still has the zing of vinegar. "I dunno. It's like Jewish *Bibaporru*, or something," Frankie says. *Bibaporru* was what my mom used to call VapoRub, aka the Latin cure-all. My nose opens, and as the tiniest burn of vinegar hits me, I immediately go from hating it to kinda loving it. I don't like pickles, but he's right. That smell is intoxicating, almost spa-like. "It kinda lifts you up, right?" Frankie holds his hands up by his chest, kind of circling them, highlighting his vinegar-infused increase in airflow.

By the time we get to Hester, the sweet smell of burning paper and incense starts to smother the bright vinegar. A few doors down from the corner, a Chinese family stands around one of those oil-drum-style trash cans, dropping incense-laden joss paper into the fire burning within, watching as the embers float up and join the soot-heavy Lower East Side air space. All around us, factories smoke, box trucks cough, outlawed apartment incinerators churn and the charred remains of ornamental money burn, all of it now broken down into floating black particles lighter than air and searching for lungs to live in. "Ghost money," Frankie says. "For their ancestors in the afterlife." I already know that, but I'm surprised Frankie does, and I immediately feel like an ass for thinking Frankie shouldn't know about other cultures.

The apartment building is about halfway down the block, smack dab between Hester and Canal and right across from Seward Park. Frankie explained his connection to the place, but it was convoluted at best. From what I can gather, it's a sublet that's being subletted from the subletter. The person Frankie knows is the second subletter. He's some sound recordist or audio anthropologist who's currently walking around Cuba recording indigenous folk songs.

"How do you know this guy?" I ask.

"How do I know anybody? He got in my van, and we talked."

Frankie says the Cuba opportunity opened up at the last minute and this guy had to leave fast. He was desperate to find someone to take care of the plants in the apartment. "There are lots." He doesn't need cash, doesn't need rent. He just needs to know that the plants will be watered and cared for by somebody responsible. "And that's gonna be you."

Frankie opens the door to the vestibule and then puts the keys into the inner door's lock. He pauses for a moment, and I feel a catch coming. The second catch. "Here's the deal." Another breath. "This building has rats. Lots of rats. But they all pretty much stay on the first floor with all the trash cans under the stairwell. So, when you walk in, make lots of noise. Rattle the keys; rattle the doors. Get 'em to hunker deep down inside those trash cans. Out of sight, out of mind, right?"

He rattles the door repeatedly and then opens it loudly. I can hear the rats scurry and hide, and I swear to fucking God, one of those black Rubbermaid trash cans under the stairwell is rocking like some invisible hand is moving it, but I don't say anything. Frankie feels like he's doing me a major solid here, and I want him to know I appreciate it, so I eat my defensive sarcasm and smile as if I'm swallowing down heartburn, and we walk up to the second floor, the sea of rats underneath the stairwell hungry and plotting.

CHAPTER ELEVEN

"I T'S FUNKY, RIGHT?" FRANKIE's smiling as he shows me around the plant-filled apartment. There's a definite island thing happening here. Lots of palms, lots of ferns, and the color scheme of the walls is very red, gold and green. I feel like Frankie may have had some plans for himself and this place that my needs have interrupted, but he doesn't say. And it is funky but also maybe a little structurally unsound. It's actually two railroad apartments side by side, but the common wall between the two bedrooms has been knocked down. There are still some two-by-fours up, but all the plaster, all the insulation—it's all been hammered away, making the two railroads one giant U-shaped apartment.

"Frankie, I'm kinda positive that this middle wall is a load-bearing wall for the rest of the building."

"Is it?" He starts walking around, hitting walls, checking sturdiness. "Seems all right to me."

"There are four floors above us. How can this be safe in any way?"

"I dunno. It's been like this for five years. You're only here for a month or so, right? You really think it's all gonna come crashing down next week? Two weeks from now? C'mon. It's not happening."

"This is a rental, right? How'd he convince the landlord to let him do this?"

Frankie's face scrunches into confusion. "Well, I'm pretty sure he didn't ask."

He gives me the 101 on the plants, reading off a crisp, water-stained piece of loose leaf with instructions for each—nothing too complex, just which gets how much water, how frequently, et cetera. I figure one to two months of me doing my best should be good enough to keep them from dying. Frankie finally hands me the keys and then splits to head back to Brooklyn as I settle in.

It's your standard old-school railroad tenement, with the one major exception being the aforementioned fact that it's actually two apartments illegally turned into one. All the plumbing is in the kitchen, and it's the bare minimum. The tub and the toilet are in a narrow bathroom next to the stove. The only sink in the entire place is the one in the kitchen, hence the subletter's toothbrush, toothpaste and dirty razor sitting in a rusty tin cup next to a moldy sponge and a mostly empty bottle of Dawn. The tiny eating area is a homemade butcher block table that's been lacquered so many times it's long forgotten its own texture. Somewhere deep below that thick amber, the personality of the wood is frozen in a medically induced coma. On the center of that smooth and permanently shiny table is an empty beer bottle with a single giant yellow daisy in it. I can't imagine this was left for me, or for Frankie for that matter, but it's kinda quietly lovely all the same, and I'm happy it's here.

I want to make some calls: Detective Hong. Wally. But I won't make them from the phone in the apartment. I'm not telling anyone where I'm crashing, and I don't want any phone numbers beyond pay-phone numbers connected to me for the foreseeable future. I grab the keys, and it takes me more than a few moments to figure out the Fox police lock on the apartment door. It's one of those industrial locks with a key right in the center of the door. It extends two steel bars into slots on either side of the doorjamb when you twist the key. I've only seen these things in movies, and I'd be lying if I said I didn't get a kick out of this being my lock. I feel less cool after it takes me more than five minutes to figure it out, but still.

Downstairs, the fluorescent bulb of the entryway buzzes as the rats hum in excited anticipation of tonight's leftovers.

—

I grab a quarter fried chicken and French fries from the Chinese take-out place around the corner and eat them at the tiny standing counter at the window that faces Grand. It's cheaper than it is good, but it's hard to complain about fried chicken, especially when you're starving. The heat from the food has warped and melted the top of the Styrofoam container, and there's no way that those chemicals are not now within me. It's depressing how quickly I move on from that thought and eat more chemically soaked fries.

One more bite and I squeeze the still-warm and deformed Styrofoam into the trash and head across the street to the pay phone to start my calls, just as the streetlights ignite. I'll call Wally first, then Detective Hong.

I get Wally's voicemail, and I keep it as vague as his job title sounds on his machine. Special advisor to the mayor sounds like it could apply to anything, and I'm guessing that's the way Wally likes it. I don't mention the Seven Five or my new digs. I just tell him to page me, and we'll catch up.

Detective Hong answers on the first ring. Honestly, it seems like it was before the first ring.

"Hong."

"Hey, it's Nico. Nico Kelly."

"Finch's PI."

"Yeah."

"How come we never talked about that?"

"About what?"

"About you being a PI. You seem a little young for the burned-out hack-investigator route. Why mess around in the minor leagues like that? Why don't you go pro and become a cop? You ever think about that?"

"I've thought about it, sure."

"So, what? Why not pursue it?"

"Well, there's that whole deeply-rooted-corruption thing permeating your organization. I see that at as a negative."

"There's a great pension, though."

"Can we talk about Finch, now?"

"You mean my suicide."

"It's not a suicide."

"Except, it's really, really looking like it is. Like, so much so that I'm about to submit it as such."

"How?"

"Gunshot residue on his hand. Angle of the wound is right for a self-inflicted wound."

"That's the type of stuff a cop would know how to stage."

He ignores me and pushes through. "He owed twenty large to his bookie; did you know that?"

I did not, but I don't let him know. "He wouldn't kill himself over a debt."

"Twenty grand is more than just a debt. It's an insurmountable debt for a ham-and-egger like Finch. Did you know he was living in that office? I talked to the landlord. He told your boss he was gonna have to be out by the end of the month. Your boy's world was falling apart."

"But the tape—"

"There is no tape. And if there is a tape, then find me the tape; otherwise, stop saying, 'But the tape.' "

"And Finch paging me? What about that?"

"Those pages came from the pay phone across the street from your apartment. It was probably the guys that robbed you. They knew you, knew your patterns and were trying to get you out of the apartment so they could roll it."

"I wasn't in the apartment."

"It doesn't matter."

"That makes no sense. You're saying they weren't related? They were totally separate? They paged me with Finch's number."

"They knew you."

"No one knows me that well."

"It's a coincidence. Nothing more than a coincidence, unless proven otherwise."

"Bullshit."

"Sometimes coincidences are just that and you gotta go with it. It's an Occam's razor situation."

Occam's razor? Jesus Christ. That's supposed to be the simplest solution, not the stupidest.

"Did you check his phone records? Who'd he call?"

"Nobody."

"Nobody? There's no way. He said he was going to call someone with the Mollen Commission. He was going to call them and give them the tape."

"If he called anyone, he didn't do it from his work phone. Maybe a pay phone, maybe someplace else, but no one had dialed out from his work phone for over twenty-four hours."

"This is fucked. You saw my apartment. All they took was the camera and the tape. There's no way that it's separate from Finch."

"I have no idea if that's all they took. I have no idea if that camera was ever even there." His tone is tenser now, threatening. I get the idea that he's dangling the fact that he can make me for this, that if I keep pushing the murder angle, I'll probably become the number one suspect—all of it to get me to back down. "Listen, I love the enthusiasm, kid, but it is what it is. I gotta boogie. You find that tape, you give me a call, all right?"

I slam the receiver down into the scratched-up silver cradle of the pay phone and give my head a shake of angry disbelief. There's no way in hell that Finch didn't call somebody. No way. Even if it was "the wrong guy," like Wally said. He still had to call him, had to call someone. I'm thinking and staring and trying to figure out my next move when I see the orange card for a 900-number sex line tucked into a seam on the inner wall of the phone booth's cubby. And then I remember.

Finch didn't just have a gambling problem or just have a drinking problem. He also had a 900-number problem. The first year I worked with him, his office phone kept getting shut down for unpaid bills. One of my jobs was to run down to the corner bodega and pay the phone bill whenever it got cut. Finch would give me a wad of cash, mostly singles and fives and change. They had a Bell Atlantic bill-paying station at the bodega, and I'd pay the bare minimum to get the phone turned back on. I finally managed to take a peek at a bill and saw the rows and rows of 900-number calls. I never brought it up; I didn't think I had any place or standing. But then it stopped. The phone bills went back to a normal amount, and the phones were never turned off again. I figured Finch had gotten over his vice or at least found some other less expensive way to get his needs met. And then one morning in the office, I picked up the phone to make a work call, but there was already a conversation happening on it.

Two women speaking rapid-fire in Spanish. In general, I can understand a lot more Spanish than Cookie thinks I can, but some conversational clips are so goddamn fast I can get nothing beyond the fact that they're speaking Spanish. This was one of those.

Finch saw my confused face. "What's the matter?"

I covered the mouthpiece. "There's someone already on the phone line."

His eyes went wide, and he practically leapt over the desk to push down on the phone switch and hang it up before they realized I was on their call. Once his finger was safely on the switch, he took the receiver out of my hand and put it down on the cradle.

"Sorry about that." I watched as he walked to a corner of the room and unplugged the phone line from the jack in the wall and walked it toward the jack closer to his desk. "I forgot to switch back the plugs last night." He explained that he'd been moving some furniture a while back and found this second jack in the wall that wasn't connected to his phone line. "I use it sometimes for long-distance calls, stuff like that."

"So, it's like a crossed line or whatever?"

"No, I think it's just somebody else's line."

"And you're making long-distance calls on it?"

"It's not my fault the phone company fucked up."

"Yeah, but that's somebody else's phone line. They're paying for your calls."

"I barely use it. And only late at night."

That's when I realized he never stopped calling those 900 numbers. He was just using this family's line so he wouldn't have to pay for it. Out of sight, out of mind and off his bill.

If Finch had the phone plugged into that other wall jack, that would explain why it rang and rang and rang when I called, never switching to the answering machine—it wasn't connected to his office line. And if it wasn't connected, any phone numbers for calls he made wouldn't show up when Hong pulled the LUDs for it.

I need to go back to Finch's office. I need to check that phone.

CHAPTER TWELVE

T HE SUBWAY RIDE IS mostly filled with anxiety over how to deal with the police evidence seal that movies have taught me will be on Finch's office door when I get there. I could try to peel it off or just slice it down the middle. Either action would be incredibly illegal. I figure they're designed to keep you from being able to peel them off, so I resolve to go with slicing and just deny I did it if the cops ever asked me.

When I turn from the stairwell toward Finch's door, I realize my problems aren't what I imagined. There's already a slice down the middle of the sticker. Somebody's been here or somebody's here right now, and both possibilities have me a little freaked out. I put my left hand on the thick wooden rail and try to offset my weight on the planked wooden floor to keep it from creaking as I slowly begin to walk toward the office. Suddenly, a large shadow crosses the frosted glass. *Shit*. I can either bolt for the upper landing or make a break downstairs. Since I'm almost there, I push forward toward the next floor up, no longer worrying about any noise my shifting weight makes as I speed-walk up the stairs and on the landing toward a safe place to hide.

Just as I tuck around the corner of the stairwell, Finch's door opens, and from the size of the silhouette and the sound of his breathing, I know right away who it is—Wally. He closes the door, does a quick check over his shoulder to see if anyone is watching and then pulls a new NYPD evidence sticker out of his overcoat pocket and places it over the old one he must've sliced through earlier. I guess being special advisor to the mayor has its perks.

Goddamn it, man. When I said everyone would have to earn my trust, I didn't expect that Wally secretly digging through the crime scene was gonna be the first gut punch I took. It takes everything for me not to scream out to him, "What the fuck, Wally?" but I swallow it down. There's a moment where I think that this might actually be a legit visit, and then I watch as he takes out his handkerchief and wipes down both the doorknob and the sticker. Shit is officially fucked and getting fuckier.

Wally leaves and I listen as he groans his way down the stairs, mouth breathing as he lumbers heavy footed to the first floor. Once the door to the street opens and shuts, I move—first to the top of the stairs to peek and make sure he's gone and then back to Finch's door. I pull out a penknife I have on my keychain and try find some air under the police sticker. Wally didn't press it that hard, and I think I might be able to peel it back with minimal damage. The sticker under the one Wally put on starts to tear off the doorframe side, but he did a shitty job of putting on the second one—he didn't push the middle of the sticker flush against the door. My plan is to lift the right side off the frame—it should be okay if it rips a little underneath—and then, when I close the door, press the still-sticky part in the middle flush against it. It should hold. It should look normal.

I get the sticker off the right side of the frame, unlock Finch's door and step into the dark office. It feels like cracking open a tomb. Like I'm the first person stepping in here in a hundred years. I take out a small flashlight and keep the light aimed low so no one can see it from the windows. Looking at the room like this, I realize that this place isn't just a theoretical tomb. It was Finch's. He lived here. He died here. I look over

to the desk. All that's left of him is the curved imprint of his bony spine
on his chair pillows and the blood and brain matter still stuck to the TV.
I shine the light on the desk phone and follow the phone cord with it.
I tense as it begins to lead me to the proper wall jack, but it continues
past it, snaking around shoes and boxes and evidence of a life barely lived,
finally connecting to the other jack in the far corner. Finch's secret jack.
I turn off the light, walk back to the desk and pick up the receiver. I
mumble, "Okay, okay ..." to no one in particular, take a deep breath and
then hit Redial.

A ring.

Another.

The click of a connection.

"This is Detective Richard Pittman at the Seventy-Fifth Precinct.
Leave your name and number. If this is an emergency, please hang up
and dial 911." The accent reeks of Staten Island asshole. I hang up
and scribble down the name onto my notepad: "Richard Pittman/7-5."
I'm guessing that's either Rangers Jersey or Kangol Hat, but either way
he's most definitely the "wrong guy," as Wally put it—the one Finch
shouldn't have called but did. I turn on the flashlight again and head to
the series of file cabinets that Finch set up to hide his cot from public
view. My finger moves along the army-green metal, looking for the right
drawer. At "L–P," I put the flashlight in my mouth and start flipping
through. It only takes a few until I find it: "Pittman, Richard." I pull
it out, and I know right away it's empty or at least emptier than it
should be. It has that hollow-shell feel—like it was once stretched out
and bursting and the folder's muscle memory wants it to stay in that
engorged shape even with barely anything inside. I take it over to Finch's
cot and sit down to look—the cabinets should block anyone from seeing
the flashlight clearly from outside the office. The only paper in the file

is the initial job order from the city. According to this, seven years ago Pittman was rear-ended in his patrol car and made a cash claim to cover medical expenses for a neck injury. The PI assigned to the case? "W. Tinderman." What's missing in the file is what came next—a slew of eight-by-ten photos from Wally's stakeouts on Pittman and whatever summary report Wally wrote. Did Wally take the rest of the file? Did Pittman?

I look around at the dark room, this cave that was the center of Finch's depressing life. This was his work. This was his home. Dump twenty large in debt on top of all this, and you've got a weight that's undeniably crushing. I get why Detective Hong is leaning toward suicide—he didn't see any other way out for Finch. No escape. Except he doesn't know about Pittman, about this file, or whatever's left of it, anyway. Finch must have recognized Rangers Jersey or Kangol Hat, remembered that he was a case from the past. I'm guessing Pittman was still wearing Rangers jerseys or Kangol hats back then. He doesn't seem like he's the type to keep reinventing his personal style or evolve in any way.

I think back to when Finch and I watched the tape together. I never saw any recognition, never saw any light in his eyes where he remembered. It must have come later, come after I left, when he was watching it alone. Sometime after he'd stumbled home from the Doray, buzzed and smiling, it must have hit him. But what was the grand plan? Blackmail? Would this admittedly very dirty cop really have access to twenty grand?

Probably. Probably that and more.

But Finch wouldn't have just invited him over. He had to have some plan to protect himself, some plan to keep what happened to him from happening to him. It must have been me and my tape. The original. "Do anything to me, and the tape goes to Internal Affairs." Or the *Daily News*. Something like that. *Well, that plan didn't really pan out, did it,*

Finch? They must have beat him up and knocked him around some to get my info. Or they could have dug through the files themselves. Seen my name on the job order for the cop I videotaped them killing.

Jesus.

I put Pittman's near-empty file back in the cabinet and head over to Finch's desk. There should still be a bottle of something in the drawer if the cops didn't swipe it. I sit in his chair, and the hard pillows mold my spine into a concave arc almost immediately. I do my best to break out of the shape and lean forward to open the drawer, the action causing the fifth of Jameson inside to roll toward me as I do. I grab it, screw open the top and pause before I sip. I look over toward the TV screen and pour a little out for him before I drink.

"Slainte and *salud*, Finch. And I'm sorry." I bring the bottle to my lips and am taking a sip when I see a bit of yellow poking out from behind his TV/VCR combo unit. Leaning closer, I can see that it's the yellow video connector for an RCA cable—the cable you use to connect a VCR to a TV. Finch shouldn't need one of those for this. Everything in these combo units is internal. Unless ...

I shoot out of the chair and go to the back of the TV/VCR unit to find the RCA cable, follow it into the closed cabinet below it and the second VCR inside. *Goddamn it, Finch. You made another copy of the tape, didn't you?* I press Eject, but nothing comes out. I pull out my flashlight and look around—no other tapes. No anything. I search the office for another hour, trying to find it, but it's not here. And if it was, Pittman probably found it. Or Wally.

Or maybe they did it together.

I call Cookie from the street and give her the detective's name. I figure she should have it in case he comes snooping around.

She seems tense. I get it.

CHAPTER THIRTEEN

S o.
   There's probably another tape. Or at least I hope there's another tape. And either it got swiped by Wally or Rangers Jersey and Kangol Hat, or Finch did something else with it. It's not in the office—there's no safe, no secret stash hole in there; I'd know by now if there was, and he doesn't have any other addresses, so I'm leaning toward his sending it to someone if it wasn't swiped. And if he sent it to someone, let's be honest: he sent it to me. I'm the only one in his circle that has even a clue about the context, so yeah, if it exists, if it wasn't swiped, if it wasn't destroyed, I think he must have sent it to me.

   Yeesh. Those are a whole lotta *if*s resulting in one *I think*, but that's all I got.

   I head back from Finch's to my Avenue B apartment to check my mailbox for the tape, doing my best *French Connection* as I do, taking trains the wrong way and then doubling back the right way, until I've ditched my imaginary Popeye Doyle on the other side of closing F train doors. I'm deep in the darkness of Tompkins Square Park now, and it's buzzing on a Friday night. Shadows and couples and drugs and dogs scattered throughout. I cut through the curves of the park, feeling invisible, *willing* myself invisible, until I get to the corner across from 7B. I've already done a couple of laps around my block and saw no undercovers, no double-parked idlers to spark any Seven Five–precinct paranoia. All I have to do is walk across B, go into my lobby and check my mail. That's it. If the tape is there, I'll go upstairs, call Hong, wait for him and hand it over. That's it. And yet ...

Five minutes later and I still haven't worked up the courage to walk into my lobby. But then some drunken screams of happy youth at the other end of the park give me the adrenaline push I need, and I cross, keys in hand, eyes square on the front door lock, purposeful footfall after purposeful footfall. Curb. Sidewalk. Lock. Twist. Push. Groan. And I'm in.

And once I push into the foyer, I see it—my mailbox pried open, half of the mail spilled out onto the penny tile floor, the other half barely fighting the gravity that wants to pull it down. No tape. No bulky envelope. No easy fix to my current situation. And as much as I'd like to think it was left open by a lazy mailman or simply burst at the seams on its own, I know better. They've been here. They did this.

I scoop up the mess—mostly Associated Supermarket circulars and a few bills and then decide to head upstairs. I'm here already. Why not see what's doing in 3R? As I get to my door, I realize I should have put some Scotch tape on the frame and door or maybe tucked a wad of paper into the crack of the doorjamb—one of those low-tech, James Bond, "did anyone that wasn't me open my door?" moves. But I didn't and I should have, and maybe I'll remember to do it before I leave but probably not. I push open the door and plow back the surprisingly large number of menus that has accrued in my two-day absence and flip on the light.

It's quiet. And a little weird—it feels like I'm walking into someone else's apartment. The idea of Rangers Jersey or Kangol Hat being in here, touching my stuff, taking the camera and the tape—I don't like it. And I don't want to be here long. I head to my fridge and check for the spoilt or the soon to turn and am pouring the liquids down the drain and stuffing the solids into the trash when I notice that my answering machine is blinking pretty rapidly. In all the chaos, I haven't been calling to check it, and the messages have piled up like so many menus behind a closed apartment door. I figured important reach outs would go right to the pager, but who knows? I know Finch probably isn't on there, but I take a deep breath, make a wish to hear his tape-recorded voice and press Play.

"Nico. Call me. Please." It's Tommy. He paged me a couple of times a few days ago, but I ignored it.

Delete.

"Nico, man. I *need* to talk to you. Like, now. Some shit has happened."

Delete.

"Why aren't you answering your pages? What's the point in having a pager if you don't answer your pages? Call me. Please."

Jesus. Are all these from Tommy? Delete.

"I inhaled crack smoke, okay? I inhaled crack smoke. I know it went inside my lungs, and I need you to call me back. I don't know if I'm addicted now or what."

Delete.

"This guy got in my cab, all right? I hailed a cab on Twenty-Third, and then he just pushed in right behind me, and before I knew what was happening, he lit up a crack pipe and started smoking it *in the cab*. I mean, the windows were up; the cab had its plastic separator thingy up. It was a contained space. There's no way I didn't inhale some smoke. No way. Call me back."

Delete.

"Nicholas. It's Ruby." My great-aunt. My dad's aunt. The last of that side of the family if you don't count me. "Come out for dinner next

week. Also, I wanna give you something of your father's. Call me." The
Queens in her makes "call" sound like "cawl." I'm not thrilled at the idea
of an evening with Great-Aunt Ruby, but the idea of getting something
of my dad's—that intrigues me. She knew it would take a little extra to
get me to Sunnyside, and she dangled just enough to make it happen.
Smart.

Delete.

"And get this. When the cabby finally stops, and I tell him what this
guy was doing? He starts yelling at me. Like, why would I let a crack
addict in his cab? Don't I know what they're capable of? And on and on
... I tell him I didn't let him in! The guy shoved his way in right behind
me! But the cabby didn't give a fuck. Man, he was so pissed at me. Oh,
and this guy, the crack guy, when he leaves the cab, he turns and thanks
me, like I was doing him a solid on purpose or something! It was all so
weird. He was Black but, like, crazy well dressed and well spoken, you
know? Like a Wall Street guy. Like Gordon Gekko but Black. Fucking
crazy. Anyways, I thought maybe 'cause of your dad and stuff, maybe
you knew about stuff like this. About secondhand crack smoke and its
addictive properties and things like that. Anyway, call me."

Jesus. Delete.

"Okay, um, I'm feeling weird about how I worded the fact that he was
a Black Wall Street guy. Like, I don't know why I said it like that. I should
have just said Wall Street guy or Black guy, maybe? I dunno. But you
know what I mean. It wasn't a racist thing. I'm not racist. I'm just— I'm
worried about having inhaled that crack smoke. I'm all over the place,
man. Call me back."

Delete. That's all of them. And no, I'm not calling Tommy back. By
now he's probably gone to a clinic or called his old pediatrician or moved
back home and checked into rehab just to be sure. Regardless, I don't

want to hear about it—the well-spoken crack man or how Tommy isn't racist.

I turn off the lights and lock up, somehow actually remembering to tuck a little piece of paper into the doorjamb. If I come back to the apartment and the paper is on the ground, that means someone opened the door and let it fall. Then I'll know if someone has been here. Someone who isn't me.

—

I convince myself that some pinball at 7B wouldn't be the worst thing and head across the street. While I'm waiting for quarters, I see Susie walk in with a girlfriend. I give her a smile and a nod and watch as she grabs her friend aggressively by the arm and U-turns it right out the front door the second she sees me. I haven't spoken to her since Detective Hong called her to confirm my timeline. It's looking like giving a homicide detective my sex partner's phone number to confirm my whereabouts and solidify my alibi for a murder isn't sitting too well with her. I should have called her, warned her, explained it to her, but we never call each other. We never really talk all that much at all.

Shit.

I burn through my two dollars in quarters and two pints pretty quickly. I thought playing would clear my head, relax me, but my fucked-up situation is making me lean wrong, or maybe the table is leaning, or maybe there's a magnet in my pocket, 'cause ten seconds into every fucking ball, it gets sucked down the right-side gutter.

I stop the bleeding and call it a night, heading out the back door of 7B, and then hoof it back to the Chinatown crash pad. In the foyer, the trash rats are mostly silent while I climb the stairs, probably in some MSG-induced coma, sleeping, building muscle, *evolving*. I flip on the kitchen light after I open the door, and a giant cockroach on the lacquered kitchen table begins to scurry, not sure which way to go, which direction to head to find some darkness and escape my reach. It chooses foliage, running up the side of the beer bottle and onto the long stem of the sole daisy that sits in it, finally nestling in the yellow center circle of the flower. The stem immediately begins to bend from the weight of the water bug, the back of the cockroach lowering closer and closer to the table till it's eventually pressing against it, the daisy's stem forming a thin green arch.

If a cockroach's face can have an expression, this one's is "Oh, fuck." I roll up a *NY Press* and fuse flower and insect into one and then put everything into the trash can.

I'm getting that unraveling feeling again. That helpless feeling I had the morning after the cop and his wife got shot. I need to try to take back some control. I need to start turning this boat now, or it's going to be too late.

CHAPTER FOURTEEN

"**I** DON'T LIKE COLD soup."

Detective Hong leans back from the table. "They got a hot version, too."

"I'm just gonna have the pierogies."

"Don't do that. Don't do that. That's like getting pad thai at a Thai place. It's the default; it's cliché. Get something genuine. Live a little."

"I *like* pierogies." I also like pad thai. But I don't like beets. I don't like them hot, and I don't like them cold. The *Green Eggs and Ham* vibes are unintentional, and I'm very happy I didn't say that part out loud.

"Beets are very good for you. Very good for you." He looks up at the waitress. "Right?"

She gives her best "I don't give a fuck" look and then reconsiders when she realizes which person at this table will be paying her tip and says, "Sure." Poor thing has been standing here this entire time.

"All right, so borscht for me, pierogies for young master Nico."

We're at Veselka. I called Detective Hong first thing in the morning and told him about the other phone line. I didn't tell him that I peeled off the evidence seal or that I hit Redial on the phone myself, but I told him about the phone, told him what Finch used it for, told him he should check it out. He was intrigued and called me a few hours later asking to meet here. Said he didn't want me inside the station house. The waitress takes our anticlimactic order back to the kitchen as Hong leans back and crosses his arms, giving me a hard stare.

"So. Interesting stuff happening, huh?" I figure the question is rhetorical hot air, so I take a sip of my water and wait for the rest. "We ran the LUDs on that other phone line, Finch's party-time line. You're right. He did call someone. But you already know that, right?" He leans in, his forearms on the table. I'm suddenly very aware of my hands. What do I do with them? How do they work? I take another sip of my water to give them an activity.

"Somebody used that phone line again last night. I'm assuming they just hit Redial to see who Finch called last, but regardless, they called the same last number as Finch."

Shit. I should have realized that his pulling the LUDs would also show my call last night. "Wow. What number did they call?"

Hong doesn't answer right away. He just looks at me, working me. It's hard to tell with this guy. I feel like he flipped through his Rolodex on how to get suspects to admit to wrongdoing, and seeing me he lands on the very undramatic disappointed stare? First Maggie's saying I "look like a George" and now this? I tighten up my face and give him the same stare back. *Sorry, bub. It's gonna take more than that to get me to admit to openly breaking the law. I can take unblinking eyes just fine. Flip to some other card.*

I keep staring silently back at him, waiting for him to change it up from his sad eyes, which, in turn, makes "Sad Eyes" by Robert John crawl into my head as I look at Hong. I'm practically mouthing the words to the song as I look back at him and almost totally crack up, but I somehow keep it together. Sidenote: my dad used to do an amazing cover of "Sad Eyes"—he slowed it down by about 25 percent. Really held on to the emotions of it, really made the whole thing resonate. It was devastating.

He only played it live. Anyways, Detective Sad Eyes' stare is thankfully interrupted by our food arriving. I guess it doesn't take that long to ladle out some cold soup and plate some pierogies when they're 90 percent of what people order here.

Hong seems to forget why he was staring at me and becomes genuinely excited about the food. He takes a spoonful, enjoys it and then turns his attention back to me. "I'm not gonna tell you the phone number for two reasons. One, because I don't have to fucking tell you anything. I'm the cop. You're not the cop. I'm the cop. Secondly, I'm not gonna tell you, because I have a deep suspicion that you already know it." I spread some sour cream onto a pierogi and take a bite. Can't talk with my mouth full, right? "Be careful, Nico. Whatever you're doing, be careful about it."

"I am careful," I mumble, breaking my no-talking-with-my-mouth-full rule right out of the gate.

"No you're not. You should have just told me about the phone line and let me do my job. Keep your duck out of the mud and leave the investigating to the professionals."

I ignore the "duck out of the mud" comment, wipe my mouth and sit back. "That's weird because I have this thing in my wallet that says that I'm a state licensed investigator. I mean, that's *very* professional, right?"

"Relax."

"I mean, I'm not in a union or anything, and I don't think I get a pension, but my job is literally to investigate things."

"Whoop-de-doo. So, you have a laminated license in a wallet. Great. What do you do with it? From where I sit, all you to do is hide in the shadows and take creepy pictures of folks who don't realize you're standing there. That doesn't make you a cop."

"Who said anything about wanting to be a cop?"

"Fine. An investigator. A license doesn't make you an investigator."

"Are you trying to inspire me to become a cop, or are you just trying to make me feel shitty? Just a heads-up, neither's working."

He takes a moment to wipe the beets from his lips and gather himself before responding. "All I was trying to say is in my job, I have protections. You don't. Things are going to get complicated from here on out, and I'm concerned you're not aware of how complicated they're gonna get."

"So, tell me then."

"That's what I'm doing."

"And yet, you still haven't."

He leans back and sucks at his teeth. Did I piss him off a little bit? Yeah, I pissed him off a little bit. He takes a deep breath and continues. "Complications in regard to the number Finch called and the people on the other end of the phone ... that's what worries me. That, combined with what you told me you saw."

"The tape, you mean."

"The tape that doesn't exist, yeah. Anyways, taking both those things into account, things will get more complicated. Internal Affairs may get involved. And I just want you to watch your back."

"For what?"

"For lots of things but mainly in case parts of the investigation that shouldn't go public, well, you know, go public."

"Like my name gets out there or something?"

"Yeah. Like that."

"And how would that happen?"

"It's a complicated case. Cops protect cops. It happens."

"Even when cops shoot cops?"

"Listen, just be prepared, all right? Always be prepared."

"Right. Semper Fi."

"No." He shakes his head annoyedly, and I try to hide my smile. "That means 'always faithful.'" He's ready for this conversation to be over. "Just keep your eyes open."

Twenty minutes later and I'm doing exactly that when I see Maggie walking down Second Avenue as I'm about to push open the glass door of Veselka. The idea of chasing her down and tapping her on the shoulder will come across as totally creepy, so I do something that's essentially ten times creepier. I cross the street and jog a block ahead of her, then start walking uptown toward her on her side of the street so running into her seems happenstance.

I know there are other things I should be doing right now, but Hong's warning freaked me out more than my bon mots probably revealed. I guess I'm gonna respond by ignoring it for a little bit and pretending that Rangers Jersey and Kangol Hat aren't potentially just around the corner waiting for me.

I need a break. I can have a break, right?

—

Maggie says she's headed to Astor Place to buy some mixtapes, and I play along like I know what the hell she's talking about. I figure she means DJ mixtapes, but she doesn't seem the type. We stop on the north-side sidewalk of Astor between Fourth and Third Avenues, and it takes me a minute to process what I'm looking at before I figure out that she was talking about *actual* mixtapes.

It's that spot where folks sell the shit they steal from unsuspecting and far-too-trusting students at the NYU library when they get up to go to the bathroom or leave their desk to flirt in the stacks. If you leave that bag, you lose that bag. Before you know it, someone slinks by and snags it. Five minutes later it and its contents are laid out on the sidewalk just a few blocks away. It's all such obviously stolen stuff that there's something totally refreshing about the absolute lack of desire to hide that fact. Everything is out: the book bag they stole, the books from inside the bag, the Walkman, pens, pencils—really *anything* that was in the bag is for sale. I mean, it's possible that a very homeless looking guy is looking to offload his copies of *Truffaut by Truffaut* and *I Lost It at the Movies*, along with his used 1998 *Manhattan Diary* and last month's *Sight and Sound*, and honestly, based on what research I've done into film school, that might be what caused the homelessness, but I'm guessing this stuff just comes from an NYU library snatch. Mixed among all that film-school-related detritus are the mixtapes Maggie came for.

"How do you decide which ones to buy?" I ask.

"What do you mean? I pick them up and I look at them. This isn't Tiffany's; this shit isn't locked up behind glass." She picks one up—a boring-looking one, just black ink on white paper. "See, this one's gonna suck. No cover art. No collage. No nothing." She looks inside and winces at the horror. "Eagles. Steve Miller Band. This is basically the cursed eternal soundtrack of a freshman dorm. No thanks." She puts it back down on the sidewalk and picks up another, more colorful cassette with some sort of collage on the cover.

"Look at that. I don't even need to open it to know it's gonna be good." Except she immediately opens it and pulls out the cassette. "Side one is called 'Johnny LaRue,' and side two is called 'Lyndon LaRouche.' See, this is quality." I don't get the Johnny LaRue reference until I see the collage on the cover—a cutout of John Candy's head as Johnny LaRue from *SCTV* and a cutout of Lyndon LaRouche's head as, well, Lyndon LaRouche, all made to look like the two are running for public office together.

"So, you just listen to them? What's the appeal? I mean, you don't know the person who made it, and you don't know the person it was made for."

"That's *exactly* the appeal. You try to figure those people out. The one that gave it and the one that got it."

"Huh. Okay." I get it, I think. I mean, I get why it's interesting, but I wouldn't have enough gas in the tank to pursue it myself.

"I've got some good ones at home. The best are the obvious attempts to win back lost loves. There's always an agenda, always a purpose. Like, look at this one. All late-seventies and eighties indie stuff. This is definitely some grad school TA creep trying to fuck one of his younger undergrad students." She switches to a mocking, deeper voice. "Oh, you've never heard of Television? They were seminal." She drops the fake voice and switches back to her own. "Those dudes call everything seminal. They love that word." I grab the mixtape and check out the titles, letting out an uncontrollable guffaw when I see my dad's name. She notices. "What?"

"My dad's on here."

"What? Get out. Wait. Who? What? Who's your dad? And why didn't you ever tell me who he is?" She grabs the cassette from me, scans it, looking for something, and I see her face as she recognizes the name, probably more from his OD than from his work. "Shit. You told me your dad OD'd, but you never told me what he did."

"Besides the coke and heroin, you mean?" She looks at me with some surprise at the comment, so I backpedal. "Sorry. Bad joke." Emotion successfully deflected. "I didn't tell you because ... I dunno. It didn't come out naturally? It would have seemed like a stretch to bring it up? Like a brag, or something? It always feels weird and clumsy to bring up, so I don't. But yeah ... that's my dad."

She hands two bucks to the guy selling the book bag contents and slips the cassette into her back pocket. "Adult relationships with your parents are messy. I haven't talked to my dad in two years." She pauses for just a moment. "We sort of talk. It's complicated."

I say let's get a drink and talk about it. She counters with let's get a drink and talk about something completely different.

Sounds good to me.

CHAPTER FIFTEEN

THERE'S THAT EXCITING NEW-FRIEND feeling kicking in with Maggie. When you're hanging out with someone you barely know and the more you talk, the more you realize how much you enjoy talking with them. The conversation just goes and goes and goes and never feels like it's going to lose momentum. It doesn't have that potential-hookup feeling, and that's fine. I know that ship sailed away a while ago. Honestly, the ship probably only ever existed in my own head.

We're sitting in the back at International Bar, near the jukebox. It didn't take long for her to go back on her word and start talking about her dad. They evidently had their split over her choice of acting as a career—he wanted her to go to grad school, study law or medicine or something else endless and painfully reliable. She refused, and somewhere in there, stuff was said, mostly about her dad's new wife and her very badly done fake breasts. "They're crazy eyed," she says. "One goes like this." She points up with her right index finger. "And one goes like this." She points down with her left. "It's like talking to someone with a lazy eye the size of a watermelon." Since then, it's been nothing but silence for a few years, but about six months ago her dad sent her a copy of Victor Hugo's *Les Misérables*, his favorite book. Inside it he wrote, "Read this and we'll always have something to talk about." Maggie did and responded with one of her own.

"*The Great Santini*," she says. "I know—it's like painfully on the nose, but I couldn't help myself. Not that he was an abusive fighter pilot or anything, but he was, you know, a sort of tough guy. I figured if he sent me a book back after that one, we might actually talk again."

"Did he?"

"Yeah. *To Kill a Mockingbird*."

"A much warmer take on fatherhood."

"There's a lot of daylight between Atticus's and Bull's parenting philosophies, yeah. We still haven't talked, but I guess the books are sort of like talking. We'll talk eventually."

She asks me about my dad, and I tell her about him as we drink. How young my parents were when they had me. How he was a shitty husband and an okay dad, but I admittedly tended to grade everything involving him on a curve because of his addictions and because everyone else was constantly shitting on him. "Like, he was able to be there sometimes for me, even with everything going on." The moment I say "sometimes," I know how delusional I sound. The way he treated me didn't feel that good at the time, so why should I pretend it felt good now? I dunno. I know he sucked. But he was also great. When I started getting into film, he used to take me to revival double features at Theatre 80 on St. Marks Place and the St. Marks Cinema on Second Avenue. Maybe that's why going to movies calms me. Resets me.

I can tell she's surprised at how together I'm able to seem when I talk about it all, but I'm mostly waiting for the subject to change. If I have a tactic, that's it—just be quiet and wait for the conversation to move on. It always moves on. Somewhere in there she asks me about my work, and for a minute I try to come up with some quick brush-off like I usually do. My regular *say something shitty about how boring it is and then move on*, but I think about everything going on and realize ... it's not boring? Jesus, it's anything but boring. I take a deep breath and a swig of my beer, and before I know it, I've told her everything. I mean *all of it*. It kind of feels like I'm revealing my secret identity for the first time, and it's insanely good to tell someone not in the day-to-day mix of it about it all. I watch as Maggie's eyes get wider and wider. At one point she finally begs me to pause so she can pee, but when she comes back, I get right back to it. When I finish, wrapping up with my late lunch at Veselka with Detective Hong and skipping the creepy part where I ran out of my way to bump into her, she just leans back slowly, shaking her head in disbelief.

"Holy fuck," she says. "*Holy fuck.* I mean, I know that horrible things happened and there's that whole fearing-for-your-life-and-safety thing as well, but that is the best story I've heard since I moved here."

"Thanks."

"So, why are you wasting time with me tonight? Don't you have, like, crimes to solve?"

"I needed a break from the stress of it. I needed to do something else. A distraction."

"And instead, I made you tell me the whole thing."

"Well, I spilled it willingly. And it honestly felt good to let it out."

"Well, I'm sorry you had to relive it to tell me, but I'm not sorry I heard it. Shit, man, that's just, like, an epic tale." She takes a deep swig.

"And it's not over yet."

"Fuck right, it's not over yet. This is just like act two or some shit."

I smile and bask in the praise. Everything she's said is true. If I survive this, I'll have a great story to tell for the rest of my life. I feel immediately guilty about this feeling of pride that's linked to Finch's death, so I bring my beer to my lips to cover my growing sour stomach smile.

"All right. So, you want a distraction, huh? A night off?"

"Sure."

"Then we're gonna get good and ripped, right? Because this is your night off ... *from murder*." She says "murder" exactly the way you'd expect, and yeah, it's predictable and cliché, but it's still funny, goddamn it, so I laugh.

—

First stop is Marion's Continental. A theme-y cocktail bar and restaurant that seemed out of place on the Bowery until B Bar moved in next door. It's the type of place you can go and watch the band Spacehog drinking for free at the bar, if you're the type of person that could actually recognize members of Spacehog. Maggie worked at Marion's briefly and can still talk her way into a comped round or two and the occasional free appetizer.

"But we still have to leave a tip. Always leave a tip." I nod, understanding. I'm not a monster. "Oh, and for the rest of the night, I'm going to introduce you as my brother. That's really the only way anybody is going to agree to buy you drinks."

Mildly emasculating, but free drinks are free drinks.

From Marion's we move on to the Scratcher, an Irish pub a block away and around the corner on Fifth Street. Before we walk down the stairs to the entrance, she tells me we're not going to stay long. "Drinking free means we gotta keep moving, we can't outstay our welcome and we can't stay long enough for it to be our turn to buy. As far as everyone is concerned, we're always on our way somewhere; we're always late. 'We'd love to stay for another, but we can't, and we swear we'll be back soon.' Got it?" I nod, acknowledging that Maggie is definitively behind the wheel on this and I'm just going along for the ride.

Inside, she's recognized immediately by the bartender and pulled in for cheek kisses. This was her go-to every night after getting off from Marion's, and it's clear that she has some fans. I'm introduced as her visiting brother from ... LA? It's said by Maggie with about as much confidence as I'd have answering any questions about any West Coast city, but it's enough to get us two pints of Guinness and a ham and cheddar sandwich. We split it, down our pints and make a quick exit.

A brief discussion of bars we've never been to results in us heading to McSorley's, and I'm ready to leave almost immediately. It's not a bad scene; it's just not my scene. It's brightly lit—not as bright as Max Fish, but there's no real place to hide in the shadows. The place is almost entirely male, and while it's definitely multigenerational, everyone somehow looks upper middle aged. A pandemic of unhealthy ruddiness on capillary-studded noses has spread from face to face, as have toothy smiles, loud single back slaps and rugby shirts. My dad could fake his way through this, and I know I'm half my dad and half my mom, but I still feel itchy, sorta like I'm behind enemy lines. And I don't know exactly how not paying for any drinks became the theme for the night, but I'm starting to find the entire thing incredibly chaotic. This is not the night off from anxiety that I was hoping it would be. My original plan was to see *Happiness* at Angelika at 7:00 p.m. Maybe I could split off at some point and still make the 10:00 p.m. screening. Maggie disappears for a few and then reappears with two old-school mugs in her hands.

"We have to chug these and then split." More chaos. Fantastic.

"Split? Chug and split?"

"Yeah."

"If there's a problem, why don't we just *not* chug and leave right away?"

"That would be a waste. Chug it." She says it as forcefully as those two words can be said and I oblige. She begins to chug hers, but I can see her eyes continually looking back over my shoulder toward the bathrooms. They go wide for one second, and she immediately puts down her beer and grabs the mug from my hand. "We gotta leave." She pulls me through the multigenerational musk toward the door.

Outside on Seventh Street, I ask her what the rush is about, but she just keeps pulling me toward Third Avenue. There's a moment where we're walking under a streetlight and both of us are turned, looking back at McSorley's with some fear in our eyes, and all I can think of is how we must look like an alternate version of the *Into the Night* movie poster, except she's Jeff Goldblum, and I'm Michelle Pfeiffer, and we're standing next to trash cans in the East Village, not in a perfectly dramatic shot of the Hollywood Hills. I've never actually seen *Into the Night*, but I'm fairly certain that there's a tattered poster for it in every video store I've ever entered. I think B. B. King did the song. Real phoning-it-in type stuff with lyrics that put a painful emphasis on the movie title whenever possible: "I'll go out of my mind or ... *into the night*."

"Have you ever seen *Into the Night*?" I ask Maggie as we run.

"I don't think so. Why?"

"No reason."

"Shit. He sees us."

Back at McSorley's a stocky brick wall exits the bar and begins to look around frantically, smiling and waving at us when he sees us. As we make the turn up Third Avenue, I try to get the story on who this Bob Hoskins stand-in is.

"He's a guy who's obsessed with me. He'd come by Accidental whenever I worked there, trying to force me into conversation, refusing to leave. He's off a little bit, you know? And every time I reject him, he thinks I'm just flirting. That I'm being cute or coy or some internal-dialogue-fantasy bullshit. The last time he came by, he kept touching me, trying to pet my hair and shit. Real total creep stuff. I had to go inside and lock myself in the bathroom while my boss called the cops on him."

"What did the cops do?"

"Nothing. They just told me not to engage with him, like I had any fucking say in any of it. He's tried to follow me home some nights, but I always saw him and managed to give him the shake."

After the turn north, I see a karaoke place I've been to before—the kind with private rooms in the back. I tug on Maggie's jacket and pull her toward the entrance and past the flashing red Open sign. I figure we can bluff our way into the back rooms and disappear for ten minutes while this bulldog loses our scent.

Inside we smile and wave at the young woman behind the counter. "We're meeting friends," I offer up as we dart past her. She's not convinced and stands, waving one arm in protest, but Maggie and I run up the stairs two steps at a time and toward the shoddily carpeted white corridor of private rooms. It's closed door after closed door, with muffled laughter and off-key singing bleeding out from inside each.

At the end of the hallway, there's a door that's about halfway open. We head for it and try to slide into the already-overcrowded space without getting any attention but it's near impossible. There are two doors to the large room, and the open one we walk through is right next to the five-foot-tall singer currently belting out "Fantasy" by Mariah Carey while standing on one of the benches that lines each wall. It's a square room that's probably made to fit about fifteen people, but there are easily twenty-five in here, making it crowded as hell, especially because one of the people is the New York Mets mascot Mr. Met, and he and his giant baseball head are taking up a lot of real estate. It's a hometown crowd of almost all college-aged-looking kids, with some of them definitely leaning closer in age to learner's permits than legally drinking. We smile and nod and act like we're supposed to be there, and then sit down on the bench on the other side of the standing singer. People seem fine with it, everyone assuming the other knows who we are. I turn to the guy next to me. "Is that really Mr. Met?"

"Yeah." We're shouting. It's loud.

"How and why is Mr. Met here?"

"You can rent him out for parties and stuff. You just gotta make sure the door is big enough, you know, for his head. They send someone in advance to measure the entrance to make sure."

On the other side of me, I feel Maggie lean in. "Did you mean the movie with Jeff Goldblum?"

"What?" I say.

"*Into the Night.* That's Jeff Goldblum, right?"

"Yeah."

"Not a great movie."

"Never saw it." I start to explain the poster image and us and how our body language outside McSorley's under the streetlight made me think of it, but Maggie's eyes are focused past me on the open door.

"Shit."

I turn toward it and see Young Bob Hoskins in the hallway. We lock eyes almost immediately, and he smiles in a way I imagine Bob Hoskins smiles just before he sticks his thumbs about two inches into your eye sockets. I grab Maggie by the hand, and we quickly cross the room toward Mr. Met just as the beginning of "Barbie Girl" starts. The Eurotrash rhythms and whiny vocals rip right through my head, but Mr. Met and the crowd love it, and everybody's immediately up, immediately dancing and scream singing as we swim upstream through them, circumventing Mr. Met's giant head to get to the other door. Behind us, Bob Hoskins has worked his way into the room and doesn't seem to realize there's a second door on the other side. As we exit the room, we get a glimpse of Mr. Met getting the business end of Hoskins's Long

Good Friday, and a scuffle quickly ensues. Maggie and I hit the hallway and sprint down the corridor, jumping down the small stairwell and pushing out onto Third Avenue, where an empty cab magically awaits. We both dive in just as Bob Hoskins emerges through the glass door of the karaoke place and defeatedly runs out onto the street. As our cab pulls out, Maggie and I are both laughing that insane, exhilarated laugh of those who have just barely escaped physical harm. It's a bit like the end of *The Graduate*, but instead of a church shrinking in the distance behind us, it's five and a half feet of solid creep.

Sitting in the back of the cab next to Maggie, everything inside me tells me to kiss her at this moment, but I don't. It's just the adrenaline, just the excitement, I tell myself. But it's probably my last justified moment for it before the two of us calicify into friendship. But why's that bad? I honestly don't think I have a friend that I enjoy hanging out with more, and I hope the feeling is mutual. Who knows? Maybe she's having the same exact conversation in her head.

We drive around for a bit and then decide to head to Motor City Bar on Ludlow. Maggie knows the DJ tonight, and it's sort of her home drinking base in Manhattan, so it feels safe on paper.

We don't see the cab pull up behind us moments after we stop. We don't see the out-of-focus Bob Hoskins exit its back seat, saunter up and put his arm on Maggie's shoulder. I'm exiting our cab street side, and when I do see him, she's pulling away and screaming as he's digging in. Our African cabby sees it in his side mirror and gets out of his car immediately, trying to put himself between Hoskins and her. One punch from Hoskins's cement-block hand and the cabby goes down. I'm moving. I'm still at the trunk of the cab, and I can see the moment when the cabby loses consciousness. It's almost immediate, just a split second after the knuckles hit his face and his brain starts rattling around in his skull. I watch as his body releases itself from perception and gives itself up to gravity as he buckles to the ground. It's good that I see it. This way I know what it will look like when it happens to me.

Which it does about three seconds later.

—

When I come to, I'm on the sidewalk, propped up against the wall in front of Motor City. I can feel the muffled percussion of the song getting played inside, and it becomes immediately, drastically important for me to remember the name, but it's hiding in the dark and concussed corners of my head. I squint thinking it might help, but it doesn't. Maggie is talking to a cop near the bouncer. She sees me and comes over, and I try to stand, admittedly pained. She reaches out an arm to support me, and with her help, I slowly manage to get vertical.

"Easy, bud," she says. I can see that she's got some contact marks on her face, but she doesn't look as bad as I'm guessing I do.

"Did he hit you?"

"Just barely. Marc— That's Marc." She points at the bouncer. "He was able to get to him just as he was swinging. He barely grazed me."

"Oh. Good. What song is this?"

"What song? Inside, you mean?" She listens. "Um . . ."

"It's the Shangri-Las, right?"

"Oh, oh, I know it. I know it ... It's, uh ... 'Sophisticated Boom Boom.' Yeah. Good one."

"Yeah. Solid track."

My legs go wobbly just as the streetlights of Ludlow begin to get very bright and white in my eyes. I can suddenly feel sidewalk under my palm, which is weird because I'm standing.

Oh.

CHAPTER SIXTEEN

I LEAVE BETH ISRAEL'S ER just as dawn is cracking the east side. No concussion but lots of pain, a black eye and a prescription for very strong ibuprofen in my pocket. I figure I'll save time at the pharmacy and just double or triple up on the dosage of some Advil and call it even. I don't know what happened after I left Motor City, but it seemed like the cabby was going to press charges against Bob Hoskins. Maggie stayed and dealt with the cops, and I took my blurry cab ride to the hospital. Now that I've been released, I head back to my plant-filled jungle room on Essex Street, close the curtains, and promptly fall asleep.

It's just before 6:00 a.m. the next day. Is that how I say it? It's the morning after the morning I left the hospital—*there, that's clearer*—and I'm sitting in Seward Park eating my second bialy from Kossar's and sipping some bodega coffee. I woke up about two hours ago to a dumpster filled entirely with glass and metal getting emptied into the back of a very sound-conductive garbage truck outside my bedroom window. Up to that point, I'd slept through the day and most of the night, so the chances of slipping back into a slumber were pretty much nil. Fresh bialys are one of the few benefits to being up this early, so I took advantage. It's crisp out, but the cold feels good on my swollen face, so I take it.

A day and a night have been wasted, and I feel the guilt of an ignored to-do list weighing down on me. I need to get back on track. Wally's not calling me back, and me calling him again just to leave another message would be a continued waste of time. A lot more waiting as the clock moves forward. Nope, I'm gonna go to him. I dropped him off a few times at his place in Hunters Point in Long Island City back when we worked together. I figure he's still as cheap as I know his rent was then, so hopefully there's a chance he's still there, even on a special advisor to the mayor's salary.

If the fight won't come to you, go to the fight. But as I've said before and my swollen face proves, I'm not very good in a fight. So maybe forget that I said anything about fighting. If the fight won't come to you, bring it a fresh bialy, and just hope it appreciates the gesture.

—

The idling black Lincoln Town Car with NYC official license plates outside of Wally's place gives me some confidence that he's still upstairs. I'm in the tiny diner just below his apartment, not drinking the bad coffee that's grown cold in the chipped mug in front of me as I wait for him to show. I'm not exactly sure what the play is with him, but I'm leaning toward honesty—at least honesty about everything except seeing him leave Finch's office.

I see the driver get out to open the back door before I see Wally, but I know that means he must be coming, so I drop two bucks on the table and head street side.

"Wally!"

He turns about halfway to the car and gives me a squint. "Nico. I know I owe you a call, but ... Jesus, what happened to your face? Who did that?"

"Wrong place, wrong time. It's not Finch related or anything."

"I should see the other guy, right?"

"Uh, no. The other guy looks fine. Very fit and very good at punching faces. You got five minutes to talk?"

He ponders that, shifting his weight as he does. "You okay talking in the car? My guy can drop you wherever after he drops me downtown."

"Sure."

"What's in the bag?"

"A bialy."

"For me?"

"Yeah."

"Where's it from?"

"Kossar's."

"You should have led with that."

He holds open the door for me, so I get in and slide across the back seat, which then rises from the weight of Wally's giant body as he sits down to my left. Seconds later, we're off, speeding through the industrial streets of Long Island City, heading for the Midtown Tunnel.

"Your guy drives fast," I say.

"The mayor's office has its privileges." Right on cue, we buzz past the Queens Midtown Tunnel tollbooth, barely even stopping long enough for the toll worker to read whatever official logo is on the windshield that gets us waved through. Wally gives a shrug, like none of this is his idea, he just goes along with it. *Sure, bud.*

We hit the tunnel at a good clip and then slow as we catch up with morning traffic. Wally takes a bite of the bialy but doesn't let a full mouth stop him from talking. "So, I'm afraid I don't really have any new news on my end re: Finch."

I tell him that's okay, that I've got plenty. I go deep—the camera and tape stolen from my apartment, the LUDs on Finch's secret phone line, that Rangers Jersey or Kangol Hat is probably Richard Pittman of the

Seven Five. I pause and wait for some response from Wally, some reaction at the name, but his face remains agnostic. I leave out the empty work folder with Pittman's name on it and the possibility of a second copy of the tape; oh, and I especially skip seeing Wally fucking with a crime scene.

He processes it all with slow nods as he finishes off the bialy. "You've been busy."

"I've been doing what I can."

"Did you hear about Finch's gambling debt? Twenty large."

"Yeah. It was big."

"With that in the picture, the suicide angle makes some sense to me."

"Him getting his legs broken or even getting killed cause of a debt? Yeah, that makes sense. Him giving up and doing it himself? No." Still. I make a note that I should look up his bookie. Have a talk with him and see what comes of it. Maybe Detective Hong could tell me. Or Mikey.

"His health hadn't been very good. You know that, right?"

"His health was never good. It never stopped him from living his life." I carefully avoid discussing the *quality* of said life.

"Well, that's the thing about health. When it stops, it stops."

Yeah. And when it's stopped with a bullet, it stops real quick.

The Town Car exits the Manhattan side of the tunnel, and the dappling morning sunlight begins to flicker across us as we head down the FDR. Wally's doing his best to lean into this suicide angle without trying to seem like he really is. I play the conversation like it's just that, a conversation, and keep my pushbacks casual. I let him know Hong is leaning toward my way of thinking and that Internal Affairs might be getting involved.

"IAB, huh?"

"Yeah."

"What about the tape? Did it ever turn up?"

I tell him no but that I'm working on something.

"And what's that? Specifically."

"I'd rather just work on it and let you know when it comes together."

Wally gives an audible grunt of an exhale—he doesn't seem too happy about my vagueness, but that's sort of the point. All I have is vagueness. I wanna see what Wally does, see if he gets curious and starts snooping. I wanna see if that little piece of paper falls out of my doorjamb sometime soon.

"What's happening with the body?"

Wally looks confused. "What body?"

"Finch. Jesus, who do you think I'm talking about?"

"Oh yeah. Sorry. Just ... He has a sister in Atlantic City, but I couldn't track her down. Unless she shows up soon, the city'll probably cremate him."

"What about a memorial? A wake? Something?"

"Who would come? Besides you and me, I mean."

"We gotta do something." It too depressing otherwise. The idea that a life can just end, even Finch's, and nobody gives a shit—that's too much.

"We could just meet up at the Doray. Drink for him. Buy a few rounds for the regulars. See if anyone has any stories they wanna tell, et cetera, et cetera, et cetera." Wally's recommendation is the obvious choice, and it annoys me that I didn't think of it before him.

"Yeah, yeah ... That's good. It's something at least."

"Well, pick a date and let me know. I'll make sure I'm there."

As we pull up to City Hall, I remember the big question I wanted to ask when I first called Wally's office and left a message. "Hey, I don't think you ever really explained—how'd this special advisor to the mayor thing ever happen?"

"Hizzoner and I knew each other from high school, Bishop Loughlin. We weren't tight, but we were cordial—you know, friendly. Anyways, he kept seeing me at these Mollen Commission–related events, and we eventually got to talking." The idling Town Car rocks as Wally scoots his way to the edge of the back seat and pulls his body up.

"And what exactly are you advising the mayor on? If I can ask ..."

He leans down into the car with one hand on top of the door to keep his balance as he gives his answer. "I didn't tell you? Shit. I figured with all the cops around, I would have. I'm sort of the liaison between the NYPD and the mayor's office."

"Wouldn't that be, like, the chief of police? Or the head of the union?"

"Eh, the chief is the chief. The union boss is the union boss. I'm something different. Lemme know about that thing you're working on when you've got something."

"And the memorial for Finch. At the Doray."

"Yeah, yeah. Definitely." I give him a nod, and he shuts the door solidly.

I gotta say, his being "something different" doesn't seem like something friendly. And his commitment to a Finch memorial was thin soup, at best.

The driver asks where I want to be dropped just as my pager buzzes. It's Frankie's number plus 911.

That's never good.

CHAPTER SEVENTEEN

"**C**ookie's a mess. You gotta get out here."

That was the gist of what Frankie said to me on the phone, and it was enough to get me on the L to Williamsburg. He meets me in front of the bodega at the corner of North First and Berry, a few stoops down from her apartment building.

"What's going on?" I ask.

"What happened to your face?"

Oh, right. My face. He puts his hand on my cheek and roughly turns it to get a better look. "Sucker punch," I tell him. "The guy surprised me." I guess that's what it was. In my blurry memory, it sort of feels like I ran willingly *toward* the fist, so maybe it's more like I'm a sucker who got punched? "You should see the other guy," I say, lazily borrowing Wally's joke.

"Knowing you, I'm guessing he's fine. It is a he, right?"

"Yes." *Yeesh.* I wasn't expecting zings from Frankie.

"Why didn't you call me?"

"It wasn't really a planned thing ..."

"Just promise you'll call me next time. You're no good with the fists."

I know this. Apparently, everyone else does as well. "If there's time to prepare, sure. I'll call you."

"Good." He gives me a paisan clap on my cheek, and I wince from the pain.

"So, what's up with Cookie? What happened?"

He takes a deep breath and releases a few headshakes before he tells me what's what. "Her girlfriend OD'd. Like, died OD'd. They found her a few days ago near the waterfront."

"Jesus. That's awful. They were close?"

Frankie looks at me like I'm an idiot. "What do you mean 'close'? I just told you she was her girlfriend!"

"Girlfriend girlfriend? Like … Cookie's a lesbian? That's what you're talking about?" It's hard not to look stupid when you're saying what I just said, and I'm fully aware of exactly how stupid I look the moment the words leave my mouth.

"Do you not know your *tía* at all?"

"Well, I mean, I didn't know *that*." I didn't.

"Why do you think your mom doesn't talk to her?"

"I just thought they didn't like each other."

"Well, yeah. They don't. But her being gay is kind of at the center of all of it."

"Jesus."

"You really had no idea?"

"No, none."

"I mean, you lived with her, and you had no idea?"

This isn't saying much for my general investigative skills, but I was admittedly younger then, and the most recent stint at her apartment had its own distractions.

"Well, I can't sit with her anymore. I got routes with no one driving. You're family. You gotta take over from here."

I thank him, tell him I'm on it and head to Cookie's. Frankie gets into his dollar van and goes off to drive his routes.

Cookie doesn't answer her buzzer, but I still have a key, so I let myself into the building and climb to the second floor. I take a deep breath and then give some light knocks on her apartment door, hoping she'll answer, call out, say something, but mostly I'm just giving her a warning that I'm entering. I unlock the door and open it slowly. It's dark inside her place. Musty.

"Cookie?" I wait at the half-opened door for a few beats, but there's no response. "Cooks, it's Nico. I just spoke with Frankie. I'm coming in, okay?" I step in, my foot making the floorboards of the hallway entrance of her apartment creak. I turn the corner into the kitchen, and it's still mostly dark—some light bleeds in from around closed living room curtains but not much. My eyes adjust as I push deeper. "Cookie?" I take one more step. "*Tía?*"

The bedroom door that's open a crack gets quickly shut. At least I know she's alive in there. I try to connect with her a little more through the closed door, but it's a one-way conversation. I open her curtains, and the spilling light reveals the usual distraught mess of those left living when another has moved on. Empties, both cans and bottles, takeout not eaten or barely eaten and not thrown away, glasses sunk in gray stagnant water in the sink. I take off my pea coat and start to do what I can to clean it all up.

A few hours later and I'm sitting on the couch flipping through an *Entertainment Weekly* from two weeks ago—the one with a giant Alanis Morissette head on the cover—when Cookie slowly opens the door to her bedroom and sits down next to me. I don't want to smother her with compassion and sympathy—people did that to me after my dad died, and it never felt good to receive. What was meant as selfless always rang as selfish in my ears. It always felt like it was being said to make *that* person feel better, not me. It takes a minute or two for Cookie to say anything, and even then, she stops and starts a few times before she can get the single word out of her mouth.

"Thanks." She says it small. Quiet.

"Don't mention it."

"What happened to your face?"

"It was just me being stupid." She nods slightly, agreeing, fully understanding the stupidity of which I'm apparently capable.

The quiet in the room is broken by Cookie's taking a deep breath in through her mouth, holding it and then letting it shiver out through her nose. Her lips are pursed tightly, trying to keep the tears from coming back again. I'm not looking at her, but I know her eyes are raw and red from days of crying. The only move for me is to be here for her.

"Do you ... do you think it has something to do with the tape?" She stares straight ahead as she asks me. "You know, like ... with the cops?"

"What do you mean? You mean what happened to your girlfriend?"

"Yeah."

It never dawned on me that they could be connected. "Why do you say that?"

"She didn't OD. She didn't. Something else has to have happened."

"What do you mean by 'something else'?"

"She didn't smoke; she barely drank. There's no fucking way she did heroin, and there's definitely no fucking way she would shoot that shit inside of her body. Something else happened to her. Somebody did that to her."

It's obvious we're firmly in that denial stage of grief, but there's no fucking point in telling Cookie that. Whatever she wants to talk about, whatever she wants to say, I'll roll with it for a bit. Let her talk it out until she realizes what the truth is. Let her come to it on her own.

I decide I'll try to push her a little toward positive memories. "How'd you two meet?"

"At the Bum Bum Bar."

"Where's that?"

"Woodside."

"Cookie in Queens? Whoa. That's the real scandal here." Probably poorly timed levity on my part, but she still gives me the slightest of polite smiles before continuing.

"It's a safe place, you know, for me. It's mostly Ecuadorian and Colombian women from Woodside and Jackson Heights, but it was still worth the trip from Brooklyn. Especially on dance nights." She met her there on one of those nights. "She was this super pale white girl. Like translucent, out there dancing. Like a light was on her all the time." Her name was Katie. From Orange County, California. "I assumed that meant she grew up out, you know? That she grew up in a ... in an accepting environment and all. But she didn't. It's like a super conservative part of California, Orange County. Like *viva Reagan* level. I didn't know California had that. I just assumed it was all like San Francisco, you know?"

Their first date lasted about seventy-two hours. Their second date the same. "I didn't take any shifts at the beginning with her. I didn't want to."

"How long were you seeing each other?"

"Two and a half months."

Inside I twitch. Two months isn't very long. You can keep secrets from someone for two months. She picks up on my pondering.

"I know what you're gonna say."

"I'm not gonna say anything."

"Two months isn't long, but it *is* long. We spent a lot of time together. I know her. She didn't use. She wouldn't use."

"Still ... It could have been her first time. You never know."

"No. I know."

"But—and forgive me—can you really know?" I know I'm walking the line of civility here, but it seems like she needs to think about this. "Can you ever really know for sure? I mean, did you even have conversations about that stuff?"

"Yeah."

"When?"

"When I was telling her about you, and we were talking about your father."

Ah, okay. Still with the judgment about my dad, even when your girlfriend OD's. I take a deep breath. I get that she's emotional, but being supportive is becoming irritating. I try to keep my tone calm. "Well, then you know. Addicts lie. All the time. If she was using, she wouldn't have told you."

"No. She wasn't using, and if she was, she *would* have told me."

Fine. I'm not fighting this wave anymore. I float with it. "So, tell me why you think whatever happened is related to Finch and the tape."

Tears begin to well up in her eyes. She wants to answer, but I can tell she's hesitating. Once she opens her mouth to speak, the crying will start again. She locks her jaw and tries anyway.

"Because she didn't deserve that. She didn't deserve to end like that. And I can't come up with any other explanation."

I put my arm up and around her for maybe the first time in our adult relationship and lightly pull her toward me. To my surprise she lets it

happen and leans into my shoulder. I can feel the steady flow of tears
running off her cheeks and onto my shirt.

"Can you look into it? Try to find out what really happened? Please?"

I tell her yes I will, and we stay seated and silent, her going in and out
of crying and me watching as the moving sun slowly pushes shadows
across her apartment walls. I wanna ask why she didn't trust me with
telling me that she was a lesbian, but I know the answer is right there in
the question. She didn't trust me.

—

I call Hong and beg for any info on Katie's OD. He makes it clear that
if he does this, it will result in me owing him a favor, which I figured
going in. He calls me back a few hours later and tells me what he could
find out.

"Why do you hate cops so much? I mean, what's with your obsession
with crashing autopilot cases? Are you really that hell-bent on making
our lives more difficult, or what?" He tells me she was found at Williamsburg Beach—which isn't really a beach, just a small outcropping of sand
just south of the Williamsburg Bridge. There was a needle in her arm and
lots of heroin in her body. "Lots and lots of it. She OD'd. She got too
much, or she got a bad batch, and it did her in."

"Did she look like a user?"

"What does that mean? Nobody looks like a user, and everybody
looks like a user."

"No, I mean, other track marks, sores, bruises, stuff like that?"

"How do you know about that stuff?"

I'm not getting into my dad's addictions with Hong. "I watch TV."

"Bah. TV. There's nothing in her file about any of that. She was fresh.
If this wasn't her first, it was maybe her second time. Maybe third. She
got unlucky. Or maybe she knew enough to shoot-up between her toes.

Or maybe it's just that bad things sometimes happen to folks right outa the gate, you know?"

Yeah, I'm aware.

He gives me as much information as he can, which honestly isn't much at all. Her father is flying in to collect the body and clean out her apartment in a few days. After that, her file goes in a drawer, and the case is, as they say, closed. I don't even bring up the possibility that Katie's OD could in any way be related to Finch. The longer I can leave Cookie's name officially out of the Finch mess, the better. But I do selfishly shake the tree a little bit. "While I got you, what's going on with IAB and our case?"

"Our case? That's cute. That's real cute. It's *my* case, Nancy Drew." He goes on to tell me that his afternoon meeting with IAB got canceled. He's not sure what's up, but when it gets rescheduled, he'll keep me in the loop as much as he's able to. He says keep my nose clean, and I tell him to keep his duck out of the mud, which I think he forgot he originally said to me at Veselka.

"What the hell does that mean?" he asks.

I dunno. Maybe I misheard him the first time he said it.

—

I go back to the jungle room to get a few things and then back to Cookie's. I'm going to stay there till she gets herself back into some sort of functional mode. I'm pretty certain Katie's death is in no way connected to me and Finch, but I owe it to Cookie to do what I can and at least look into things. If anything, I'll learn more about her, and she'll learn more about me—for better or for worse.

CHAPTER EIGHTEEN

I START WHERE IT ended for Katie.

Williamsburg Beach is actually just the remains of some nineteenth-century piers left over from a long-gone ferry system just south of the Williamsburg Bridge. All that's left are dots of decayed wood that bob above and below the waterline as the river rolls in and out against a small patch of sand. It's all just behind and down from Giando on the Water at Broadway and Kent. Every neighborhood in every non-Manhattan borough has at least a few Giando-type places—event space Italian restaurants specializing in confirmations, weddings, anniversaries and funeral receptions (chronologically). Each of these places generally has a tall white stucco facade with its name looming high on the wall in oversized black cursive letters. Below, red-coated valets give and take tickets for leased Cadillacs and Town Cars. And inside each of these life-event-centered restaurants, a maître d' named Bobo or Puco or Geno awaits to guide you to your white-tableclothed table complete with a view to the skyline of a borough that most of the patrons wouldn't step foot in if you paid them.

I walk around Giando's parking lot and find the path down to the water, squeeze through a hole in a worn plywood fence and walk to the drop a few feet from the waterline. A moisture-rotted ancient wooden ladder sort of leans against the steep incline. I decide if the ladder is going to break, I'd rather it happen on the way back up, so I jump the six feet down and aim for the softest-looking sand I can reach. As I land, I roll forward a bit too much, and my hands land in the cold shallows of the East River, somehow missing the glass, the metal, the rocks, the syringes, I know are hiding just inside the gray murk.

Standing, I can see the remains of some police tape flapping in the river breeze about ten feet away. The whole scene feels a little too TV heroin to me, a little too perfect a location for an OD. There are many better places to shoot up. Safer places. I could see coming here with the intent to dramatically end it all, but that doesn't sound like this situation. It wouldn't be that hard to drag a body out here and dump it. Yeah, there's the six-foot drop, but you could easily let a comatose body simply fall into the sand with minimal damage to it, minimal bruising. Then you just drag it over here and set up the hipster death scene and wipe your footprints on the way out. And I'm not saying she didn't OD. She still could have, and the person she was shooting up with could have chosen to leave her here. I don't think I'm stretching reality with either of these takes, so I log them inside my head and move on with my night.

Katie bartended at Honey and Milk in Carroll Gardens the night she died, but I don't want to head over there just yet. I want to be there about the same time she would have been, so I climb up the wonky ladder and take the long walk up Broadway, eventually cutting left to Kellogg's Diner to eat an overly toasted bran muffin and kill some time. I wish this part of Williamsburg had a movie theater. I could use a movie in a large dark room right about now.

—

The vibe at Honey and Milk seems forced and unnatural for this part of Carroll Gardens. It's a gaudy Manhattan square stuffed into a run-down Brooklyn circle. I can see this place in Bay Ridge or Brighton

Beach even, but not here. And judging by its emptiness, the locals can't see it here either. There's an *A Clockwork Orange* Milk Bar thing happening with the aesthetic, but it's cheap and poorly done. The walls look like the dorm-room walls of a weed-obsessed freshman—Woolite-painted mushrooms luminesce under the purple beams of head-shop-bought black lights. Some of the black light spills out onto the edges of the white couches, highlighting the constellation of stains on the fabric. Behind the bar, a barely dressed female bartender flips through a water-splotched *Daily News*. A steroid-pumped goombah on the last stool sucks on a Heineken while his fat fingers skim a copy of *Maxim*. The high BPM of the Chemical Brothers' track on the stereo gives the absolute lack of action in this mostly empty space a bizarre fever-dream vibe.

I take out the photo of Katie that Cookie gave me, getting it on deck to show, and then motion toward the bartender. She lazily walks over to me, rubbing her sore neck as she does.

"What do you have on tap?"

"Budweiser."

"What else?" There are two taps at the bar.

"The other one is our Honey and Milk Pilsner. But it's actually just Budweiser. Same keg, different label, different tap. And it costs a buck more."

"Michelle! Jesus Christ. What did I tell you about that?" The *Maxim*-reading man is pissed. I'm guessing he's the owner or the manager. Probably both.

"I guess I'll have the Budweiser, then," I say. "The cheaper one."

"Coming up."

"She's bullshitting you. She's just trying to piss me off." He walks over and takes the stool next to me. "I'm Bobby. I'm the manager. I'm also the owner. The owner/manager, I guess. You just stopping in? Meeting friends? I'm only asking 'cause we're having some problems keeping the stools filled, ya know? I figure if I know why people come in, then I can try and focus on that aspect of the business and try to promote that, push that and so forth and so on."

"What do people normally say when you ask them?"

The bartender puts my pint in front of me. "That they came in to use the bathroom."

"Michelle! Honestly!" He turns toward me. "That's not what they say. I swear. I mean, sure. Some people need to use the can. Sure. I'm not gonna lie. People gotta use it. It's a biological function. But not everybody that comes in here. Not everybody."

I grab the pint, and the cold beer inside makes me want to press the glass against my swollen face, but I opt not to highlight my injuries and just take a small sip. "Well, I'm not here for that, but I'm also not really here to drink." I slide Katie's photo across to Bobby. "I'm looking for some information about an employee of yours—Katie. She used to work here, correct?" He looks at it and gives the usual "what a shame" headshake as he does.

"Yeah, but not much. She had other gigs, mostly."

Michelle picks up the photo and looks at it sadly. "*Better* gigs, you mean. She was nice. Are you a cop or something?"

"No, private investigator. Hired by a friend of hers."

Bobby leans toward me. "She ... OD'd, right?" His voice drops to a whisper when he says "OD'd," and then he looks around nervously like it's going to have some negative effect on the nonexistent clientele.

"That's what they say. Was she the type? Did she seem like she used?"

Bobby leans back and ponders it. "I dunno. But you can never tell."

"No, she didn't," Michelle jumps in confidently. "I've worked with a whole range of junkies. Light to heavy and back again. They all could hide it for a while, but eventually, I knew when each one was fucked up. They slide. They get lazy. Katie never did that. She was reliable. Always reliable."

"Okay," I say. "Well, I'm just trying to retrace the steps of her last night. What time did she get off?"

Michelle hands me back the photo. "She split around three a.m. She was supposed to close, but I covered for her. She was meeting someone in Williamsburg."

"Did she say who?" I ask.

"No."

"Does the name Cookie sound familiar?"

"No. Sorry."

"How'd she get there?"

"Car service."

"Do you know which one?"

"We always take Arecibo. They're good. Safe."

—

Bobby lets me use their phone as long as I promise to say good things about his place and come back sometime with friends. It seems like an easy lie to tell, so I tell it. I call Cookie to see if she's friendly with any drivers at Arecibo, and she says yes and then tells me to meet her there. I push back on her coming in person as much as I can without pissing her off—she hasn't really come down yet—emotionally, I mean—and if she goes off, she could stir things up. She pushes back harder, so I fold. The reality of the situation is that we need info from a driver, and if it takes one hack's trust in another hack to get the info, so be it.

I call Arecibo for a car and give my drop-off as the intersection nearest their dispatch office on Fifth Avenue in Park Slope. The dispatcher says five minutes, but the car doesn't show up for about fifteen. By the time I get there, Cookie's already standing outside, laughing it up with another driver. They look like old friends. Maybe she can hold it together. She sees me, says good-bye to the other driver and heads my way.

"I got it. Let's go." She taps me on the shoulder as she passes by, heading to her double-parked Town Car.

"You got what?"

"The info. The address where they dropped Katie off." She opens her door. "C'mon, let's go."

Shit. Okay. Maybe Cookie's got it together more than I thought. Purpose seems to have given her clarity of thought, at least in the moment.

We drive by the Doray on the way to the BQE, and I remember that I need to swing by and talk to Mikey about some sort of a memorial for Finch. I'll do it tomorrow. Maybe the day after. I think about killing time on the way to the address by filling Cookie in on what I've learned so far, but she seems so focused and solid that I don't want to rock that. I decide to wait till she asks me about it.

In Williamsburg, we cruise down Metropolitan, and I see the same septuagenarian pair seated outside the Sons of Verona Social Club as we pass. At Berry we hang a right, and Cookie smoothly slides into the first parking spot she finds.

"This is it?" I ask.

"It's a block ahead."

"What is?"

"Kokie's Place."

"Oh. Right." *Great. Another coke bar.*

I've never actually been to Kokie's. When I was fifteen and my mom and I lived with Cookie, I avoided this part of town and mostly stuck to the Northside. Back then Kokie's was a Puerto Rican social club and kinda gang-y, if I remember correctly. I stayed away for obvious reasons. From what I've heard, it's still pretty heavily Puerto Rican, but its after-hours coke reputation has spread to NYU and Parsons kids and is now being passed around between them like a precious secret. Slowly it's becoming a late-night destination for many a pale-faced undergrad from the other side of the river. None of this bodes well for the idea that Katie didn't OD, though, and from the look on Cookie's face, she's thinking the same thing.

I try to recenter her by doing the opposite of what I said I'd do earlier and tell her what little I know from my day—that Katie's dad is coming in the day after tomorrow to claim her body and pack up her apartment and the whole too-perfect TV chicness of the waterfront as a shoot-up spot. Cookie takes it in, nodding as she ponders it all.

"You ever been?" I ask. "Here, I mean?"

Cookie holds on to the lingering thought occupying her brain for a moment longer before answering. "A few times. On salsa nights. But not for years." She turns off the engine and keeps staring forward. "It's so weird. I haven't even dropped anybody off here in ages. What was she doing here?"

"Let's try to find out, huh?"

A block ahead at Berry and North Third, white block letters on a dirty red awning let you know where you are—KOKIE'S PLACE. It's actually pronounced coqui, like the tiny Puerto Rican frog, and originally had nothing to do with cocaine. I guess it just eventually grew into its name the way some folks grow into a nose or a chin. The windows on the street are blacked out from the inside, so it's hard to get a vibe, but it's totally dead outside. We head toward the bouncer, and with Cookie in the lead, he doesn't give us any grief. She looks local; shit, she *is* local. The moment the door opens the scene changes.

The reggaeton hits first. The speakers throb with static—they're too weak for the bass, too tight for the treble. Inside, we scan the room. It's mostly Puerto Ricans and Dominicans, with random Caucasian smatterings of Greenpoint Poles, liberal arts undergrads, and Brooklyn artists, of both the genuine and the poseur variety. It's more brightly lit than I imagined it would be—there's no attempt to hide in the shadows here. In the back left corner, a small line has formed of folks leaning against the wall near a shower curtain. At first, I think it's the bathroom, then I realize, with all the nose wiping of those leaving the curtain, that it must be where you buy and do the coke. Look at me with my insanely perceptive investigative skills. Cookie seems overwhelmed with it all, so I take the lead. "Let's start with the bartender. Katie was a bartender, right? They might have known each other."

"Right, right ..."

We belly up to the bar, and I shout an order of two Buds to the bartender. She comes over with a pair of tiny bottles—ponies, they're called—I remember Finch used to get them sometimes in between booze at the Doray. She puts them down and says, "*Seis.*" I pause for a moment, maybe a little too proud that she assumed I speak Spanish. And as I dig for a ten, Cookie leans in.

"*Mijita*, can I ask you a question?"

She incorrectly predicts what she's about to be asked. "Ask one of the folks in line how it's done."

"No, not that ..." She pulls out a photo-booth-strip photo of Katie and her. "Have you ever seen her here before?"

The bartender takes the photo strip and looks at it as I down my pony beer in a few gulps and move on to Cookie's. The bartender looks up at us and notices my black eye and hesitates for a moment. "What's this about? Who are you guys?"

She's nervous. Doesn't want the law sniffing around, doesn't want to be dragged into anything requiring statements and depositions. I jump in. "We're her friends. She's missing and we're worried about her. We know she came here a few nights ago—we're just trying to retrace her steps and hoping we can find her."

She eyes me a little warily, but it seems like she may have bought the story. "Okay. Yeah, she comes in here about once a week. What's her name? Kay something?"

"Katie." Cookie says it small. I think she was hoping we'd strike out. Any positive connection to this place makes Katie OD'ing more likely.

"Yeah, she, like, gets sponsorship for parties, right? She'd look for clients here."

"Clients? What do you mean?" I say.

"All the gringo kids that have been coming by. The white kids moving into the Northside."

"But how are they clients?"

"I dunno the specifics. I just remember the bits she sometimes talked about when I was serving her." Down on the other end of the bar, somebody fights for the bartender's attention. She gives a wave and starts to lean that way.

"My photo?" Cookie says.

The bartender stops, not even having realized she still had it in her hand. "Oh. Sorry." She hands it back to Cookie.

"One more question ... Do you remember ... did she ... like, did she ever go behind the curtain?" I'm surprised Cookie was able to keep it together long enough to get the entire question out.

"I don't think so, but I really have no idea. But she never orders alcohol. Only Diet Cokes."

A small smile forms on Cookie's face, and she goes distant, remembering something private with Katie, something sparked by what the bartender said. I'm about to recommend moving on when a firm white hand comes down on my shoulder.

"Where the fuck have you been?"

I turn and am surprised to see a flush-faced Tommy standing a little too close to me. "Tommy. Jesus. What are you doing here?"

"Yeah, I could ask you the same thing. I thought you kept it clean. I mean, booze, yeah, smokes, yeah, but not, you know, this kinda stuff."

"I'm working."

"You're working? Where's your camera?" He looks around the chaotic room. "Who's the unlucky MTA grunt about to lose their fat insurance payoff?"

"It's not that kind of case." He's a bit saucier than usual tonight. A bit pumped, a bit energized.

"No? What? So, you're like a real investigator now? You doing real PI shit?"

I think on that and then realize, yeah. *Fuck, yeah, I am.* But I play it calmer. "Sort of, yeah." I like this moment of quiet confidence on my part, but I don't want to dwell on it. "Sorry I didn't call you back after your cab thing. I've just been insane with work."

"It's all right. It's all right." He puts a finger up to the bartender for a pony and gives his nose a fast wipe. "It all worked out. It all worked out." He drops a five and takes a swig. "Ends up I'm not, like, an addictive type of guy. I felt nothing after the crack thing, you know? Nothing. No cravings. No desire to get more or anything."

I could say I don't think secondhand crack smoke really works that way, but I don't think it would matter. I also have no idea.

"Yeah, so anyways, since I now know I'm not the addictive type, and I've always wanted to try this, you know"—he nods toward the shower curtain queue—"it seemed like a sign or something. Like, just do it. Just go ahead and do it. Just *do it*. So ... yeah. Here I am."

Oh boy. "And how's that working out?"

His face goes red as a Robert De Niro smile forms on it. "Fucking great, man."

"Well, good." *Yeesh.* I give him a slap on the shoulder. I gotta end this. "It's good to see you, Tommy."

"Yeah. Yeah. Same. Same." He's already mentally moved on from the conversation, plotting his next bump or his next bump buddy. I give Cookie a quiet nod, and we make our escape.

Back in her car, Cookie gets lost in thought the moment she closes the door. I try to bring her back. "What do you make of all that client stuff?"

She shakes her head lightly. "I don't know. She bartended; that's all she ever told me. Said she worked at a few places across Brooklyn." She finally turns the ignition. "At least we know she probably didn't use."

Do we, though? I'm not so sure. I don't outwardly agree with Cookie, but I don't fight it, either. Instead, I present her with the truth of what Katie's not using means. "So, about that. Let's be clear about something. She *did* die of an overdose. That's a fact, right? So, that means it was either her first time using—"

"She didn't use."

"Right. Okay. But what I'm trying to say is, if she didn't use, that means she was murdered. Somebody held her down and shot heroin into her. Is that what you're saying happened?"

"She didn't use."

"Okay, okay. I get that. But I'm asking if you can wrap your head around what accepting that fact means. You're saying somebody killed her. Do you really see that? Do you buy that happening?"

"More than her willingly shooting up, yes."

It's starting to seem like it's going to take more than actual facts to get Cookie to change her mind. I wish we could get into Katie's apartment. Dig around. I know all the places my dad used to hide his gear. If I could look, maybe find her kit, that would end this quick. "You don't happen to have a spare key to Katie's place, do you?"

"No."

"But you've been there before, right?"

"Of course. She's in South Slope, close to the park."

"I wish there was a way to get in there before her father gets here."

"You could break in." She says that faster than I would have imagined. She must have already been pondering it herself. I turn to see if she's serious. She is.

"I wouldn't know the first thing about breaking into an apartment, Cookie."

"Yeah, me neither." She clicks the Town Car into drive and pulls out. "But I bet Frankie does."

Shit. I bet he does.

CHAPTER NINETEEN

I WAKE UP ON Cookie's couch the next morning and almost immediately start trying to figure out how to back out of this proposed
break-in. Since Katie's dad is coming in from California tomorrow, it
would have to happen today; Frankie's already agreed to help, and he
and I are supposed to do a preliminary scout of the place during the day,
then regroup tonight.

I don't know if "Fear loves company" is a thing, but once the B-and-E
fear enters my mind, several more push through behind it, the first being
about my diminishing bank account. The selfish harsh reality of Finch
being dead is that I'm out of a job. I've avoided thinking about it—it
seemed self-centered to worry about not having a job when Finch doesn't
have his life anymore—but the realities of New York City will start taking
their toll on my existence, even without rent to pay. I have the monthly
co-op fee of the apartment and city taxes. The checking account is down
to under three hundred bucks, and the three thousand I have in savings
will go quickly without anything new coming in. With Finch's case and
now Cookie's, I have a lot to be thinking about, but if I run out of money,
I'll have a lot more.

Cookie's still sleeping, and I can't find any coffee in her kitchen, so
I head out in search of some. As I leave her place, my pager gives me a
buzz—it's a number I don't recognize. It looks like it came in at 1:00

a.m. last night and I didn't see it. Maybe it's Finch related, maybe not, but I'm curious, so I step up to a pay phone on Bedford Avenue and call. The voice that answers is barely awake. It grunts what I assume is a hello.

"Yeah, this is Nico. I was paged."

"Hold on." She covers the receiver and proceeds to cough her way toward coherency. It seems to do the job, although she's still a little froggy. "Georgie boy! How's your face?" *Ah, Maggie.* I haven't thought much about my face since last night, and the mention of it brings on the throbs. I need more Advil. I tell her I'm on the mend, and she brings me up to speed on what happened after I left. She's pressing charges against Bob Hoskins, the cabby is pressing charges against Bob Hoskins, and I don't need to get involved if I don't want to, but a detective may or may not be calling me sometime.

More cops. Great.

My need for caffeine is crawling to the front of my brain, and I quickly regret not getting it before I returned this page. I try to wrap things up quickly so I can take care of it. "Was the cop stuff why you paged?"

"Oh, no, actually ... I wanted to bounce something off you."

"Okay."

"It's a TV show idea."

All around me people walk on the sidewalk with coffee in their hands while I stand here with none. *Wait. What?* "Why would you call me for that?"

"You're smart. You watch things. I figured, why not?"

"Okay. But does this have to happen now?"

"Yeah, 'cause I met this guy, this TV producer guy, last night, and we sort of connected creatively, and he told me to pitch him some ideas today. I need to get them fleshed out." *Connected creatively.* Yeah. I'll have to remember that one. She goes on to ask me if I've seen that HBO show.

The one with horny ladies. *No.* Then she asks about the NBC show. The one with the couch. I tell her I'm not sure.

"Wait, you don't know if you've watched it?"

"I'm sure I've seen some episodes, yeah."

"How could you not watch it?"

"I dunno, Maggie. I mostly watch movies, reruns of *Barney Miller* and the Mets."

"Movies are like TV. I mean, the qualities that make them good are like TV. It's essentially the same thing. You know what I mean."

I don't want to get into this philosophical conversation right now, so I push past it. "Okay. Just bounce it off me." She goes into the pitch immediately, fast-talking past my sleepy ability to comprehend, but somewhere in there I realize she's pitching her own life, her own experiences. "So, it's basically your life?" She says yeah but with comedic embellishments and exaggerations. "So where am I, then?" I'm joking, but she actually answers.

"You're, like, established, with a career and everything. This is supposed to be about people who have no clue what they want to do with their lives."

Huh. If I'm established, that's news to me. Do I look like I am? I don't feel like I am. If I look like I am, I'd really prefer to feel like I am as well. I tell her to break a leg and let me know how it goes, hang up, and then brave the scene at the L Cafe for my coffee. By the time I get back to Cookie's, Frankie's already there, sitting in his double-parked van outside of her place.

"Let's go, let's go, let's go." He's slapping the outside of the driver's-side door repeatedly as he says it. The difference in our moods about the plan for the day is as vast as his neck is wide.

I pour an inch of my coffee out onto the street so it doesn't spill all over me while we drive and then get in. Frankie grabs the Club that's on the passenger side seat and tosses it to the ground. "Goddamn things are better weapons than they are locks."

What am I doing? It's feeling like every time I try to regain control, something else is taking over. I need to hit Pause—sincerely this time. I need to stop and regroup. After this, though. Get through this day, and then it's back to Finch, back to Rangers Jersey, back to Kangol Hat.

I wish that fucking tape would show up. It would make things a hell of a lot easier.

—

The scout was pretty quick. We buzzed every buzzer in Katie's building till the front door opened and then did a brisk walk by of her door—Frankie immediately said, "Nope" when he saw her setup, and we headed downstairs.

"That's too much work. Too noisy. It's gonna take too much time." His plan B was more complex "but quieter," he said. We guesstimated which building was behind hers on the parallel street and blind buzzed our way into that one, this time heading up to the roof. Across the way, over the weed-filled backyards, it looked like Katie had at least one window with a fire escape. But to get there, we'd have to climb down past two sets of windows since she was on the third floor of five.

"How do we get by their windows without being seen?" I asked.

"Time Warner, baby."

I didn't know what that meant, and I very much didn't like how it sounded.

—

We split up with plans to regroup at midnight. Frankie goes to take care of his workday, and I go back to the Avenue B apartment to see if there's any sign of the tape in my mailbox. Nothing. I run upstairs to check the paper I left in the doorjamb, and to my surprise it's still wedged in there. I grab some black jeans and a dark sweatshirt for tonight and then reposition the doorjamb paper and skip down the stairwell toward the street. I still have to head over to the jungle room on Essex Street and water the plants. It's been a couple of days.

Halfway down the last flight of stairs I freeze—goddamn Kangol Hat is standing in the vestibule, trying to close a broken mailbox that I'm assuming is mine. *Shit.* He doesn't see me, or he plays that he doesn't see me. If I stay here on the stairs, it's going to bring attention to my hesitation. If I turn around, it's worse. I decide to push on down the stairs and open the vestibule door, squeezing past him with my head down. As I grab the handle of the door to the outside, I see his left arm move out of the corner of my eye, and I can't help but flinch as I step through to the street.

On the sidewalk, I can see that he wasn't reaching for me. He was reaching out to stop the door to my building from closing so he could go in. Basically, I just helped him break into my own place. Brilliant. I mean, he's a corrupt cop, and he would have gotten in eventually, but me helping was really kind of spot on for how things have been going. As I'm standing there pondering my idiocy, Rangers Jersey pushes by me and into my building, and both of them start jogging up the stairwell toward my floor. I'm pissed at myself and pissed at them, but I also realize something pretty great—these assholes don't know what I look like. I assumed they would, especially if they pulled the photo from my PI license. But if they pulled the photo from my 1994 driver's license, they'd be looking for a platinum-blond-dyed-unfortunate-Caesar-cut-wearing kinda guy. It was a brief look that lasted less than a year, but thanks to the New York DMV, it lives on forever in my wallet. At least for a few more years, anyway.

This is good. This helps me. I can watch them with a little security. I see one of their shadows pass by my living room window upstairs and my anger blossoms.

Enough of these assholes going in and out of my place whenever they fucking feel like it. I need to make things more difficult for them.

I have no idea how this will play, but I walk over to a pay phone, dial 911, say that I live in 3F and that someone is breaking into 3R across the hallway. I give it some energy, some mania. I hang up and take a seat on a bench in Tompkins Square Park to wait and watch.

It takes about five minutes for the cops to show up. A cruiser double-parks in front of my building, and two uniforms get out and enter the vestibule, blind buzzing their way inside, just like Frankie and me this morning at Katie's. A pang hits me when I see one pull his gun out as he enters the hallway—I didn't process things to this point, didn't imagine it could turn into some sort of a shootout. Another cruiser pulls up as I stand. Two more cops head inside. It's all too late to stop now.

Fuck. I may have seriously fucked this up.

I stare. I wait. Nothing. After five minutes, the last two uniformed cops to arrive walk out—quietly, calmly—get into their cruiser and drive off. Then the rest exit—the first two uniforms walking out with Rangers Jersey and Kangol Hat, talking and laughing it up. Everybody friendly like. Fucking assholes. I'm pissed at myself for worrying about any of them. As the uniforms get into their car, a black Town Car pulls up in front of my building, and Rangers Jersey and Kangol Hat get in it. The car idles as it sits double-parked. I can't see who's in the back seat with them, but I can see the driver—it's Wally's guy. I realize if I can see them, they can see me, so I start to pull back deeper into the park. Maybe

Rangers Jersey and Kangol Hat can't recognize me, but Wally can, and he's sure as fuck in that back seat.

I don't need to stick around anymore. I turn and head across Tompkins and start cutting down to the Lower East Side.

On the bright side of all this, at least I have clarity. Wally is officially bad news. I felt it, I thought it, but now I know it. I need to protect myself better around him or avoid him entirely. I'll need to find another escape hatch, another means of protection from all this. If the cops can't help you, if your government can't help you, if your priest or rabbi can't help you, what else is there? The press? Do I know anybody in the press?

—

I meet Frankie at midnight at Jackie's Fifth Amendment on Fifth Avenue and Seventh Street in Park Slope. He's at the end of the bar, leaning over a metal bucket full of ice and Budweiser pony beers. When did ponies get so trendy? He looks up as I walk in. "It was on special." The tiny bottle looks ridiculous in his giant fist. He hands me one and raises his to cheers. "A little courage never hurt, right?"

I don't like the need for courage, but Frankie has repeatedly assured me that this will be smooth and stress-free. We'll see. I called Cookie earlier to tell her I wouldn't do the break-in, but she immediately said if I wouldn't, she would. I've dragged her into so much shit lately, I felt like I kind of owed it to her, so I conceded. "All right," I told her. "I'll do it."

Two beers later and Frankie and I are walking south on Fifth toward Katie's place. I ask him again how we're going to get past the fourth- and fifth-floor windows without being noticed, and he tells me it'll just be easier to explain when we get there. Not a good sign.

—

"You're joking," I say.

"No. It's sturdy. Don't worry about it."

We're standing on Katie's roof. Frankie rigged the vestibule door earlier so it would be able to push open—something he learned somewhere from someone—and he's just explained the plan to me.

"Of course I'm going to worry about it. We're on the fifth floor."

"This is how it's done. People do this every day all over the city."

"By 'it,' you mean breaking into apartments?"

"If you're going from the roof and then through a window? Yeah. It is. It's also a good way to get from building to building. You just swing. Like Tarzan."

Jesus.

The plan is to shimmy down one of the many coaxial cables that hang down the back of the building. Frankie has wrapped one around the cable box a few times, and he swears that it'll be enough to hold us. We'll stay clear of the windows as we go, and then at Katie's floor we'll do what Frankie affectionately calls the "Time Warner Swing" over to her fire escape. From there we'll try to get in through that window.

The idea of hanging and being able to hold my body weight with *only my arms* seems an absolute impossibility to me. Frankie could probably hold us both if he needed to, but personally, I can't remember ever successfully doing more than one pull-up in my life, so I'm admittedly nervous. "Frankie ... I'm not like ... I mean, my upper body, it's, uh ..."

"It's twenty feet. We're shimmying down twenty feet, then we're swinging over five feet to the fire escape."

"That's more than twenty feet."

"Fine. Twenty-five, then. Thirty at most. *Maybe* thirty-five. Maybe. You seriously don't think you can do it?"

I never made it up the rope in gym. Never rang the bell. Not once. I tell him.

"That's what? Twelve years ago? You're a man now, Nico! Come on. I know you can do it." He's all smiles as he gives me a reassuring slap on the shoulder. "Anyways, it's way easier going down than it is going up. And you'll be surprised how strong you can be when your life is depending on it."

I know that last bit was meant as comedic encouragement, but it really felt more like a warning of impending doom, like beware the ides of March, and remember to respect gravity at all times. I don't know what to say. I just stare at him waiting for this not to happen. Waiting for something to intervene.

"I'll go first. I'll show you how to grip it, how to use your legs. Using your legs makes it easier. Come on. Watch me." He gets to the edge and gives an intense tug on the coaxial cable. "See? Totally sturdy." Before I know it, he's over the ledge, his legs out but bent at the knees. He sort of looks like that bit when Batman and Robin would climb up the side of a building on the old TV show, except he's going down. He shimmies down a little farther, then easily swings the five feet to the fire escape. The whole thing takes less than ten seconds. "Okay, come on. I'll hold the cable so you don't have to swing. Just come on down to me."

I grab hold of it and give it my own tug. It does seem secure, but I know that's the least of my worries. I put one foot over the ledge, take a deep breath and put my trust in Frankie's trust in me. *Just hold tight. Hold tight. You can do this. Hold tight.*

Jesus Christ, five floors up is high.

I slide the other leg over and try to get in that same position Frankie was in—and it works for a few feet, but my foot slips on the dusty brick, and my whole body goes vertical, my hands squeezing the cable, my legs immediately twisted around it tightly, in a panic. "Shit, shit, shit ..."

Below, Frankie calls out to me quietly. "It's fine. Just relax. You got it. You're holding."

"I'm slipping." *I am. Fuck.*

"That's great. That's fine. Just slip on down—but slowly. Just slide down toward me. I'll get you."

I'm terrified to do it, but the longer I stay still, the sooner I'm going to get too tired to hold on, so I let myself slide down slowly, and it's honestly easier than I thought it would be. I can hear activity bleed out of the cracked window to my right—cooking, chatting and the harmonized CBS-FM call-letter radio ID as I slowly pass by. Right when I feel my grip start to weaken, I feel Frankie grab my belt and pull me onto the fire escape, to temporary safety.

Jesus.

Jesus Fucking Christ.

Frankie gives me a minute to catch my breath. "Good work," he says.

"That was terrifying."

"You did great."

"You know, one day you've gotta tell me what you've been up to since juvie. I mean, you've learned some new skills."

"I thought that was basically what I was doing now."

Fair enough.

He goes over to the window, looks in and stops for a moment. "Fuck."

"What?"

"I think there's an alarm on this window."

"What? How can you tell?"

He shows me the connectors inside, one on the pane, one on the sill. "It might not be turned on, might not be set. But if it is, we probably don't wanna risk it." Frankie looks past me at the side of the building, toward another window—a smaller one. "It looks like her bathroom window is open."

I look. It is. But it's also about fifteen feet away.

"One of us could swing over—get in through there."

One of us? "There's no way I'm doing that."

"Well, I'm too big. I'll get stuck."

"Then why'd you say 'one of us'?"

Frankie gives me a long look and then a smile. "I know you can do it."

"I can't."

"Yes you can. I'll show you how. It's easy. You just wrap the cable around your arm a bunch of times, see?" He shows me. "And then hold tight at the top. You swing, you get your legs in the window and you kinda pull yourself in with them."

"How often have you done shit like this?"

He nods back and forth like he's making calculations, carrying ones, et cetera, and then just says, "Enough times to know you can do it. C'mon." Before I can protest, he's wrapping the cable around my right arm, over and over and over again, and then once around my palm. Even if I don't fall, my arm is probably going to rip right out of the socket.

Like he's reading my mind and knows I'm worrying, Frankie tries to give me some advice: "It's easy as long as you're quick. You gotta be quick. Gotta be quick. You just step off the ledge, and you just do it. If you're in trouble, I'll pull you back, okay?" He looks at me face-to-face. "Okay? I'll pull you back."

"How?"

"I'll pull up some slack from below you, hold on to it, and if you're in trouble, I'll pull you back in. Easy."

"Okay."

All right. I can do this. I need to do this to move on. Fuck. I stand on the railing of the fire escape, give a hard tug up top to make sure it's still secure. It is. *Okay. Okay. Deep breath. Okay. Deep breath.*

"It's gonna be over in five seconds," Frankie says.

Maybe not the best wording, Frankie, but right, I get what you meant. Fuck. Okay. I count down. "Three. Two. One."

I jump and I feel Frankie's hand on my back, giving me a push, but I wasn't expecting it, and the extra energy makes me brush the wall of the building and immediately start spinning from the contact. Once my weight starts pulling on the cable, the pain in my arm and hand is immediate and excruciating. I'm in pain, I'm spinning and I'm swinging above darkness, but I know what's down there—cement to crack me open and rats to eat what spills out. It's not just that I'm spinning, though—it's that I'm spinning in the *bad* direction, the unraveling direction. I'm like a top spinning out as the cable around my arm comes unwound with each turn.

Fuck. Fuck, fuck, fuck.

I can see the window getting closer, so I stick out my right foot and somehow manage to get it wedged in. I pull up on the cable for leverage and use my other foot to push the window open more and then start to shimmy inside. It's not graceful. My feet are knocking over shampoo bottles and soap and other toiletries—things are falling and breaking as I'm doing my best worm imitation with my body to move to safety. My shirt comes up from the friction, and I feel the metal of the windowsill scratching and scraping my stomach and my ribs as I go in, but there's no fucking way I'm stopping until there's a building underneath me and a wall in front of me with me on the correct side of it. The side with a floor. I relax a bit once my torso is inside the dark bathroom, and I unwind what's left of the cable around my arm, letting it drop out the window.

Jesus.

How fucking stupid am I? I look out at Frankie and give him a wave and realize he wasn't even holding onto the goddamn cable as he said he was going to. Goddamn liar couldn't have pulled me back if I'd needed it.

I shimmy farther backward and blindly try to step off the small sink and counter and immediately slip, panic reaching out, managing to grab hold of the shower curtain for support, but each of the plastic ringlets connecting the curtain to the bar releases in rapid fire, one after the other, pop, pop, pop, pop, pop, until I'm flat on my back in the bathtub, looking up at the ceiling, reflecting on what, up to this point in my life, is definitely the stupidest thing I've ever done.

As the blood begins to flow back into my right arm, a second wave of intense pain hits. Every part of my body that got scraped, every part that got scratched, every part that got bruised, starts to sting and throb.

It's not just that I did this very stupid thing. It's that I did it and I knew that I shouldn't have.

"Get it together, Nico. Now."

I say it out loud, as if hearing it outside my own head is going to help. I hope it does.

CHAPTER TWENTY

B ACK AT COOKIE'S, WE say good-bye to Frankie, and I wait for him
to leave before I start going over what I found at her girlfriend's
place. Twice while we were there, I had to remind Frankie that this wasn't
an actual robbery, that we were specifically looking for things that might
help explain *how* what happened to Katie happened to her. Honestly, I'm
not even 100 percent positive he didn't manage to lift something when
I wasn't paying attention, but I'm not gonna piss him off by patting
him down looking for loot. Between that, his not holding the cable and
the fact that there actually wasn't an alarm on the window, I need a
Frankie break. I'm a little pissed. Also, the window to the fire escape was
unlocked. So, yeah. I'm not in the best mood about Mr. Frankie Balls.

When he's finally out, I go over everything with Cookie.

At Katie's I started with the search I had seen my mom do a thousand
times with my dad's stuff when they were still married—the old "where
are you hiding the drugs?" exploration. I began in the bedroom—first
between the mattress and the box spring, then looking in the mattress for
a slit, for a hidey-hole. There was nothing. Then the two stuffed animals
on the bed. Nada. Then the nightstand—no drugs, but a selection of
vibrators and a sleeping mask. I tried to keep things neater than my mom
did when she would tear into my dad's stuff—with her it was more like
a jail cell inspection, flipping mattresses and leaving things broken and

chaotic. It was as if beating up his stuff was as close as she'd get to beating up his body, so she needed to make it count. I didn't want Katie's dad showing up tomorrow, seeing a mess and then calling the cops about a break-in, so I searched with some care.

At her desk, I opened books, unscrewed pens, opened drawers, and flipped through notebooks. I found a folder marked "taxes" and paged through it to see what I could see. Mostly just the usual pay stubs from bars with the pitiable pre-tip hourly rate that bartenders and waitstaff are paid. And then two more pay stubs—one from something called "The ILA" for $1,200 and the other from UNITE for $400. Both said they were for "consulting fees." The ILA one had a subheading memo referencing the labor—"Red Hook"—but it didn't make sense to me, at least in terms of a job description. Maybe the job was located in Red Hook? Maybe there's a bar called Red Hook somewhere? I dunno. No memo on the UNITE pay stub. I tucked both into my pocket and moved on to the kitchen to check jars of dry powders—flour, coffee, sugar. Nothing. The only books around were all paperback sci-fi from the Park Slope Library, so no thick Bibles or dictionaries to flip through looking for chunks of pages cut out. Finally, I went to the bathroom, where I checked everything, pulling out the stick on her deodorant, a spot my dad loved using to hide his stash—he'd break the deodorant stick in half, toss the bottom half, stuff drugs into the plastic deodorant holder and then put remaining stick back on top. I looked everywhere and found nothing. Except ... behind me, the toilet was running—that hissing, constant bleed of water without pause, without collection. I wiggled the handle and it wasn't catching. Something was off with the mechanics on the inside. I didn't start at the toilet tank, because it's so obvious, so common. Maybe I didn't want to find the drugs right out of the gate?

I think I wanted to hold on to the hope that Cookie was holding on to. For Cookie's sake, I wanted Cookie to be right.

I took the top of the tank off, the condensation dripping as I set the porcelain rectangle down on the toilet seat. Looking inside, I fully expected to find ziplock baggies of heroin and shooting gear. But I didn't. I *did* find a plastic bag—a large one at that—but no drugs, no needles.

—

Back at Cookie's place, I put it down in front of her. "I didn't really know what to do with it. I didn't want to tell Frankie about it. And odds are her father doesn't know about it, right? So, if I leave it there, it's just gonna be found by the landlord or a plumber or the next tenant, and that seemed wrong somehow."

"How much is it?"

"About fourteen thousand dollars."

"Jesus."

"I want to be overtly clear—I didn't take it to take for me or for you to keep. I just ... Like I said, I didn't know what to do with it."

"I get it, I get it." She looks up at me. "You didn't find any drugs, though, right? No needles, no pills?"

"No."

"So, I was right."

"It seems that way."

"But ... that much money is weird. Right?" I can hear the concern in her voice. This is an entire new oddness, a new unknown, a new secret, kept from her by Katie.

"It might be. It might not be. Bartenders have a lot of cash from tips. It's possible she didn't want to report it all, you know? If she doesn't report it, she can't deposit it, so she's got to put it somewhere safe." Is that the tank of her toilet? I dunno. Maybe.

"Yeah. That's probably it. Yeah." She pauses, pondering something else. "The pay stubs are also weird, though. Like, odd?"

Maybe, maybe not, I tell her. Let's look into it and see.

We grab Cookie's Yellow Pages and look up both the ILA and UNITE. The only ILA we can find has an address that matches the pay stub, in Red Hook, Brooklyn, at the old shipping terminal. So there's that Red Hook reference from the stub, not that my understanding of it is any clearer. UNITE is in Manhattan, in the Garment District. I tell her I'll hit up both tomorrow. She pulls me in for a long hug, and when it's over, she says a very sincere *"Gracias, mijito"* and then turns and heads for bed. The action, the words, her body language—she seems so much older and fragile in this moment than she ever has before. I can tell she's spent. We both are.

It's been a long day and a long night.

—

I start my morning heading for the no-man's-land between Cobble Hill and Red Hook. Most of the shipping industry moved to Jersey years ago, but there's always at least one container ship dropping off and loading up here on any given day, sometimes two. The Newark, New Jersey, port has dozens of looming container cranes, moving, loading, working, twenty-four seven, but Brooklyn's Red Hook Terminal is now down to just three. They pop up in the distance on the low horizon between the brownstones as I walk through Carroll Gardens, walking down the arcing hill of Union Street toward the waterline.

As I cross Columbia Street and enter the shipping port, the giant ninety-foot cranes tower above me, their massive gears spinning as they glide, slide and effortlessly lift container after container. It's all kind of transfixing. I lose some time as I stare at their movements, until I get abruptly brought out of it by a stevedore asking if I need help, except he says it in the same tone as I imagine he says, "Fuck off, shit bird" or maybe "Eat shit, asshole." I look over at his round bowling-ball head and decide he's definitely more of an "eat shit, asshole" guy and then ask him where the offices are.

"Which one, dick wad?" The "dick wad" is silent. I mean, he doesn't actually say it. I'm just trying to capture the tone here.

I think on it for a moment and decide to go with staffing. Something with files. Information. "Personnel?"

"Yeah, that's easy, dick munch. Walk straight ahead and turn left at the next goddamn trailer office; it's gonna be the one just past it. That clear, asshole?" Again, that's tone. I'm just trying to capture the tone. He's actually very helpful. I thank him and follow his directions to the personnel office trailer.

The inside is faux wood paneled and run down. File cabinet after file cabinet line one wall, while the other is covered in OSHA posters, safety info and for some reason instructions on how to perform the Heimlich maneuver. The lone desk in the back is occupied by a blond-dyed-bee-hive-hairdo-topped sixtysomething woman who's aggressively punching numbers into an old adding machine, the gold charm tennis bracelet on her wrist shaking as she tabulates whatever she's tabulating. Her left hand holds a burning Parliament 100, a brand I can recognize at fifty paces thanks to my dad's side of the family's constant smoking of them. She looks like a lost-in-time extra from *The Taking of Pelham One Two Three*.

"Whaddaya need, sweetie?" she asks me without stopping.

"Uh, yeah. Not sure if you can help me. My sister just passed—"

"I'm so sorry, sweetie." Again, no stopping, no eye contact.

"That's okay, thanks. Um, I was organizing her stuff, settling her affairs, et cetera, and I found this pay stub. I'm just ... I dunno. I'm not sure what it is. The address is here at the terminal."

"What's it say on it, babe? Who's it from? There's lots of different corporations on the pier."

"Sure, right. It's the ILA. Do you know what that is?"

"That's the longshoreman's union—International Longshoreman's Association. If the paycheck is from them, I can't really help you. I'm with the Red Hook Terminal—we pay the stevedores, but the ILA, that's their union. If she got a check directly from the union—"

"You can't help me."

"Right." Her inputting continues. Just as I turn around, she jumps back in. "What's it say? The check, I mean. Like, for services rendered?"

"Ah, it says 'consulting.' That's it."

She stops her typing. "Was she a pretty girl, your sister?"

"What do you mean?"

"Attractive? Young? I'm only saying because there's been some trouble at the union—misused funds for, you know, entertainment purposes. Blue stuff." She puts her wrinkly hands up, almost in protest, like she's being forced to deliver this information, but it's clear she's enjoying it. "Look at me, talking about stuff I really shouldn't be. Just forget it."

"I'm sorry, are you implying that my dead sister was—what? A prostitute? A stripper?"

"Or just an entertainer. You never know. I'm just telling you what I hear, what I've heard around the piers. That union has had some issues, and not just with me. It wouldn't be the first time a girl like her worked her way through their payroll. But it's none of my business." And with that, she goes back to her adding machine, almost like I was never here. I'm kinda pissed off. I mean, Katie obviously isn't really my sister, but she's connected to someone I genuinely care about, and this beehived Dottie just basically called her a whore. Like, she went really far out of her way to do it. She's obviously got some beef with the ILA and wants to stir things up when given the chance. I try to tee up an insult to toss at her, but I know she won't hear it, won't register it or just won't care, so I give her a casual thanks for the info and then go off in search of the International Longshoreman's Association office.

There my request is received with a "No, can't help," then a "No, can't give out information about our employees" and then a decidedly pointed "No, and get the fuck out of my office." And that one wasn't just tone. That was tone and the actual words. Dockworkers do not disappoint.

The subway ride to the Garment District is mostly me trying to wrap my head around the possibility that Katie was, as Dottie said with heavy implication, "an entertainer." It might explain the cash. It would probably explain the cash.

I think it would explain the cash.

I get out and navigate sidewalks crowded with people wheeling clothing racks and bins of fabric. I love how sometimes this city delivers exactly what it is. In the Flower District, you get flowers. In the Garment District, you get garments. Not that anyone ever uses the word *garments* besides to say "Garment District."

The address for UNITE is easy to find, and from the sign in the lobby, I quickly realize that this is also a union office—this one for garment workers.

The person I speak to up here is much nicer, much calmer and more sensitive to my need for information considering the circumstance—my being the not actual brother of a fake sister who is really my *tía*'s girlfriend and is actually dead. She tells me Katie didn't work for them, but they paid her. It's complicated. In reality, she worked for a nonprofit in

Brooklyn called FWHS, and the union pays her for the work she does there. It's unusual but not untoward, not illegal. The woman doesn't know the specifics and recommends I speak with FWHS directly. I get the address and info for them, thank her for her time and on the way out get a massive pang of guilt when she says she's sorry for my loss.

I'm dreading that FWHS is going to be a Post Office Box for an escort agency, but the positivity of the UNITE worker's vibe gives me hope that it could actually be something different. I hope it is.

The address is on North Eleventh between Wythe and Kent in the deteriorated industrial part of Williamsburg—just a few blocks from where Katie was found. It's a small storefront on the first floor of a larger industrial brick waterfront building. The glass of the storefront is frosted and devoid of any identification of the business, the location, the address. The glass door is covered with layer after layer of social-justice-oriented stickers: "No Justice, No Peace." "Free Mumia." "End Apartheid." "Farms not Bombs." "AFL-CIO Union Strong." "Silence = Death." "Free Leonard Peltier Now!" Above the door pull handle, a handwritten sticker has the info I'm looking for: "FWHS—Factory Worker Housing Solutions." Below it another one in different handwriting: "This is the Now Films."

I try the door, and it opens with a scrape. Inside, the walls are more of the same. It's like I've walked into a travel agency but for political causes. Anti-apartheid posters. Earth Day. And reruns of all the ones stickered on the glass door I just stepped through.

My plan was to be honest, show the stubs, not even pretend to be Katie's brother, et cetera, but the second I see the dude inside I know that truth is probably very rarely rewarded by him.

I'm gonna lie. I'm gonna lie very much.

—

I've met people like this guy plenty of times before—mostly around my dad when creatives and A&R types would clutter his orbit. Full-grown men with jobs that justified them staying boys. Music types, film types, artist types. Frequently the common denominator for all those lifestyle subheadings is a comfortable safety net lined with family money. Sure, there are many scrappy and immensely talented folks with no trust funds who manage to build up careers, labels and brands from nothing. It wouldn't be New York City if there weren't inspirational folks like that. But it also wouldn't be New York if there weren't a shit ton more who have managed to fluff out a career with consistently below-average work—on Daddy's dime. Sometimes these guys will hit a vein and find some gold, somehow stumble onto some talent—theirs, or they'll leach off someone else's—but mostly they don't. They live in a self-imposed blur of work and life, wrapped up in ego and their own shitty opinions. And they'll be the first to eagerly tell you that their job is their identity, and their identity is their job, even when it's obvious that they suck pretty hard at both.

I get that vibe from this one. A lot.

I look over at the guy sitting behind the desk, the one who made me want to lie. He's holding up a finger for me to wait while he finishes his call, and everything about his body language makes me hate him. Without words, he's making sure I know that he is more important than me. That this phone call is more important than me. And yeah, I know I'm being fairly aggressive about him, but it's his ilk that kept my dad lines deep in coke and balloons deep in heroin even when he was trying to get clean.

He's wearing a beaded and multicolored kufi cap on his head and his eyeglasses are comically small—just quarter-sized lenses daintily wrapped in thin gold frames. The sports coat he's wearing looks like it was harvested from a parachute or maybe raw canvas. I can't really tell, but that's probably the point. I can only see a bit of the jeans, but it's clear from the lab-designed weathering of the denim that they are stupidly expensive. A Spring Street boutique purchase that cost about the same as a month of most folks' rent.

A 16 mm Bolex camera sits on his desk. I can't tell if it's ornamental or practical, but I'm guessing it's left out in the open a lot either way. He hangs up and waits a beat to write something down before he even looks up at me.

CHAPTER TWENTY-ONE

"I T'S ABOUT BEING PRESENT enough to capture the real. To capture the now."

"Right, but isn't anything recorded an example of the moment it was recorded? An archive of its present? Film, video, audio? How is what you're doing different? How is what you're doing 'the now,' but what everyone else is doing isn't?"

He looks at me like I'm nuts. "Well, because I'm the one that's doing it."

He's been talking for about five minutes, but it feels easily like thirty. Everything out of his mouth is as complicated an explanation as he can whip up. A red velvet cape wrapped around hollow nonsense. He hasn't even asked me why I'm here; he just leaned right into a sales pitch for his company and himself.

He leans back. "So, how can I capture your now?"

"Um ..."

I'm not sure how to respond. I know I said I was gonna lie, but I can't quite figure out the right lie with this guy. Not yet anyways. He reads me and interprets my hesitation as a reluctance to engage his services, so he leans forward and shifts into closer mode.

"Think of it this way. You, or your brand, or your band, or your store—whatever it is you want me to film, really." He pauses, maybe shifting gears, maybe pondering a change in his approach. I stare back, continuing to give him nothing because, honestly, my brain can't muster a response. I can see him feel the sale begin to slip away from him.

"Okay. Forget that. Forget all of that. Think of it this way: You—you are a mine. But a dormant mine. You have valuable ore inside of you, but you can't find it, because you don't have the tools." He pauses again and puts his hand on top of his Bolex camera. "I have the tools. Let me use my tools to mine you. Let me mine you. Let me extract and refine your ore." He has to know how sexual all this sounds, right? "Let me use this"—he taps the Bolex camera—"to show you the gold you have inside you. The gold you didn't even know you had." He leans back, triumphant, I guess ready for me to write a check or hand him cash or kiss his feet, and he looks like he'd be fine with any of those three options.

A door scrape from behind turns us both, and we watch as the front door opens, and an attractive, overcoat-wrapped twentysomething blond woman walks in. She's wearing big over-the-ear headphones—the expensive kind—and music spills into the air the moment she takes them off and lets them hang around her neck. She walks toward the other desk in the room and heavily drops her leather satchel beside it.

"Hey," she says.

She walks over to Kufi Cap and gives him a kiss on the cheek as he stares me down with an unblinking look that very loudly says, *Yes. We fuck.*

"Sorry, I didn't know you had an appointment today," she says.

"It's a walk-in." He's still staring at me, waiting for me to give him some "nice job," bro-to-bro-type high-five look about him being with a woman half his age, but I don't know the first thing about how to make that face.

Best to end this, now.

"I'm sorry, are you not FWHS?" I ask. "That's what I was looking for."

"What?" he says. "No. Of course not. What are you talking about?"

"That's me, though." She says it as she hangs her overcoat up on a wardrobe rack against the wall. "Come on over."

I offer a "Sorry for the confusion" to Kufi Cap as I head over to her desk and sit down.

He grumpily stands as he wraps a scarf around his neck. "I'm getting a coffee." He exits with no offer to pick anything up for us.

"So, how can I help you?" she says.

Whoops. I still need that lie.

Quick, quick, quick.

Think, think, think.

"I write for the UNITE newsletter. You know, for the garment workers' union?" Okay. Impressed myself with that one.

"We haven't done any work for you guys in a while."

"I know, I just ... we're doing profiles of some projects, and my boss thought we could profile your organization. The FWHS." She takes a long suck on her teeth, and I realize how quickly this could fall apart. She could ask for ID. She could call UNITE. She could just say no. I'm not used to doing this much of my PI work face-to-face. You don't really need to talk when you're looking through a telephoto lens, but this face-to-face thing—I'm learning you to have a plan *before* you walk into a room. Maybe I could get one of those mini letterpress thingies to make fake business cards like Rockford has on *The Rockford Files*. Are those things even real?

"Is this because we're shutting down?"

"Uh, no. I didn't actually know about that. Why are you shutting down?"

"Lack of funds and an excess of exhaustion and frustration. I'm kinda worn down by it all. I'd give it to somebody, but I can't find anyone else to take up the reins. There are other groups like ours in other parts of the city that'll keep doing the work, but this one'll be shut down by the end of the month." I'd push harder on asking *why* they're done, but I still have no idea what they do. First things first.

"We'd still love to profile you. Maybe I could work some plugs for those other groups into the piece. That would help the cause, right?" Whatever the hell that cause might actually be.

She stares, and I can tell she's going to agree to it before she verbalizes it. "I mean, we're a nonprofit. We always need press. And, yeah, it would be good to mention the other groups. It would help." She pauses. "Okay. Go ahead. Shoot."

People are far too trusting. Seriously.

"Okay, well, let's start generally," I say. "In really basic terms, tell me what FWHS does."

She takes a deep breath before going into an explanation I'm sure she's given five hundred times before. "We're a nonprofit workers' rights organization that uses city zoning and occupancy laws to try to keep landlords from illegally renting commercial real estate to residential tenants."

Huh. Not the angle I was expecting. "And why would members of UNITE be interested in that?"

"Well, when real estate that's supposed to be zoned for business gets illegally rented as residences, it has a ripple effect on the rent of the apartments surrounding it. Prices go up. It happens again and again and again in neighborhood after neighborhood after neighborhood. We're trying to keep the cost of housing near factories—manufacturing or garments or whatever the respective industry is—we're trying to keep those rents down."

"I see."

"I mean, you can already look at the area surrounding Williamsburg. Have you seen what some realtors have started calling Bushwick?"

"No."

"*East* Williamsburg. They see the market growing here, so they're branding it and expanding it. In ten years, this neighborhood and everything around it'll be unrecognizable."

"Just being devil's advocate here, but won't some of those changes be good? Won't they improve and modernize the neighborhood?"

"Ha. In a word? No. I'll give you an example: This neighborhood has needed access to fresh, healthy food and produce for years. Will the improvements gentrification brings result in a conveniently placed and an affordably priced supermarket? No. What will we get? Well, currently there are plans for some sort of 'food boutique' that I guarantee no one who's lived here for longer than a year is going to be able to afford. That's what we get." She's fired up now. They may be winding down, but she still cares. I can see her flip through topic after topic in her head until she decides what to land on next.

"The really annoying thing is that it's profitable, you know? The landlords actually make more money renting a shitty, tetanus-ridden open floor of an abandoned factory to a gaggle of Parsons School of Design kids than to actual industry. And as more landlords turn toward renting to residential occupants illegally, the smaller the real-estate market gets for actual industry and manufacturing within the city. And do you know what happens then?"

"No."

"Manufacturing and industry look for other places to function. More affordable places. And those local jobs go away."

"Like to Jersey."

"I was thinking more like Mexico, but yeah, basically the same thing." She takes a deep breath before continuing. "We're not against business, not at all—but these neighborhoods have had factories and nearby affordable housing for the people that work in those factories for over fifty years. We're talking mostly about unskilled workers, mostly minorities, mostly people that society has no problem marginalizing. Lots of these folks and their families—they've only known these neighborhoods. When they get priced out, where are they supposed to go? What are their options then?"

"I suppose by that time it's too late."

"Right. So, we're fighting now."

"And how do you do that?"

"We gather evidence of illegal occupation, file reports and submit it all to the city to get the landlord fined—hopefully. Every day we can prove someone is living illegally in an industrial space can cost a landlord up to two hundred bucks. That's per person, not per apartment. Not per building. So that can add up."

"Wow."

"The city rarely lays the heaviest fine down. But still ... it does add up."

"How do you gather evidence?"

"You start by looking for industrial buildings with plants in the windows. Not many factories have plants up in their windows. Then you look for people walking into those industrial buildings with groceries or pets. We take pictures of all that stuff, folks walking in and out at all hours, personal names on buzzers instead of names of corporations. But the most damning evidence is always if you can get inside the apartment and see how they're living."

"And how do you do that?"

"Well, you socialize. You make friends. You try to get invited in."

"Like to a party or something?" The bartender at Kokie's could have misunderstood what Katie told her about why she was there, or she could have misremembered. But the basic aspect of what she described Katie doing—finding parties—it's starting to sound a lot like this.

"Exactly."

"And who does this for you? Do you have a staff?"

"I used to. Now that we're winding things down, it's just me."

"What skills do you need to do something like this?"

"It helps if you're a cute girl ... or boy. Cute and flirty and easy to talk to. Hipster-ish. You need to be able to fit in with the artsy crowd. And you need to be able to start a conversation and keep that conversation going. You need to be good at pulling information out of people. And being naturally observational helps."

"Are you hiring?"

She laughs. "You interested?"

"You basically described me."

"So, you're a cute hipster boy?"

"I was more talking about the need to be observational. And the conversation thing. Being able to pull information out of strangers. I mean, I just got you to tell me all this, right?"

She ponders that for a moment and smiles. "Well, six months ago, I would have said yes. But not now. Thanks for the offer, though."

"Have landlords ever retaliated? Tried to stop you?"

"Generally, not much beyond a hard stare. But sometimes there are some verbal altercations. It can get tense. It matters who the landlord is."

"What about tenants?"

"Most tenants don't realize that what they're doing is illegal. They think if they were able to rent it, it must be legit."

"But still, if they get kicked out of their place, they could get mad, right?"

"There's no way they'd make the connection to us."

"What's the other guy's story? The filmmaking guy. Does he work with you?"

"Martin? No, he's just borrowing some space. He needed a desk, and I had the room."

"Who started all this? The FWHS, I mean?"

"You know the Domino Sugar factory on the waterfront, right? We were founded by some employees there, specifically to help their local coworkers, then it branched off to its own thing. I interned here during college and started working here during grad school. The guy that hired me retired to Florida, and he set me up to keep it going if I wanted. Which I did, for a while. But ... it's a bit too much for me now. It's a lot. I'm spent."

"Where'd you go to school?"

"Columbia. Undergrad and grad."

"That's not cheap. Do you make enough here to cover your loans?" I know the answer before she gives it.

"I don't any have loans, but if I did? No."

"What are you doing when this shuts down?"

"I'm still working that out."

I nod to her with a smile and stand. "Well, thanks for your time." I realize I never asked her what her name was, so I ask.

"It's Rebekah. Rebekah Mason."

Nice to meet you, Rebekah Mason.

CHAPTER TWENTY-TWO

I GRAB SOME COFFEE and plan to stake out Rebekah's office for as long as I can take the cold, stomping my feet repeatedly like Sean Connery says to do in *The Untouchables*, but it doesn't do shit. Luckily Rebekah and Kufi Cap both walk out together after about an hour, so I follow, watching as he talks at her nonstop, his arms flapping around as he speaks. Rebekah's mentally somewhere else. Listening but not listening. They head inside their Bedford Avenue apartment building, and I give them a beat to go upstairs before I jog over to look at the mailbox. I see "RM" on one, jot down the info and get the hell out of there. I'm definitely intrigued about seeing where this goes, but Finch is the priority, and I need to get back on that.

I take a car service to the Doray, and the moment we pull up, sour-stomach nausea fills my gut. I haven't been in here since the day before I found Finch sprawled out on his desk.

Inside it's the usual scene—a few single barflies separated by the long dark bar top with Mikey in the middle, arms crossed, staring out at the street. It takes a beat for him to register that it's me, but when he does, I can see there's a different demeanor about him. I wouldn't say he's in mourning, but maybe he's giving me the room to be.

"Nico. Good to see you. Let me get you one." He reaches into the ice-water coffin, pulls out a dripping Budweiser and gives it a wipe down before placing it in front of me. He's never bothered to do that for me before.

"Thanks." I give a small cheers toward him with the bottle, and he gives a quiet nod back to me as I take a deep swig. I put it down and wait a beat for him to say something else, but he just goes back to his Atlantic Avenue stare.

"I've been thinking about maybe having some sort of memorial for Finch," I say.

He finally breaks out of his trance and looks down at me. "Yeah? Where?"

"Well, here, I guess."

"Who would show?"

"I would. Wally might. I assumed you'd be here."

"Matters what day it is. I'd have to check my schedule."

Okay. I'm getting the picture that the dynamic between bartender and patron with Mikey and Finch was pretty much just that—bartender and patron. I hit Pause and move on to the real reason I'm here. "Hey … any chance you knew who Finch's bookie was?"

"Why?"

"I'm just trying to wrap my head around some stuff. I heard he had some serious debt. I just wanted to ask him about it."

"Beyond the fact that he owed a lot of money?"

"Yeah."

"Well, no introduction necessary. It's me. I got my own book."

"Shit. So … he owed you twenty?"

"Basically. Twenty-three large, so yeah."

"Was he upset about it? Worried about it? That's a lot of money."

"It's the most he ever owed, but it didn't seem to stress him. He was mostly pissed off about me not taking any new bets from him till he was out from under the debt."

"But you let him come in here. You let him buy drinks."

"I keep the bar and the book separate. Business-wise, I mean."

"Do you think he would kill himself over a debt that large?"

"Over a debt? Nah. To stop living? To just, like, give up and rest? Hell yeah, sure. I could see him going for the big sleep just to relax finally. That I'd buy." He shifts his weight and crosses his arms. "The thing about money and Finch—it came and went with him. He'd be down; he'd be up. When he owed me, he'd go to another book and bet so he could win and pay me back. And when he did win, all he ever spent the money on was paying us bookies to get out from under old debts just so he could get into new ones."

"Was he any good at it?"

"He had his inside men at the track, and they'd come through with tips from time to time. Every now and then he'd get a solid tip about a fix being in. That's why I wasn't that stressed over his debt. I knew he'd hit eventually. In the meantime, he was paying me in installments. Overbilling the city on jobs here and there."

Ah, yes. My rental car fees. Now I know where they went.

He turns and pulls an envelope out from under the cash register. "Hey, I almost forgot about this. Finch left this here." It's a stained thick manila envelope. What's inside is looking very rectangular, very VHS to me.

Holy shit. The tape.

I grab it faster than Mikey thought I would, and he gives me that pissed off look that I'm more used to him sending my way. I rip it open, and boom. The VHS porno from Finch's office, with masking tape put over those cutouts that keep VCRs from being able to record over tapes accidentally. Finch covered them up and used the porno as a blank.

This is it. This is *the* tape. It's definitely stickier than I want it to be, though. Mikey notices my displeasure at the texture.

"Yeah, sorry about the soda. One of my canisters was leaking, and I didn't notice till it was too late. Some of the syrup might a got on it."

Might a? "When did you get this?"

"Finch brought it in here the night before he died. Late, like—just before closing. Said if he didn't grab it, that you would."

I stand. The old envelope crunches as I squeeze it involuntarily.

I need to watch this. Now. Immediately.

"Thanks, thanks," I say.

"What about the memorial?"

Memorial? I look up with confusion and then remember. My head is spinning. "I gotta ... I'll get back to you." I head for the exit and cram the thick envelope into my right pea coat pocket just before I push open the door and step out onto Atlantic Avenue. The cold air hits my face, and it feels fucking amazing. My anxiety is falling off me like snow sliding off a roof.

Fuck yes. The tape. I have the tape.

I have to show Hong, but I want to watch it first, make sure it's everything that I need it to be beforehand. I can't watch it at home. I can't risk that. I can see Kangol Hat and Rangers Jersey busting in on me right as I press Play. Where then? Maybe Maggie's place? I have no idea where she lives, but I'm assuming it's Manhattan and I'm in Brooklyn.

Let's keep it in Brooklyn.

Cookie.

I can give her an update on Katie, we can watch the tape and then we can talk it out. I need that. I need someone to talk this out with. Plans are important now. I need to think before I act. No more rash shit. No more surprises. Not now. Not anymore.

"Nico."

I turn to my left and see the familiar black Lincoln Town Car, the back window rolled down and Wally's smiling fat face filling it up. The car is trolling slowly next to me on Atlantic Avenue, keeping pace with my walking.

Goddamn it.

"Oh, hey. Wally. What's up?" My hand goes immediately into my pocket and involuntarily squeezes the envelope and the tape inside.

Wally's car stops and he opens the door. "Come on in. Let's talk about some stuff."

Uh ... No. No fucking way. I've seen this scene before. I know this moment. This is the Robert De Niro promising Lorraine Bracco some beautiful dresses in the back of the abandoned store moment. All she has to do is walk in. Into the dark. Into the back. *All* the way into the back, where the whispering and heavily armed voices are.

"Now's a bad time, actually," I say.

"Hmm. That's tough. It kinda has to happen now. Come on. Get in. I can drop you wherever you need to be when we're done."

Drop me? That's giving me a different visual than I think Wally wants. *I can't get in. I can't.*

And then it occurs to me: Why not just say fuck off? Say fuck off and move on, fat man? I shouldn't be afraid of saying no to Wally. He's the criminal. He's the one with shit to worry about. Shit to hide.

So, don't let him hide. Stay in public. Stay on the street. Or take him someplace safe.

"Where are you headed that you can't take ten minutes to talk to me?" he asks.

"I have to meet somebody about a possible gig. It won't take long though." The lies are flowing better out of me now. Smoother. "How about we meet in about twenty minutes? You know O'Connor's? Up on Fifth Ave?" I'm friendly with one of the bartenders, and I make a silent wish for him to be there.

"Yeah."

"I can meet you there in twenty."

"Okay, yeah, fine." He's disappointed, but he rolls with it. "Meet you there in twenty." He closes his door. "And Nico?"

"Yeah?"

"Don't do something stupid like not show. That would piss me off." He rolls up his window as his Town Car pulls out.

Was that a threat? A warning?

No. It's okay. It is. Really. It'll be fine.

I call Frankie and leave a message letting him know what I'm about to do. Maybe he can have my back. Maybe he can get there in time.

Maybe.

—

By the time I get to O'Connor's, Wally's already there, sitting in a booth facing the door. A shot and a beer in front of him and a shot and a beer across from him, I'm assuming for me, so I take a seat on the worn-down booth and make quick work of the shot.

"How'd your meeting go?"

"Fine. It was quick."

He nods and folds his fat fingers across his belly. "I thought the back of my car would be more private, but . . ." He looks around at the empty bar. The only other person here is the bartender—*not* the one I was hoping for; this one didn't even notice me as I walked in. "This seems private enough. At least this way we can talk and have some refreshments. It's more civilized." He gives me an uncomfortable smile. He seems like he's procrastinating, hesitating. I try to take the lead, take some control.

"What's so important that you followed me to the Doray?"

"I wasn't following you. I came to talk to Finch's old landlord to work out what to do with all his papers, all his files and shit. I saw you from across Atlantic Avenue. That's all that happened."

"Okay." Defensiveness comes easier than confidence with me, so I'm going to keep it brief when I can. I take a swig of my beer, and he goes for his shot. Another hesitation. "So, what's happening with his papers?"

"The city'll take them, probably shred them or burn them. I dunno."

"What are they afraid of people finding?"

"Nothing. It's just easier than storing them indefinitely." I sit and wait for more, but he clears his throat and gives a wipe of his ruddy, wet nose. It's like he's waiting for me to talk, but I didn't call this meeting, so I keep my mouth shut. "All right. Let's ..." He shifts his weight and lets out a long exhale. "Before I talk to you about what I want to talk to you about, I think it's time for me to be honest with you about something."

I keep looking silently back. I read this interview with Errol Morris once where he was asked how he gets his documentary subjects to be so honest, so willing to hand over as much information as they do when he's interviewing them. He said the key was silence. Humans are trained to hate it, to want it filled. When his interview subjects give him unsatisfying small answers, he just stares back, quietly waiting. It's like he's telling them that the simplicity of their answer has disappointed him. They see that look of disappointment and feel the uncomfortable quiet and then almost always start spilling more, just to end the awkwardness. So, I'm trying it. I'm staring at Wally like I know everything, but really, I'm just waiting. Waiting for him to get nervous and fill up this silent hole between us with information.

"The cops you've been talking about, the, uh, Rangers jersey and Kangol hat—I know them, well, one of them, Detective Pittman, Rangers Jersey. I actually tracked him once on the job. For Finch, I mean." He wants me to react, but I won't, goddamn it, not yet. *More. Give me more.* He takes a dry swallow. "Anyways, I just wanted to come clean about that, you know? It didn't feel right not telling you. It's just a weird coincidence, but I had to mention it. Seemed right to come clean." I lean back and cross my arms. "And I did look into, uh, your mark, et cetera, et cetera, et cetera. Seems he was off the job because he was about to testify about, you know, corruption on the force. It wasn't medical leave."

"So, why'd the city hire us to follow him, then?"

"You know the city. One department doesn't know what the other department's doing. Like, over here"—he leans his massive body and arms to his left—"you got IAB putting your guy on medical as a cover, complete with an insurance claim. And then over here"—he leans toward his right, the ancient booth barely able to take the weight shift—"you got a switch getting flipped at fraud and oversight because of that claim. And that results in you and Finch getting hired. It's just the regular city bureaucracy bullshit."

"If my mark was gonna flip, why'd he go out and make his pickups? If he's working with IAB, is he really gonna keep breaking the law?"

Wally puts his hands out in a "who knows?" pose and then offers up his interpretation. "I dunno. He's a bad guy. He's gonna testify about corruption, but he's a still a bad guy, and he wants his bad-guy cut. Or maybe IAB had him do it. Maybe they had him make the rounds so all the other bad cops would still think he was on their side. Who knows?" Wally takes a sip of his beer and wipes his mouth.

Is that it? Is that all I'm getting? I give a long stare, but Wally looks done—at least without some guidance and questions from me.

Fine.

"At least his making collections that night backs up what I saw on the tape," I say.

"Why's that?"

"Well ... why would he collect if he was planning on killing himself?"

"He wasn't planning on killing himself. But he did." He looks at me with a forced confusion that bleeds into some confidence below the surface. Whatever he's about to tell me, it's the kicker. "He put it in his note. Did you not know? About the note?"

"What note?"

"The suicide note. They found it later; some uniform misfiled it or something, but it lays it all out." *How goddamn convenient.* "Your mark got drunk. He got depressed. Started spiraling. Feeling as if he had let his brothers down and he couldn't live with it anymore."

"Let his brothers down? How?"

"By his flipping. It's pretty common. I mean, IAB had his back against a wall for something, right? His career's over, he's looking at jail time, et cetera, et cetera, et cetera. So, he flips. And sure, he gets out from under the jail time, but his life is over. And the further and further he gets from that original cornered moment, the more and more he can't believe what he did. He can't believe he gave up his brothers in blue, be they corrupt brothers or not. He drinks more, he gets more depressed and then pop, pop."

"Yeah, that ... that's not what's on the tape."

He sits up a bit, intrigued, his fat jiggling under his suit as he does. "So, you *do* have the tape?"

Fuck. "No. No. I just ... I mean, I saw it. Watched it with Finch that night. And anyways, I was there. I was the one recording it. I remember."

"Listen, I'm getting sidetracked here. I want to get back to what I really wanna talk to you about." I give him a silent "okay, lay it on me" look. "I talked to Detective Hong. He told me how you were really pushing back hard on the suicide angle on Finch." *Yeah, 'cause he didn't kill himself.* "While we're talking, he starts asking me questions about you—like, out of concern. He's a good guy, and, uh, I think he's—you know—worried about you. Anyways, so, I'm telling him about you, and I remembered your dad. And what happened to him."

Oh, man. Do not take it there, Wally. Do not.

"I was thinking ... the way you would talk about him with me—not all the time, right? But sometimes, on stakeouts or at bars or whatever ... There was always this heavy sadness in how you talked about him. And listen—of course, I know there's gonna be sadness when you talk about losing a parent. I get that. But with you it wasn't just that he died or how he died. It's that you thought he abandoned you, right? He left you here. He gave up and he left you alone to deal with the mess of life."

This motherfucker. I can feel the heat in my cheeks, in the lobes of my ears, but I can also feel the wet building in my eyes. *Do not cry. Do not cry.*

Do not fucking cry.

"And when I was talking to Hong about all that, I remembered what you said to me when I told you that I was leaving Finch to work with the DA's office. You said, 'Don't leave me here.' And I know you were being comedically dramatic and all, as you tend to be, but you were also being a little truthful."

If I say anything, tears will pour down my face. If I blink, tears will pour down my face. I try to lock them in. I clench my jaw as Wally clears his throat before moving on. He can see. He can tell the state I'm in and he pushes forward. He goes all the way. That's when I realize: This isn't about me pulling info out of Wally. This isn't him giving me what I want. This entire conversation has been leading up to this. To him feeding me this. He's in control. He wanted this reaction.

"That job offered me a great opportunity, and I had to take it. I had to take the gig. I owed it to myself. But to you, I was leaving you alone with Finch. I was abandoning you. Just like your father did. And then all this with Finch happens ... and I know he's not a father figure, but for you he's the adult in the room, right? He's your boss. You turned to him for help after a difficult night on the job; you went to him hoping he'd have an epiphany for you, right? He'd somehow fix it all magically or something. And what happened? In the end, he just gave up. He gave up and he left you holding the bag." He pauses. "So, your dad abandoned you. You think I abandoned you, and now Finch abandoned you. And that's why you're pushing back on the suicide angle. That's the real reason you refuse to see what's the most obvious solution here—that Finch killed himself. You think if Finch killed himself, that says something about you not being worth the trouble. 'Cause your dad abandoned you. 'Cause you think I did too in my own way. And now Finch. But it doesn't say that. Finch had stresses far beyond the tape and your job. He was gonna do this no matter what. The cop's suicide's probably what put it in his head. Probably what got him thinking about it that night. He didn't give up on you. He gave up on himself. Your dad didn't give up on you. He gave up on himself. And maybe it seemed like I gave up on you or abandoned you, but I never will. I promise you. I never will. None of their bad stuff is on you. And you shouldn't carry any of it. Not an ounce."

My eyes have overflowed down my cheeks, but I'm not crying, not like you normally would. I'm clenching. Holding. And I'm not making a sound. Inside I'm screaming. *Motherfucker. Mother. Fucker. Goddamn it.* I wipe my face and dig inside myself for a verbal pushback. I almost scream out, "Did the cops magically find a note for Finch as well? Something misfiled?" But I don't. I almost tell him I saw him that night at Finch's, most likely taking the missing files. I'm *so close* to screaming that I saw him with Rangers Jersey and Kangol Hat in his Town Car outside my place.

But I don't.

I can't tip my hand. I can't let him know what I know. Because what I know is all I have on Wally. That's it. I put my hand in my pocket and feel the envelope. Feel the tape. I almost forgot about it.

"When the tape shows up, you'll see that I'm right about the cop," I say. "And Finch."

"The tape's not going to show up, Nico."

I wipe my cheeks again and take a deep breath. I'm so pissed that he'd do this to me. Try to break me so he can be the one who puts me back together. He wants me to owe him. To need him.

"You seem pretty confident about that fact," I say. "Is there something you want to share with me? Some knowledge of where the tape went? Maybe some associates of yours that could help explain it?"

This is the closest I've come to tipping my hand, and Wally picks up on it immediately. He pauses. Sniffs. Scrunches his nose and his face as he ponders what to say, how to play this. Somewhere inside him, a voice tells him to relax. Not to worry. He's in charge, not me. He knows everything; I know nothing. I see his face go back to the forced sincerity of earlier—Wally as comforter.

"I wish I did, Nico. I wish I did have some info on it. But I just don't."

"I gotta go. I got somewhere to be." I start sliding across the booth to stand.

"Listen ... I'm worried about you, Nico. Hong said you're not staying in your apartment anymore. Where are you staying? Let me drop you off."

Yeah, I don't think so, Wally.

CHAPTER TWENTY-THREE

I WORRY THAT WALLY has someone following me, so once again, it's *French Connection* time. I enter the giant Atlantic Terminal and immediately do my best to sprint through the rush-hour bodies that have started to clog the station's many intersecting pedestrian tunnels. I take the Q to DeKalb, transfer to the R, take that to Canal Street in Manhattan, run topside, jump in a cab and head to the L at Fourteenth and Sixth Avenue, take it to the Lorimer stop in Williamsburg and backtrack on foot toward Cookie's.

I know I'm being paranoid, but I have to protect myself, and I have to protect this tape. And I'm not buying any of that bullshit Wally was selling packaged as caring. He can manipulate the context of the cop's and Finch's murders as much as he wants; he can throw as many Hail Mary, just-in-the-nick-of-time suicide notes at me as he wants. It doesn't change anything. It certainly doesn't change the facts. I saw Rangers Jersey and Kangol Hat go into the cop's house. I saw the light flash three times. I heard three gunshots. And yeah, Finch was in debt, but he didn't kill himself over it. He tried to blackmail the cops because of it, and it backfired. Hitting Redial on his phone and having it call Rangers Jersey at the Seventy-Fifth Precinct was enough proof of that for me. And I saw Wally leave Finch's office. And I saw him and the killer cops outside my place. And the possibility of a duplicate tape existing makes him very nervous.

Good.

Back in Williamsburg I walk around for a bit before heading to Cookie's. I'm looking for stragglers, looking for a tail, looking for anything that makes me even a little nervous. Satisfied I'm alone, I finally head into her place. Being careful adds a lot of goddamn extra time onto a commute.

Cookie's not home, so I decide to watch the tape alone. I wet a paper towel and wipe down the sticky cassette box to try and get as much of the syrup off as I can before I put it into her VCR.

"Okay."

I say it out loud to myself and press Play. It's either a one-word wish for the future or a statement about my own readiness to watch; I'm honestly not sure which. A tracking line rises across the TV screen, then the porn disclaimer about all performers being over eighteen, then a burst of static as another tracking line rolls upward and then my footage.

Fuck.

Right away I can tell that something's wrong. The quality is absolute crap—the colors faded, the image shaky. I play with the tracking, but it just makes it worse. Goddamn Finch must have recorded it at EP—extended play. High quality is SP (standard play), regular quality LP (long play), and cheap bastards trying to stretch out a tape's length record at EP. This is already a dub of a dub. And I'm guessing the original porno is probably not the first thing recorded onto this tape, either. Shit recorded on top of shit on top of shit.

Goddamn it.

I fast-forward to get to the moment when Rangers Jersey and Kangol Hat show up. I can't make out the plates on their car at all. The faces are blurs. The light flashes when the gun is fired aren't as bright as

I remember them being, and the pops of the gun firing are dull and muffled, not crisp like on the original.

My hopes for definitive evidence have degraded to a bad dub of the Zapruder film.

God fucking dammit.

I eject the tape as Cookie enters the apartment and decide it's not worth telling her about. Not yet. She'd just spiral, and then I'd spiral, and then we'll both be stuck at the bottom of a well with no one to pull us back up. I say "Hey" to her after I hear her toss her keys onto the kitchen table, but she doesn't answer. She sits heavily on a squeaky vinyl chair and lets out a long, sad sigh. I go to check on her, and she's sitting, arms folded on the pink Formica table with her head pressed down into them.

"Hey ... You all right?" I take a seat across from her. "Where you been?" She takes a deep breath, and I can tell she's trying to decide whether to be honest with me.

"You're gonna give me shit if I tell you."

"I'm not gonna give you any shit. I promise."

She looks up at me. "I went to Katie's. I went to talk to her dad."

Oh boy.

"The conservative one? From Reagan California?"

"Yeah. He was packing her stuff up. I thought that maybe he should know his daughter was loved by someone, you know? I thought that would have been important to him. I wanted to tell him how special she was. And that she wasn't a junkie. That she was a good person. She was a good partner."

I wait. I figure she'll tell me how bad it went when she's good and ready. It doesn't take her long.

"It did not go well."

"What happened?"

"He blamed me and essentially all of New York for corrupting her. Called me a lot of not-nice names. Said I was a sinner. That I was going to hell and that I helped send his daughter there, blah, blah, blah." She puts her head back down on the table. "I haven't been yelled at like that in a long time."

"What did you say back?"

After a moment, she sits up again. "I was going to rip into him, right? Really let him know what I thought of him. But I could see his eyes. They were so goddamn red and puffy. He'd been crying, probably for hours. Probably for days. Whether or not he accepted Katie at all, whether or not he loved her at all—I dunno. But he was in pain over her, and I didn't feel like adding to it. So, yeah. I just walked away. I mean, if Katie—the sweetest girl I've ever known—if she's going to hell, then I'm *definitely* going to hell, so I'll see her there, and we can talk shit about her dad together then."

She gets up and gives me a squeeze on the shoulder as she passes. "You got any *noticias* on that union stuff?"

I tell her it's nothing that can't wait till morning. Best to let her sleep and reset from this very rough day.

Anyways, I don't know what's next. Not yet.

—

In the morning I give her a rundown on everything Katie. The FWHS. Rebekah Mason. Even the creep filmmaker boyfriend.

"So, she was working for her?" Cookie asks. "Collecting evidence of illegal renters and stuff, right?"

"I think so."

"That's pretty great. That's a good thing she was doing. For the community."

I'm not sure if anything is entirely altruistic when the subject is New York City real estate, but I keep that to myself. "Yeah. Definitely."

"Still doesn't explain the cash, though, right?"

"No. But like I said, that might just be her stash of cash tips. Maybe she was saving up for something."

She downs her coffee, and then she surprises me. "Let me take over her case. You're busy; you've got the tape and the thing with your boss. I can do this. Let me do this." I dunno. She seems emotionally better, but I know it would be a lot for her to take on. But it's true—I'm stretched incredibly thin trying to work both Katie and Finch cases at the same time. "I can't just go back to work. I can't just sit in a car and drive all day. I need to feel like I'm doing something for her."

I relent. I give Cookie all the info I have on Rebekah and the FWHS. She says she's got a friend that works for the city who might be able to dig up some information for her. Shake a few files free. It makes me nervous. If I get caught breaking the law, at least it was me doing it. I don't want to get dragged down by someone else's mistakes.

"Just be careful about, you know, illegal stuff. There are lots of new privacy rules about accessing personal information. If you get caught and there's a paper trail back to me, I'm fucked." I look at her with some concern to let her know I'm serious.

"*Bueno*, baby. I won't get caught, then." She gives me a quick peck on the forehead and heads out, all smiles. She's invigorated. Purposeful. It's nice to see.

Me, on the other hand ...

I head to the New York Public Library to dig around the microfiche to see if there were any reporters that specialized on the Mollen Commission beat. I jot down the most consistent names at the *Times*, the *News* and the *Voice* and then head out to a pay phone to set up some meetings. In person, all are intrigued until the tape plays and its subsequent fuzziness quickly begins to pull down my own story. I see it on their faces the moment it starts playing. Afterward they politely write down info, take my number and listen to my last pleas, but I don't think they're necessarily gonna dive headfirst into anything. I dunno. It's hard to tell. When I get to the part about Wally, the reporter at the *Voice* gets interested.

"Tinderman? From the mayor's office?"

He gives me another name, a freelance writer named Ernie Boyd from Brooklyn. Says he's had been working on something interesting about Wally and that I should give him a call.

Ernie Boyd and I agree to meet in the park by the Old Stone House off Fifth Avenue in Park Slope. He says to sit on the bench closest to Fourth Street on the Fifth Avenue side, but by the time I get there, it's been taken over by a smoking, twentysomething dog walker and his tangle of eight dogs. He looks up and gives me a long stare.

"Nico?" He stands and the dogs immediately start frantically pulling on their leashes, barking, eager to move. "Do you mind if we walk? It's easier if we keep moving."

Oh boy. "Sure."

We head north on Fifth Avenue, clogging the sidewalk with thirty-two fast-moving, hairy legs of varying lengths.

"Thanks for meeting me out here," he says. "I'm sort of locked into my daytime schedule with these guys."

"Yeah. Okay." I watch as he struggles with a pair of tangled leashes. "You *are* a reporter, right? You're Ernie Boyd?"

"Yeah. But just call me Boyd. Oh, shit—" Two of the dogs go after each other, and he tries to pull them apart. "Can you take this guy?" He hands me the leash of a small corgi. "Little Lennie Briscoe does not like the big guys." I take it and try to separate him some from the pack. "All right. Let's keep going. We can talk while we walk."

At Second Street he tells me to hang a left. "Let's drop Lennie Briscoe off. He's kinda the instigator of the group. It'll be easier without him."

I sort of don't know what the fuck is going on, but I nod affirmatively in an effort to roll with it, trying to ignore the ridiculousness of the situation. "Your friend at the *Voice* said you were working on something to do with Wally Tinderman."

"Yeah. How do you know him? Tinderman, I mean, not my friend."

"I worked with him for a few years."

"Back when he was a PI?"

"Yeah."

We stop in front of a brownstone, and he ties the gaggle of leashes to the stoop and then grabs the corgi's leash from me. "You can come up if you want."

I hesitate. "You just leave the dogs out here?"

"Yeah."

"All alone?"

"Yeah."

"What if something happens to them?"

Boyd's head is down as he flips through a giant ring of tape-marked keys, trying to find the right one. "Eh, they're fine. Don't worry about 'em." He opens the front door and steps in as the wagging corgi leads the way. "You coming?"

He climbs the squeaky stairs in front of me, following the short-legged corgi, who hops his way up one step at a time, face planting about every third step. "Listen, I get that the dog-walking gig is maybe not the most confidence-boosting first impression of me as a reporter, but I am a reporter. And I'm a good one. But I'm freelance, so I gotta do this for the consistent check." He stops and turns toward me. "If I can't cover rent and smokes, I can't write. Such is life."

"I get it." I do. Maybe a little too much. My next check is a big, fat unknown to me, and maybe I should be thinking a little harder about that than I have been. At the second-floor landing, Boyd unlocks an apartment door, heads in and unfastens the leash from Little Lennie Briscoe, who then immediately bolts to a hair-covered couch and curls up into a circle of sleep.

"Gimme a sec. Gotta give the poop report. Brooklyn loves a poop report." He scribbles a quick couple of sentences down in a notebook on the kitchen table.

When we head back outside, I'm surprised that all the dogs are still there, regardless of what Boyd said earlier. If you leave something on a stoop, that generally means "I don't need this anymore; please take it." I know dogs are different from a stack of used breastfeeding instructional books or an ex-girlfriend's pile of CDs, but my head can't get around it.

"Have you ever lost one?" I ask.

He offers me a smoke, and I wave it off as he lights up. "No, but I gained one once. I came out of an apartment last year, and somebody had tied up their dog to my pack. No ID, no license, no nothing."

"What happened to it?"

"I kept her. Took her on my neighborhood walks, waiting for some-body to recognize her, but no one ever did, or if they did, they didn't say anything. So, she's my girl now. A total sweetie." He grabs the leashes, and we begin to head back toward Fifth Avenue. "Okay. Let's talk about Mr. Tinderman."

Finally. "What made you interested in him—as a reporter, I mean?"

"Well, he keeps popping up over and over and over again and always in the same scenarios."

"Which are?"

"Stories about cops—police brutality, wrongful arrests, straight-up beatdowns—wherever those stories start to gain a little traction, where people are about to go on record, stuff like that, he pops up, and pretty soon afterward, the story dies."

"What do you mean?"

"The people involved stop talking to the press. They clam up."

"And Wally has something to do with that?"

"I think that Tinderman—or his office or someone who works in his office—I think they're convincing these folks *not* to talk about their negative experience with the cops."

"Like, they intimidate them? Threaten them?"

"No. I think it's simpler. I think it's cash. I think he's in charge of some sort of a slush fund. Not the official one the city uses for big settlements, not what they'll be paying Abner Louima out of or anything. These are smaller payments, easier to hide."

"That Louima thing. That was so awful."

"Yeah. You can't conceal that shit. Not that they didn't try—and they always try. It's kind of connected to what I think Tinderman is doing. The cops took such a PR hit when the Louima details got out that they've been aggressively trying to limit any more bad press. I think Tinderman mops up what he can when he can. Like, his job is trying to keep as much of the mayor's favorite profession looking as professional as possible."

"Giuliani loves his cops."

"It's a little perverse, honestly. Were you around when he was running for mayor, and he led them in a riot at Gracie Mansion? It had the same energy of a Klan cross burning, except they were doing it to the African American Mayor of New York City. Do you remember that? In '92?"

I tell him I sort of do, but I wasn't paying much attention to politics then, local or national.

"Jimmy Breslin has a great piece about it. It's worth digging up. Thousands of cops at Gracie Mansion, most of them screaming about"—he leans in close—"the *N-word* mayor. I mean, they had signs that said it. *Multiple signs.* They were chanting it. Walking around with six-packs, day drunk and screaming about the N-word mayor. New York City fucking cops. And there's fucking Giuliani firing up this already-fired-up crowd of cops. Just spraying gas onto an already very hot fire and smiling like a fucking maniac as it burned."

"But how did you ever figure any of this out? Have people gone on the record?"

"That's a big negative, but it's not for lack of trying, trust me. Some people have told me things, mostly out of guilt, out of feeling dirty, out of a desperate desire to wash away the bad feeling they have from going back on what they *were* gonna go on the record about. But it's nothing that I can quote, nothing that'll get me printed. But I've got enough to know that *something* like what I'm talking about is true. Enough to know that if I'm not exactly right, I'm not exactly far off, either."

"That's a little vague."

"It is and it isn't. Like, would I love a clean pencil drawing of Tinderman? Of course. But I can't draw the actual figure with the info I have, so I start focusing on the negative space. I start filling that in with what I *do* know. Pretty soon Tinderman starts to take shape. Yeah, it's not photorealistic, it's not perfect, it's not ideal, but I can make out what I need to make out. I see what's going on. Does that make sense? Or does that sound nuts?"

"It makes sense."

We're up toward Sixth Avenue and Third Street now, and he starts his routine of fastening the dogs to the rail again. Just as I'm about to follow him up the stoop, he stops. "Yeah, you can't come up to this one. This guy has cameras everywhere."

"Cameras?"

"Yeah, like, spy shit. He owns that spy shop in Midtown. He says it's for professional use, but I don't know many spies who pay retail, you know? I think folks mostly use it to do shit like stalk their ex, spy on their wife or husband, stuff like that. Creepy shit. I'll be right back."

"Okay." Before he heads in, I bum the smoke that I passed on earlier, light it up and sit down on the stoop, killing time and taking drags until he comes back.

I'm thinking about Wally.

I'm thinking about Finch.

I'm thinking about spy shops and their small, creepy cameras.

CHAPTER TWENTY-FOUR

THE REST OF THE walk is me filling in Boyd on my side of the Tinderman story. Finch, the mark and their convenient suicides. We head back to his place in Gowanus, and I show him the tape.

"The quality is crappy, but somebody might be able to clean this up, you know?" he says.

"How?"

"I dunno. With machines and technology and beeps and boops and stuff. You know, enhance it."

"Like in *Blade Runner*."

He looks at me blankly through the rising smoke from the cigarette that dangles from his mouth. "I don't, uh ... What do you mean?"

"Like when Harrison Ford fixes the quality of a photo in *Blade Runner*. Enhances it. 'Enhance ... Enhance ... Enhance.' "

"I don't think I remember that part." He ashes his smoke and leans back on his tattered couch. I don't get how people don't remember these things. Were they even watching the movie? Were they enjoying it? "Anyways, I'll ask around."

I shake off my irritation. Can't linger on shit like that. Not now. Not with potential allies like Boyd. I need as many allies as I can muster. He tells me he wants to keep the tape, but I'm not trusting it to anybody—even in its current fuzzy state. I say my good-byes, scratch his dog and head out to call Hong from a pay phone. He doesn't answer and his message says that he's on leave, which makes me feel instantly nauseous. *Leave? Like administrative leave?* I try to ignore the film of dread that coats me and leave a message, hoping he's checking them while he's out, but I don't mention the tape, just in case somebody else is listening in.

I check my pager to see if maybe I missed a page from Hong, but all I have is a coded one from Cookie: 00413 [Cookie] 114 [meet me] and a phone number. I call the number, and it's the L Cafe in Williamsburg. That generally means she's there or near there.

I'm about to pull open the café door when I hear a light honk from across the street and see Cookie's double-parked Town Car. I open the back door and slide in, onto the soft, well-worn leather back seat.

"Cooks."

"Hey, baby."

"What's going on?"

"I'm sitting on the filmmaker boyfriend. He's been in there drinking coffee for a few hours. Tough life, that one has." She turns toward me and opens her ink-filled spiral notebook. "So, I found out some weird shit about the girl today."

"Okay. What kind of weird?"

"My friend with the city looked up both those addresses you gave me—the apartment and the building her office is in."

"And?"

"They're both owned by a real estate company called Mason Properties, which is fucking weird 'cause her name is Mason, right? So, I look up Mason Properties, and it ends up it's her dad's real estate company. Mostly they own buildings in Newark and Hoboken—they're based out of Jersey. But in the past year, he's been buying buildings in the industrial section of—guess where?"

"Here."

"Exactly here. Like, practically on every block leading down to the waterfront."

"That seems like kind of a conflict of interest."

"I know. And it makes me think that Katie found out about her dad, and Rebekah killed her over it."

"Okay, um ... that's a big jump there, Cookie."

"But it makes sense, right? Rebekah's using her gig to help her father buy buildings. Katie finds out about it, and they kill her."

"How does Rebekah's job help her dad buy buildings?"

"How should I know that? I have no idea about that shit. But it's real estate, right? There has to be something there."

"Okay, but why does she have to kill her? If she is doing all that—helping her dad and all—is it even illegal?"

"I don't know if it's illegal, but it doesn't seem right."

"I don't think there's much morality or ethics in real estate, Cookie." She's annoyed that I'm not immediately all in on her theory, so I try to soften my skepticism. "How about I go in and see if I can pull anything out of the boyfriend?"

"Yeah, okay. That's more like it. Now you're talking."

Inside the café, Kufi Cap is doing his best to stay creepy by reading *Tropic of Cancer* as visibly as possible. I get a coffee and take a seat at the wonky table behind him. I think about making a Griffin Dunne in *After Hours* reading *Tropic of Cancer* in the diner reference just to break the ice, but I assume it'll land flat, so I just pretend I'm surprised to see him.

"This is the now, right?"

He looks up from his book, and his eyes hold on me for a beat. "Have we met before?" The move feels like some weird power play, like something Kufi Cap does to everyone, forcing them to reintroduce themselves to him, his little way of letting you know that remembering you wasn't worth the trouble.

I remind him.

"Oh, right. Yesterday." *Yes. Less than twenty-four hours ago yesterday. Asshole.* His eyes go back to his book. I want to grab it out of his hand and hit him over the head with it. Repeatedly. But I need him to like me. I definitely need him to like me a little more than he seems to right now. I figure the one thing he wants to talk about is himself, and based on that cocky look on his face when Rebekah kissed him in the office, I'm betting he *really* likes talking about his ability to date below his age. So I choose my lane and move in.

"Can I, uh ... can I ask you a personal question? And if this is crossing a line, just let me know and I'll shut up, but I gotta ask ..." I motion for him to lean in closer to me, and he does. "How did you hook up with Rebekah?" He smiles knowingly, content that this life victory of his is finally getting some recognition. I notice, so I lay it on thicker. "I say this as a compliment, not to be rude or anything, but—aren't you almost twice her age?"

He closes the book and scooches his chair closer. "Almost." He crosses his legs and leans in again. "She's not the youngest I've been with, either. Honestly, Rebekah's at about the top of my bracket—age-wise, I mean."

"So, there have been others?"

"Of course."

"And you're saying you have, like, a cutoff age?"

"An approximate one. Twenty-eight is about as old as I'm willing to go. Anything older is too much trouble—too opinionated, too much of a sense of self, you know? It gets more difficult the closer to thirty they get."

"And how do you swing this as consistently as you seem to be swinging it?"

He licks his lips and ponders whether to tell me before giving in. "This is going to sound a little crass, but I actually have a technique."

"A technique?"

He nods eagerly. Now that he's all in on telling me, he's loving it. "Would you like to hear it?"

"Of course, I mean, if you're willing to share." *Ugh.*

"Well, you know that I'm a filmmaker, right?"

"Yeah, I remember." I'm honestly surprised he didn't bring the Bolex camera from his office and plop it down on the table next to his cappuccino.

"Well, being active in the arts—*as I am*—I get invited to parties with lots of younger folks. And because of my career and my accomplishments, they naturally want to know more about me. They see me—my success, I mean—and they want to know how they can get to my level."

He might as well have said, "Women love me, and men want to be me."

"Anyway, when I'm talking to these girls, these up-and-coming young artists, I try to find some moment to slip in a question about their background, specifically about their father."

"Their father?"

"Yeah. Did they come from a happy family or a broken family? Did Daddy leave early? Did their parents divorce? Did Daddy die tragically?"

Please stop saying "Daddy."

"If they say everything was great—happy childhood, loving parents, blah, blah, blah—I get the hell out of there. Any conversation past that point is a waste of my time. But if they say their father died, or left, or—even better—was abusive in some way? Then I zero in. Then I know I have a shot. I have a chance to fill that empty hole."

Good God. "And that works?"

"Most of the time. But it does have a shelf-life. About six months. A year, *maybe*. Then they generally move on. But it's fine. I lose interest, too, you know? It's not always them moving on. Sometimes it's me."

"And that's how you first connected with Rebekah?"

"Pretty much."

"She and her dad aren't close, then?"

"It's complicated, like most things. She's been chasing his validation and affection her whole life. I just stepped in and gave her mine."

"And where in the process of it all are you guys right now?"

"We're basically past tense. It's overdue to be over. She's actually with her father right now. In some ways, I think I gave her the tools to reconnect with him, you know?" He has a moment of reflection. "And I feel good about that. That I could do that for her." *Creep. Creep. Creep. King Creep. King of* all *the creeps.* I don't know what to say, so I nod knowingly at him, and he does the same back at me, seeming content that his generosity has been recognized and validated.

I need to pull more out of him, find out what he knows about Katie, but I need a change of scene and maybe a little bait. "Are you free this evening? We could get dinner, maybe? Or just some drinks. Talk some more."

"Sure. Why not?"

"I just have to make a call real quick." I head out to a pay phone on Bedford and call Maggie, describe the scenario and offer her a role in it.

"Is this a paid gig?"

"Um, maybe?"

"How much?"

"I dunno. Twenty bucks? Thirty?" I hear her exhale as she ponders it. "And I'll pay for dinner and drinks and all that."

"And this is an offer, right? A straight offer?"

"I don't know what that means."

"Well, actors either audition or they get offers. If it's an offer, it's up to them to decide if they want to do it."

"Oh. It's an offer. A straight offer."

"Well, that does intrigue me ..."

"So, you'll do it?"

"Tell me why you thought of me for this role?"

"You're the only actor I know."

"I respect that. I do. Okay, Georgie. Let's do it."

I give her a quick rundown of her backstory and the goal for the evening: pull information about Katie out of Kufi Cap. Find out everything she can about her. If he knows it, learn it. Maggie agrees to meet us outside Peter Luger's in about forty-five minutes. I pop over to Cookie's car and bring her up to speed, then reconnect with Kufi Cap.

The run-in goes a little awkwardly, but Kufi Cap is so self-absorbed that he doesn't notice anything odd about it. I invite Maggie to join us, and she quickly agrees. Inside, they seat us upstairs in the run-down, overflow dining room for non-VIPs that looks like what I imagine the upstairs residential area above a funeral home must look like.

When the menus arrive, Maggie leans in close. "You're not leaving till you pay, right?"

"Correct," I say.

"Solid."

We order, and the steaks come out almost immediately. In between bites, I let Kufi Cap know that Maggie is an actress, and I let Maggie know that Kufi Cap is a filmmaker. I finish my steak, pretend to get a page, excuse myself for a bit and come back saying I have to split, but why don't you guys stay out, blah, blah, blah? Kufi Cap thinks that's a great idea. I pay the tab and head outside to Cookie's waiting Town Car.

Cookie turns as I get into the back seat. "What now?"

"I guess we just wait for Maggie to page me."

"Well, I don't wanna wait here." She clicks the Town Car into drive and pulls out.

Cookie's talking to me about Katie and about real estate theories and about how it's actually way easier to fake an OD than I think it is, but I'm not paying attention. I'm staring out the window and thinking about what Boyd said about Wally, trying to feed back that new knowledge into everything that's happened so far.

Okay.

So, Wally runs a slush fund. For the cops. Tries to clean up their smaller messes. The mark was a dirty cop and was about to turn evidence over on some other dirty cops. Rangers Jersey and Kangol Hat are obviously dirty cops. They're probably who the mark was gonna flip on, right? That's why they killed him. But how does that jibe with Wally's slush fund? All that shit seems way bigger, way more criminal, than small cash payoffs would be able to handle. And what about Wally? When he was with the Mollen Commission, he was investigating corrupt cops. How do you go from investigating them to defending them? To covering up for them? What causes that flip? It makes no sense.

"This is where they found her, right?"

I look up.

Oh, shit. We're double-parked near Giando's. Right near where Katie's body was found.

"I wanna see it," Cookie says.

She doesn't wait for me to push back. She gets out of the car and heads down toward the small path that leads to the river. I get out and follow.

"Cookie? Maybe let's come back during the day, all right? What do you say?"

She ignores me and disappears into the darkness as she squeezes through the small hole in the fence.

Fuck.

By the time I catch up to her, she's sitting on the edge of the six-foot drop and looking up at the lights of Manhattan across the East River. I take a seat next to her.

"I didn't trust that ladder," she says.

"Yeah. It's pretty untrustworthy, as ladders go. Especially at night." I watch as her eyes go from the skyline down toward the yellow police tape, still visible in the darkness of the tiny beach. She takes a deep breath and lets it out loudly. It's a desperate sigh, a resetting sigh. I reach out my left arm and give her back a light circular rub of support.

"Your mom used to give me crap for sighing when we were kids. She hated it. I dunno why. She either didn't like the idea that I wasn't happy, or maybe she didn't think I had a right to complain about not being happy? She was weirdly obsessed over it. She had a sigh jar in the kitchen—like a swear jar—and she tried to make me drop a quarter in it every time I sighed."

"And how'd that go?"

"I told her to fuck off, mostly. If I didn't get to sigh, I'd explode or I'd crack, or I'd probably just punch her in the face. I couldn't not do it. It resets me."

"Well, it's weird that she hated it so much, because I've heard that same sigh lots of times coming out of her. Generally bookended by long looks of disappointment. My dad got it more than me, but I got it plenty."

"Yeah, well. Your dad deserved it."

I wanna say, "I know" to Cookie, but I still can't verbalize agreeing with what a shit my dad was when people feel the need to point it out. It's an unnecessary action. Nobody needs to say overtly that he was a shit. It's like saying he was a musician. It's just a known fact. If anything, they should point out the positives. The warmth. The love he sometimes expressed. How sweet he sometimes was.

Ugh. "Sometimes." Always with the "sometimes" when I'm trying to say something good about him, even to myself. What's wrong with me?

"When was the last time you talked to your mom?" Cookie asks.

"Oh boy ... uh, maybe three weeks ago? Four weeks ago?"

"*Mijito.* That's too long."

"Well, when was the last time *you* talked to her?"

"*Carajo.* Maybe a year ago? Probably more."

"So, you're saying that you're a hypocrite for criticizing me about it."

"Uh, no, I'm not. She's just my jerky sister; I'm allowed to avoid her. Especially considering our history. But you? She's your mom. *Tu madre.* You're not allowed to ignore her. You're not allowed to. You need to call her, baby. Promise me you'll call her."

"Of course I'm gonna call her. It's just been hard with everything going down."

"Life will always give you an excuse not to do the right thing, to pull you away from what matters. It distracts you and tells you that there's plenty of time to do what you need to do. Don't listen to it, baby. Find the time. Call your mother before you can't. Don't regret not having at least one last conversation with her." She looks back toward Manhattan. "Find the time."

—

The page comes in from Maggie, so we head to Kellogg's to get some coffee and wait for her to show. When she finally arrives, she looks worn down, like she's been through it. I give her a wave, and she responds with a wince as she heads over and sits down with us.

"That wasn't cool." She digs her eyes into me after she says it.

"What do you mean?" I ask.

"You could have warned me about him."

"I told you he was creepy."

"He's assaulty."

"Oh, Jesus. I'm sorry."

"What were you thinking? You know my history. You know about my stalker. Why would you think it was okay to just throw me into that situation like that without any heads-up? Without any warning?"

"I didn't ... I dunno. You're a strong-minded person. I wasn't worried about you or anything. I knew you could handle yourself."

"*You* knew? Oh, well, thank you *so* much for making that decision for me. My little female brain couldn't have handled it." *Oh boy. I fucked this up.* She takes a deep breath and ponders whether I get it or not. She doesn't think I do. "There's enough daily shit, all right? Catcalls. Creeps. Boners on the subway. I don't need any more, you know?"

Wait. What was that last one?

"Boners on the subway?" I ask.

She looks at me as if my question is absolutely the stupidest thing she's ever heard. "Yeah. Boners on the subway."

"What do you mean boners on the subway?"

"What the fuck do you think it means? Somebody with a boner on a crowded subway train grinds up against you."

"That happens?"

She looks over to Cookie with a "can you believe this guy?" expression and then back to me. "Yeah. On the regular."

"How regular?"

"I dunno, a couple of times a month—"

"A couple of times a month!" I pretty much scream it. I'm in shock. "At least."

I look over a Cookie for confirmation. She nods slowly and then says, "I don't ride the subway that much, but yeah, it happens."

"Jesus Christ." Now I feel extra awful about forcing Kufi Cap on Maggie. But also just awful in general. About men. And humanity as a whole.

Cookie's tired of waiting. "What did the creep say?"

Maggie rubs her eyes. "Can I get a coffee or something?" I put my hand up to signal the waitress and point to Maggie. The waitress gets the idea and comes back with a too-full cup spilling over into its saucer. "Thanks." Maggie lifts the cup and puts napkins down on the saucer to sop up the overflow.

I can tell Cookie is champing at the bit, so I give her a silent "relax" look, but she doesn't care. "Okay, you have coffee. What happened? What did you learn about Katie?"

Maggie looks annoyedly at Cookie, then back at me. "Who is this?"

Oh, wow. I never bothered to introduce them. *Crap.* "This is my *tía*. Katie was her girlfriend."

Maggie straightens up her posture. "Oh. *Perdón. Lo siento.*"

Cookie gives a quiet nod back and bites her lip. "Gracias." Then glares open-eyed at me—"*Blanquita* speaks better Spanish than you."

"Great. Good for her." I don't want to wait on this, but I gotta be honest—I'm still thinking about random dudes rubbing their boners on women in the subway. How the fuck does that just keep going on and nobody does anything about it? It's nuts.

Cookie keeps the conversation on point. "Now that we've all met, please tell us what you figured out."

Maggie takes another sip of her coffee, lets out a content gasp from the caffeine delivery and then back up toward us. "Okay ..."

She tells us that Katie did work at FWHS for a while, off and on, until she was fired by Rebekah a few months ago.

"Why?" Cookie's shocked, almost personally offended.

"She was on the grift." She looks at me. "Am I using that right? On the grift?"

"I dunno," I say. "What are you trying to say?"

"All right, I don't quite understand the context of everything, but the creep said she was taking cash from landlords? Does that make sense? She was getting paid off to not do her job or something like that, whatever that job was. Something to do with zoning, I think. I couldn't totally grasp it."

It makes sense, but Cookie's not having it.

"She wouldn't do that," she says.

Maggie winces down another sip of coffee. "Well, I don't think that the creep cared one way or the other. He was just spilling it like it was old news. He said Rebekah told her she had to quit, or she would call the cops."

"If she quit, then she wasn't fired."

Cookie's really struggling to find the positive in all this.

Maggie leans in. "No, she was told to quit, which is basically being fired, right?"

I turn to Cookie. "It would explain the cash. The payoffs from the landlords."

She eyes the table and shakes off the thought. "No. No, that's not right. She wouldn't do that." She looks up at me, and we lock eyes for a brief moment before she stands abruptly and leaves the diner.

"Did I fuck that up? I feel like I fucked that up." Maggie asks me with concern.

"No. You didn't. It's just ... she's wound up. I'm just gonna check on her, okay?" Maggie gives me a nod and returns to her coffee. By the time I get outside, Cookie and her Town Car are long gone. I could follow her to her place. I could talk to her some more, try to work through it with her, but that look she gave me, that moment she looked in my eyes—I think she knows that it all makes sense. That it all fits together. She needs to process all that. She needs to be alone until she's ready to talk.

I head back in and dump a series of apologies on Maggie for what I did to her as we finish our cups of coffee and start on our refills. She generously absolves me and then fills me in on the rest of her night with Kufi Cap, aka the creep.

"He is truly, unbelievably and undeniably full of himself." Maggie's smile fades as her mind shifts to another thought. "The thing is, the other directors I've met in film and TV? The successful ones? They all have that, too. They all have that bloated sense of self. That sense that everyone is here to sacrifice themselves toward fulfilling their vision. The pomposity of it always gets me. Why do I want to be in a business that requires you to be a total selfish shit bag in order to be a success?"

I dunno. But I'm not really listening anymore. I'm thinking about how to resolve both these cases. Katie and Finch. I'm looking to end them and move on.

I need to do some shopping.

CHAPTER TWENTY-FIVE

A FTER ALL THAT, I somehow manage to get Maggie to agree to meet Kufi Cap one more time for coffee. I should say she agrees to *invite* him to coffee, but she isn't planning on showing up. I've been hovering around Rebekah's office, waiting for a chance to talk to her alone, but Kufi Cap wasn't budging. Maggie calls him and sets up a meeting with him and her at Cafe Gitane in Nolita, repeatedly mentioning that it's really close to her place. That bit of innuendo should get him out the door and quick. The commute alone from the Bedford stop should give me a good chunk of undisturbed time. I wait till he splits, and then I give him five to get to the L before I head over to talk with Rebekah.

I shove open the glass door and step into the storefront. Rebekah looks confused at first, leaning back with a squint as she tries to place me. Then she remembers and relaxes. "Newsletter man."

"That's me. I was hoping you had like fifteen minutes to talk. I had some follow-ups if that's okay?"

"Follow-ups? For a quarterly trade newsletter?"

"I'm very thorough."

"That seems exceedingly thorough."

I sit down across from her desk. "Could you tell me about your staff?"

"Hmm ... That's not really a follow-up question."

"Well, you said you used to have one. A staff, I mean. How many was it?"

"One or two people at a time, not that any of that should matter to you or your readers." She thinks about my question more, and I can see her get a little pissed off. "Are you implying what I think you're implying?"

"What am I implying?"

"That we're wasting UNITE union dues money? Because we're not. No one makes much of a salary here. And we're incredibly thrifty with the little money that we spend on expenses." She gives me another squint. "Don't you want to take out your notebook? How are you gonna remember all this?"

Whoops. "I left it at home. It's okay. I'll remember it."

"You forgot the notebook, but you'll remember the notes that you should be writing inside it?"

"Yeah."

"I guess you could always follow up again, right?" She's annoyed. She can tell something's up.

"Sure. If you had the time. I wouldn't want to impose."

She locks a hard stare deep into me. "What else do you need?"

"I read somewhere that one of your employees died recently, I think?"

Her head goes sideways as she ponders the weight behind that sentence. "You think you read somewhere that one of my employees died? What the hell kind of publications are you reading?"

"Newspapers, magazines ... the usual."

"Yeah, I don't think I know who you're talking about."

"Katie Richards? She was found pretty close to here, I think. Just on the waterfront a few blocks away."

"You're not from UNITE."

"No."

"Who do you write for?"

"Nobody."

"So, who are you, then?"

I decide to keep pushing forward with questions. If I pause, she might stop talking. "What do you know about Mason Properties?"

"I'm guessing by your tone that you know plenty, so why don't you tell me?"

"They own this building. And the building you live in."

"And most of the buildings from here to the waterfront. What of it?"

"Well, it's your father's company."

"It is."

"And how do you explain that?"

"My father's a businessman. He's heard me complain about the losing battle I've been fighting in this neighborhood for years, and he saw the tide turning before I did. While I was idiotically and repeatedly pushing a rock up a hill, he sniffed out a good deal and started buying buildings. It's honestly not as titillating as you think it is. It's just capitalism. It happens every day."

"Isn't that a conflict of interest?"

"With me? Not if I'm not involved in his business. Which I currently am not." *"Currently." Huh.*

"Have you gotten him fined? As a landlord, I mean."

"No."

"Why not?"

"Because he hasn't broken the law, yet."

"Did Katie find out about your dad? About Mason Properties?"

She gives me another long stare and shakes her head when she figures out what I'm getting at. "Whoa. Okay, wait a second. If you're even slightly saying that my father or I had anything to do with Katie's death ..." She shakes her head again, pondering my accusation. "I'm not saying anything else until you tell me what's really going on here. Who are you?"

"I'm a private investigator. I've been hired to look into what happened to Katie. How she died."

"Who hired you?"

"A concerned friend of hers."

"A friend? Of Katie's?" It seems hard for her to comprehend that, like it's an impossible concept. "What's confusing about how she died?"

"Well, this friend is pretty adamant that Katie didn't use. That she wasn't a drug addict. So, the idea of her dying from a heroin overdose—it seemed pretty farfetched to her."

"Farfetched? They must not have known Katie very well."

"She did, actually."

"Well, maybe tell this very close friend of Katie's to go have a chat with Katie's junkie girlfriend. That might make things a little clearer to her."

I sit up in my chair. "Girlfriend?"

"Yeah, girlfriend."

"Were they serious?"

"They've been dating for years, so, yeah, I'd say there were serious."

Years. Oh man.

"And she did use. Katie, I mean. Not as bad as her girlfriend, but she used. Both of them worked for me. I fired the girlfriend first because she was basically an awful person and totally unreliable. Katie seemed nice enough and was working out fine for a while, but then I got tipped off that Katie and her girlfriend had been taking payoffs from landlords instead of actually filing the paper work that would have gotten them fined. They even started taking assignments from some of the landlords. Like, if one landlord wanted to damage another landlord financially, they'd overwhelm them with fines. When I found that out, I told Katie to quit or I'd call the cops."

"Who tipped you off to it?"

"My father. They approached one of his property managers with an offer."

Shit. This is gonna kill Cookie.

"My dad might not be the greatest guy, but he's honest, and I trust him, and I believe him. He was looking out for me when he let me know what they were up to." She pulls out an American Spirit and lights it up. "And just for full disclosure, when I shut this place down, I *am* going to go work for him. My dad, I mean. He's agreed to let me bring a percentage of low-income housing into his new constructions. I'm gonna try to do what I can from that side, from the money side."

"Okay."

"I don't need your judgment. Don't fucking stare at me and judge me. I could have made money on this place, but I never did. I tried to make things better. I really tried. But I can't change what's already happened. And I'm not going to waste any more of my years trying."

"I get it." I do. You can either fight the current, or you can steer with it. "I got no judgments on you." Who knows? Maybe she'll do good, or maybe she'll do just enough to feel good about herself. I adjust myself in my seat. "But ... do you think you could possibly give me the junkie girlfriend's info?"

"Yeah. Sure. Why not?" She writes it down on a piece of paper.

"What's happening with your filmmaker friend when you shut everything down?"

She hands me the paper with the girlfriend's info. "He'll be fine. He always is."

—

The girlfriend's name is Jenn Lapham, and the address is in Bushwick. I head right over there, thinking of Cookie the entire time. Whatever happens here, whatever Jenn says, I'll need to find a warm spin, something to ease the blow of all this for her.

Jenn's building is a run-down four-story gray brick apartment building. I climb the chipped stoop and press her buzzer, wait a few and then press it again.

Nothing.

"Who you looking for?" The super comes out from under the stoop wearing a tight white T-shirt tucked into tan Dickies and a nosy attitude. He pulls a smoke out from behind his ear and lights it up while I decide whether to tell him. He seems like the curious type. He might have some info.

"Jenn Lapham? In 2C?" I say.

"Oh. Yeah. She's not there anymore. I cleaned out her place yesterday."

"Do you know where she went? A forwarding address or ... "

He leans against the front of the building and takes a drag. "Well, yes and no." The raise of his eyebrows lets me know he's looking for cash. I pull out a ten, lean over the rail and hand it to him. He looks at it pitifully for a moment, then relents, pocketing it like he's doing me a favor. "Normally I'd ask for more, but my answer isn't gonna be very satisfying to you, so ten is fine." He takes another drag and exhales as he talks. "She's dead."

"Dead?"

"Yeah. Dead as in dead."

"What happened?"

"She fell off a building."

"What? Where? How?"

"Somewhere in South Slope. A couple of nights ago."

"Jesus."

"Landlord had me clean out her place last night. She was a pain in the ass, honestly. A real slob. I don't know your connection to her, so I apologize, but me—I'm glad to see her go."

Katie's place. It had to be Katie's place near the park.

I call a car and head over there as fast as I can. It takes a few blind buzzer rings to get in, but I get inside and head to the roof. Looking down, I have a hard time telling if anything happened below. Just under me, I see the pale, chalky and wrinkled arms of an old lady in the back fourth-floor apartment watering the dead plants on her fire escape. "Excuse me?" I say. Her arms freeze in position, then she goes back to watering. "Excuse me? Ma'am? *Señora*? I'm above you, on the roof."

"What the hell?" She leans out and cranes her neck to look up at me through the slats of the escape. "What the hell are you doing up there?"

I ask her about a woman falling a few days ago, and she confirms it a second before she threatens to call the cops on me. I thank her and bolt back down the stairs and out onto the South Slope street.

Walking down the sidewalk, I slip into a daze thinking about it all. Jenn has to have been looking for the stash of money, right? The ziplock bag of cash. But wouldn't Jenn have had keys if she and Katie were together? Maybe, maybe not, especially if Katie was trying to keep the cash away from Jenn and her habit. Maybe Katie had big plans for that money. Saving up for something.

Rehab. Escape. Anything.

I stop short. Did I lock the windows in her place when I left? I did, didn't I? I don't know. I wanted to leave the place looking right for Katie's dad, and I bet I locked the goddamn windows. But not the bathroom one. I never shut it. So maybe she tried the fire escape window, but it was locked. So she tried to get over to the open bathroom window like I did. She swung over to get in through there. Except she didn't make it. *Fuck.*

Fuck. Fuck. Fuck.

It's my fault.

It's not my fault, but it's still my fault. I mean, it feels like my fault.

Oh, man.

I decide to keep topside as long as possible, and I walk all the way to the Smith–Ninth Streets G station before I head to Cookie's. Hands in pockets, mind spinning, I keep walking, waiting to land on it, waiting for the dial to hit an explanation, waiting to figure out how to frame all this for Cooks.

And then I get it. I see the lie.

—

I sit Cookie down in the kitchen. I make some tea for us. I sit across from her, and I offer her a lifeline. I spin a good lie based on a few truths and a lot of assumptions, and I make a quiet wish for it to be enough to pull her out of her darkness. It's thin soup, but I hope it's enough for her to wrap her head around and move on with her life.

"So, this girl Jenn," I say. "She was the real manipulator. She was the one that was kind of masterminding the scam with the landlords." Cookie gives me a small nod. "The other thing about her—she's a junkie. A full-on addict."

"Were they close? Jenn and Katie?" She smells the truth in there. She's circling it; she's nervous. I gotta redirect her.

"No. It was strictly professional. Katie was the one who told Rebekah Mason about the scam, even. She was trying to do right. Trying to repair what she and Jenn did." No, she wasn't, but they're not here anymore, so I get to decide what happened. At least for Cookie.

"Okay." She says it quietly. Maybe Cookie wants the lie. Maybe she wants a soft pillow to rest Katie's memory on. I'm trying hard to sound sincere, but I dunno how it sounds outside my own head. I need her to want the lie for it to work. I keep going.

"Jenn must have found out about what Katie did and taken revenge on her. Shot her up. Dosed her." I watch Cookie process my words, my very big assumptions.

"If that's true then we should go to the cops, right? We need to get this Jenn person arrested."

"Well, the thing is ... she's dead. She died two nights ago trying to break into Katie's place. She ... she fell off the roof while she was going for the money."

"Fell off the roof?"

"Yeah."

"And she was definitely going for the money?"

"That's what my cop source told me." *Shit.* If Cookie and Hong ever cross paths, she might ask him about Katie. *Please don't ask Hong about this.* He's the only person I could possibly be getting this info from—that is, if I actually was getting this info from someone and not from my own head.

"And she's dead?"

"Yeah. She's dead."

"But the money. All that cash ... is that all bribe money?"

"No. I asked Rebekah about that." No I didn't. And there's no way to really know for sure. But this is the truth now. Cookie's truth. I lean into it. "Rebekah said that Katie turned that money in to her. She didn't want anything to do with it anymore. She didn't feel good about taking it." Everything I say sounds so obviously made up to me as I go. But it's only Cookie that matters. As long as she buys it, it'll become the truth.

"Then where did the cash come from?"

"It had to be tips, right? It had to be from her bartending, just like we thought it was originally." I make a silent wish for her to forget that I originally thought it was a lot for tips and wait to see if the lie takes. I watch Cookie process it all. She's not sure. Logic is pulling her away from my story, but her heart is pushing her back toward the lie. I see her going from thought to thought. Katie's not coming back. Not ever. Why not let her memory be positive? Why not let it be warm?

She looks up at me and puts her hand on top of mine. "I told you she was a good girl, didn't I?"

You did, Cooks.

"*Gracias, mijito.*"

She gives me a smile, and I'm only able to hold eye contact with her for a moment before the lie behind my eyes makes me break it.

She notices and tosses me an out. "So, what about you? What about your problems? What are we doing about your old boss and the tape?"

I look back up to her and smile. "If you can believe it, *tía*, I've actually got a plan."

CHAPTER TWENTY-SIX

I TOLD WALLY TO meet me at 4:00 p.m. at the Doray. He showed up thirty minutes early. That's okay, though, because I showed up an hour earlier. I wanted to make sure I was here first; I wanted to be seated before he got here. I wanted to watch him walk toward me. We're meeting for two reasons. Firstly, to offer up a few drinks to Finch and send him off into the afterlife. Jameson and gingers in his good name. Secondly—and most importantly—because I let Wally know that I had the tape, and I wanted him to see it.

Wally stops short when he sees me already sitting down at a table in the back. Surprised but not surprised. He nods toward me and then waves toward Mikey.

"Long time, no see, big man," Mikey says.

"Been busy, Mikey. Been keeping the peace, et cetera, et cetera, et cetera."

Wally makes his way toward me and takes a seat.

"You're early, Wally."

"Yeah, well ... I wanted to get a buzz on before things got too serious. It's been a shitty day." He turns to get Mikey's attention, but he's already arrived, Jameson and gingers in hand, like I asked him to do beforehand. He puts two drinks down on the table in front of us.

"Thanks, Mikey." I pick up my glass. "To Finch."

"To Finch," Wally says. "Slainte."

"*Salud.*"

We both drink. I know there's business to be done, but let's pause and take a moment to appreciate the Jameson and ginger. Goddamn, it's good. Finch was onto something with this as his usual. Not too sweet and easy to drink. I wanna swallow the entire thing, and I honestly have to force myself to put the glass down and release it from my hand after my first sip. Gotta keep my head straight for this. I can't get tight.

"So, the tape actually showed, huh?" Wally says. "How'd that happen?"

"Are we already done memorializing Finch?"

"We can do that while we do the other thing." He takes another sip of his drink. "So, again. How's that happen? How does the tape magically appear?"

"The same way the drinks did." I point toward Mikey behind the bar.

"What? Mikey?" He looks at him with annoyance and then turns back to me. "Fucker. I asked him if Finch left anything here."

"Well, he did. He just didn't leave it for you."

A small grunt from Wally. "So, let's see it." He takes another pull on his drink, and when it comes back down, it's nothing but ice. I give Mikey the sign for another round.

"What? You think I brought it here?"

"If it's not here, where is it?" There are just the beginnings of anger starting to bubble up in Wally's voice.

"In my apartment. On the coffee table." I added that last bit to speed things up and maybe cause as little damage to my place as possible. I watch Wally's face as he processes the information—the exact location of the tape that he very much wants in his plump hands. The second he heard me say where it is, his weight shifted; I could see him press down on the arms of his chair for a moment, about to push himself up, about to stand, but then pause and think better of it. We stare quietly at each other for a beat, and then he shakes his head, mumbling something unintelligible while he rethinks not doing whatever he originally wanted to do. He decides to do it.

"Excuse me a minute; I'll be right back." Wally stands with a groan and heads outside. I watch him overpull on the door to Atlantic Avenue, slamming it into the wall as he walks out. Mikey winces from the noise and brings over another round. I have him take away my barely touched first drink, along with Wally's empty. I want Wally to think I'm keeping up with him.

Outside, Wally's idling at the corner waiting for something, looking south on Third. Then I see it—the unmarked cop car, Rangers Jersey and Kangol Hat's car. It pulls up to Wally, who leans down to the open driver's side window. They talk for just about five seconds, just long enough to say, "It's at his apartment," and the unmarked car peels out, Rangers Jersey placing an already-spinning gumball light on top of the roof as he turns left toward the Brooklyn Bridge and, I'm assuming, my place.

A moment later, Wally waddles back inside and takes a seat. "Sorry. Just had a little mayor's office business to deal with." He gulps down half of his new drink, and I nod to Mikey for more.

"No worries." I fiddle with my glass and offer him a long stare. "So, are we gonna go get the tape, or ... ?"

Wally gives me a calm smile back. "There's no rush. Let's have some drinks for Finch first. We'll go after."

Yeah. Let's.

Wally downs the rest of his second drink, and Mikey's ready with his third. "Mikey, I'm not used to this level of service. You're gonna spoil me."

Mikey puts a full glass down in front of Wally. "Don't get used to it or anything. This is strictly a one-time thing. For Finch."

"For Finch." Wally raises his glass.

I do the same. "For Finch." I take out my pager and put it on the table. Wally doesn't seem to notice, or he doesn't care. "While I got you here, Wally, I was wondering if you could help me with something. With a case I'm working."

"Of course." He downs half of his third round. "I didn't realize you started taking other gigs."

"Nah, this is old business."

His face gets a little more serious. "Okay."

"I've got these two things, and I know they're connected, but I can't make the connection. I can't find the link. It's killing me."

"Tell me about it."

"Well, okay. The first thing is you. There's you and your slush fund. Your little gig with the mayor's office." I wait for a moment, giving him time to respond, but he just holds his stare. No emotion. No edge. "And then there's Rangers Jersey and Kangol Hat and the business of Finch. And I know you're all connected. I mean, I have eyes; I just saw it with my own eyes, right? You just went out on the street and talked to them. But even that's not the connection I'm looking for. That's physical. I'm looking for some logic, some motive, some reason for you all to be together on this. Et cetera, et cetera, et cetera." It's hard not to smile when I give Wally's catchphrase right back to him, but somehow I manage to keep the smartass joy I'm feeling hidden.

Wally clears his throat and takes an uncharacteristically small sip of his drink. "You think I'm hiding them from you? I'm not hiding them from you. You said it yourself. You saw it. I just did it right in front of you. Hell, I already told you I knew Rangers Jersey when we chatted at O'Connor's."

"I don't think you're hiding it from me. I think the opposite. I think you feel so good about your position that you're gloating about it."

"You're delusional, Nico."

"I'm not. But I have thought that. I have thought I might be seeing things. Especially when I saw you come out of Finch's office and then put a fresh evidence seal on the door, you know, to cover up the one you cut open. I also thought I must have been seeing things when Rangers Jersey and Kangol Hat broke into my apartment last week. Just to make sure that I wasn't seeing things, I called the cops. And then I sat in the park and watched as they came and went and then watched as you eventually rolled up. And then I rubbed my eyes when I saw them get into your back seat."

"I guess that explains why the guy in 3F said he never called the cops."

"Yeah, I guess that explains that." I take a quick look at my pager. Nothing yet. "So, how are these things connected, Wally? How is your slush fund and those assholes killing Finch connected?"

"First off, who told you about the slush fund? Not that I'm confirming the existence of a slush fund."

"A source."

He sarcastically tosses it back at me. "A source."

I allow myself a small sip of my drink and wince a little. This one is stronger. "Wally, help me understand. I know why those cops want the tape. It shows them committing a crime. What I don't get is why you want it. Why would you wanna protect the guys that killed Finch?"

"You're right about one thing. We got two things going on here. We got my thing, and we got Finch's thing. And I hate to disappoint you, but they are not connected."

Yeah, except for the fact that you're involved with both, Wally. "So, tell me about your thing first."

"What do you really know about what I do?"

I tell him what Boyd the dog-walking reporter told me. "I don't get how you go from investigating corrupt cops to protecting them. How does that work?"

"Like most things, it's more complicated than a pithy, one-sentence moral judgment outa the mouth of a youth such as yourself." He takes a deep breath. "I learned something pretty quickly working with the Mollen Commission. Something as true and as certain as death and taxes." He clears his throat. "You can't have cops without some level of corruption. Now, that can be vice squads on the take, like the gentleman you were following on the night of the taping, or that can be a jacked-up, steroid-addled twentysomething uniform with a gun and a nightstick who's sick of being called pig every time he goes to work, who—one day—snaps. He's had enough, so he uses the stick, or he uses the gun, or he uses the fists." He takes a sip. "It happens again and again and again. As long as we have a police force, there's gonna be bad eggs. Some'll be little bad eggs. Some'll be extra-large. But there's no way around it. There's gonna be corruption. Any police, in any city, it's the same thing. It's the side effect of policing. But corruption is bad, right?" He smothers his words in sarcasm. "And people want purity; they want a police force totally free of any illegal activity. But ... I'm sorry. It's an impossibility. It can't happen. If you want that, if you demand that, well, then you can't have a police force. You can't. So, to be corruption-free, we have to be police-free. And what do we have without cops? Fucking *Escape from*

New York, that's what." I can't help but let out a small guffaw at that. "You're laughing, but it's true. Without cops that's where we'd be."

"You're oversimplifying the choice. You're justifying corruption. It's not an either-or situation, Wally—"

"It is. It one hundred percent is. With cops you're gonna have some corruption; with no cops you're gonna have chaos. You have *Mad Max* and all the postapocalyptical nightmare shit that comes with it. Chain fights, fallout, shit like that." Wally's point of view has been deeply fucked with. His perspective hasn't just shifted. It's been perverted. I know it's him saying it, but I'm having a problem believing it is. Working in this mayor's office has made him go full fascist. "And if it were pre-sented to the public that way, as that real choice, most folks would say, gimme the cops, corruption and all. Gimme the beatdowns, gimme the frame-ups, gimme racial profiling, gimme law enforcement occasionally exceeding their legal boundaries. I mean, they might not say it publicly, but they'd say it privately."

"Yeah, because they don't think it's ever gonna happen to them. It's always gonna be the other guy that gets a stick up their ass."

"Right. And when it does happen to them, I step in. I float some cash, they sign some NDAs and restitution is made. I keep the cops looking as clean as possible, and people can keep believing in the system. That's what I do. I help people believe in the system. That's what the public needs. The corruption is always gonna be there. But the perception of corruption, that's the big bad. That's what I fight. I make sure the public can believe in the cops, even when the cops are shit. Which, let's be honest, lots are."

"That's like accepting a cancer 'cause it's a side effect of being alive. That's nuts, Wally."

"What's nuts is that most of these cops are basically kids, and we give them weapons, and then we punish them if they use them. Shit builds up inside them, anger and resentment, and eventually all that needs to be released. And in order to keep them from doing something really bad, we gotta let them loosen that valve every now and then; they need to bust a head, crack a skull—"

"Kill another cop."

"You were right before about that. That isn't the type of thing I normally handle. That is most definitely out of my jurisdiction." He reaches into his coat pocket and pulls out his pager, giving it a squint and then puts it back in his pocket.

"And your boss approves of this?"

"Of my thing? The mayor doesn't know anything. Well, he knows I'm supposed to help manage the public image of the cops when things get sticky, and he gave me the budget and some blurry lines to do it with. But he's not involved. Not in the day-to-day."

"Plausible deniability."

"I wouldn't know about that." I hear a muffled buzz from Wally's pocket. He pulls out his pager again and reads the message. "You probably don't realize this, Nico, but my involvement here, my activity with that pair of cops, with the tape and all? I'm doing it to protect you. I'm going above and beyond for you. Not for anyone else. For you. That's the only reason I'm involved."

And now we're on to the second thing. "Oh yeah?"

"Yeah. That tape existing is not healthy for you. So, I made a deal—if the tape goes away, then they back off you. You'll be safe. You'll be left unharmed."

"Do you honestly believe that?"

"I have leverage over those two idiots. If anything happens to you, I'll use it and they'll go down."

"And then what? Finch and I are dead, but we're at peace because we've been avenged?"

"I won't let it come to that. Well, I can't do anything about the Finch part, but you? You I'm keeping alive."

We both jump from my pager vibrating on the table. I pick it up and give it a read. "Why not just have them arrested for killing Finch?"

"Do you know how hard it is to put a cop away for murder *with* evidence? All you have here is circumstantial. There's no way to truly pin Finch's murder on them."

"But you think they did it?"

"I know they did it."

"Did they admit it?"

"No. But I know. But I also know why they did it. Finch fucked up. He should have called me, but he got greedy and tried to make a profit off your tape instead of doing something that would have protected you both. Finch made his bed, and he got fucked in it. That's the only reason those two clowns got involved in all this. Finch invited them to the party. It's Finch's fault."

My pager vibrates again. I read the code. "I'm guessing your page and my page are saying the same thing."

"And what's that?"

"That they got the tape."

He gives me a small smile. "You knew they'd go over there."

"I figured they would."

He leans back and squints as he processes my angle.

"So, you did something. You set something up ... cameras?"

"In the hallway. And inside my apartment." I maxed out my credit card at the Spy Shop yesterday. That shit isn't cheap. Hopefully I can return some of it or I'm fucked. "And I had my people outside on the street documenting them entering and exiting the building." My people is Frankie and Cookie. The sum total of my people.

"Hmm …"

"There wasn't a search warrant issued or anything, was there?"

Wally smiles wide. "Oh, no. This was a totally illegal affair. As you correctly assumed it would be."

"Seemed to fit the previous pattern."

He looks around. "You got cameras in here?"

"One."

"Microphone?"

"Yeah. And a witness." I point to Boyd at the end of the bar. He's been listening in this entire time. He gives Wally a wave and then points to his earpiece.

"Oh, that asshole. I know that guy. The reporter that's been up my ass for months. Hello, Mr. Boyd. Finally struck gold, I see."

Boyd gives another wave, but he keeps both his distance and his silence.

"So, what's the play here? What are you hoping is gonna happen?"

"Well, I want Rangers Jersey and Kangol Hat to pay for killing Finch."

"They will. I have plans for them. I do. They'll be dealt with. But I had to get them off your back first. And I had to clean up some business on my end, involvements I've had with them that would not reflect well on me or my office." He swigs the melted ice and turns toward Mikey. "Gimme another, Mikey. And skip the ginger ale, this time." He stares at me for a long hard moment. "Tell me that the copy of the tape they grabbed from your place is the last copy."

"Of course it's not."

Mikey puts the Jameson down in front of him. Wally takes a fast slug and messily wipes his lips with the back of his sleeve. "Who has it?"

"I have one. Boyd has one. Hong has one."

"And they've all watched it?"

"Yeah."

"Jesus, Nico. You've put them all in a really dangerous situation. I hope you realize that." He ponders it all some more. "Has Hong taken it to IAB yet?"

"I dunno."

"So, what, then? Hong goes to IAB? Boyd gets some big article in some shitty rag? My world comes crashing down? If I lose my job, I can't protect you anymore." He looks up toward Boyd. "I can't protect any of you." I take a sip of my now watered-down drink while he glares at me with annoyance. "How is any of that good for anybody? Why couldn't you just let me take care of this? The tape, Finch, those two assholes?"

"Why should I trust you? What have you done to make me trust you?"

"I dunno, Nico. Years of friendship? Years of looking out for you? Years of guiding you through your career? I care about you. I feel a responsibility for you. I do." He finishes his drink and starts crunching on the ice in his mouth. "Jesus. I was all set to have a relaxing night tonight. Now I gotta deal with this."

He stands.

"I've been looking out for you since you called me, Nico. This entire time I've been looking out for you. You can't see it, but one day you'll figure that out."

He turns and waddles toward the exit. Mikey had been doing his best to not pay attention, but he gives Wally a "See you later" when he gets to the door.

"Probably not anytime soon, Mikey."

CHAPTER TWENTY-SEVEN

I LIE LOW AT the jungle room on Essex Street for a few days, waiting to hear from Hong, waiting to hear from Boyd. I want to read the article. I want to watch the arrests. I want everybody who owed a debt to Finch, to me and to the citizens of New York City to pay it, publicly and painfully.

I'm sitting on the couch, flipping through the *Daily News*, and I'm surprised to find something in the paper written by Boyd, but it's not the article that I was expecting from him. I put down my bagel and read it with shiny, butter-coated fingers. Near the inner fold I see a pair of familiar cop faces—Rangers Jersey and Kangol Hat—but it's their formal, blue-uniform NYPD pictures, side by side, with identifying captions. Their faces seem so much more innocent than I'm used to seeing, and maybe they were more innocent when these photos were taken. Before the job did what it did to them. Or before they did what they did to the job. The article says Kangol Hat is dead—he was first through the door on a raid that went very wrong. Rangers Jersey was shot up but survived—he was second through the door. The backup they called in, the backup they expected, well, it didn't show for reasons not explained in the article. It says Kangol Hat is survived by his wife and kid. I can't imagine that guy having a family. Rangers Jersey is currently occupying a

bed at Long Island College Hospital in Brooklyn Heights and is expected
to recover from his wounds.

Fucking Wally went full *Serpico* on them. He got them to bust down
a door with no backup that they'd never survive busting down. Except
Rangers Jersey did.

I call Boyd a few times, first at his home and then through the general
number on the *Daily News*'s masthead. They connect me to his line, and
I nearly choke when I hear the recording. "This is Ernie Boyd, staff writer
at the *Daily News*. Please leave a message at the beep." I don't bother
leaving a message. I can smell the shitty under-the-table arrangement that
was made to give this fucker a staff job. I call Wally to confirm it.

"You made Boyd a deal, didn't you? You got him a job at the *News* to
get him to forget about my story."

"I did what I had to do to protect myself. And to protect you. It wasn't
easy—I have more pull at the *Post*, but he didn't want to write for those
guys."

"I guess I shouldn't hold my breath waiting for an article about your
slush fund, should I?"

"I don't know what slush fund you're talking about. I mean, I guess
there might be something about me in the *News* one day. I think they've
been talking about doing a profile on me. That'd be nice, right?"

Goddamn it. I gave everything I had on Wally and the cops to Boyd
for his article. I bet everything is long gone.

"Who has the recordings?" I ask.

"Which ones?"

"Please. Of you at the Doray. Of the cops breaking into my place."

"Oh, those. I'm not exactly sure, but if you really want to try and
track them down, I recommend looking on Staten Island. The dump,
specifically."

Shit.

"I read what happened to Kangol Hat. Did you just recently rewatch *Serpico*, or has that plot point always stuck with you?"

"I don't think I know what you're talking about." He takes a very Wally wet breath before continuing. "Although, I will say, it seems like sort of a poetic end for him, doesn't it?"

"I don't see the poetry in getting shot to death."

"It's how you look at it, I guess."

"What about Hong? What about IAB?"

"Detective Hong has received a much-deserved promotion from detective third grade to detective first grade, complete with all the benefits of both rank and salary that come with it. I don't believe anything is happening with IAB."

Fuck.

"So that's it then? You wrapped everything up pretty perfectly, didn't you?"

"I'm just looking out for the people I care about. Which includes you, Nico."

"What about Rangers Jersey?"

"Unfortunately, he's gonna pull through, so something else will have to get figured out. But don't worry. I'm on it." *Man.* "Let's get some lunch sometime, Nico."

So that's it, then.

He hangs up and I slowly do the same. I push myself far back onto the couch and take a long look around me at the overgrown plants and the insanity-inducing bright colors on the walls.

I gotta get outa here. I decide it's time. It's got to finally be safe enough to go back to my place.

So I pack.

—

A few nights later and I'm fully moved back into my Avenue B apartment. I meet Maggie for dinner at Milon, that Indian restaurant on First Avenue in the East Village. It's the one with all the red Christmas lights—the entire thing is a twinkling red cave of both cozy and crazy. And it's cheap, so that's good, even though I'm not buying. Maggie leaves for Los Angeles in the morning, and she wanted to take me out before she went. She has meetings about that TV thing she was circling ideas on, and she's not sure when she's coming back. If it goes well, she might not ever.

She's also buying because she wants an entertaining wrap-up on Katie, on Cookie and on Wally and Finch, so I oblige, in between gulps of Kingfisher and forks full of curry and rice.

"So, what ever happened to the money? The ziplock bag from Katie's place?"

I give my mouth a wipe before answering. "Cookie donated it to this gay and lesbian teen shelter for homeless kids. She did give me a little to cover some of my expenses, though."

"That's nice. Both of those things."

"Yeah."

"If this thing works out for me in LA, you're gonna have to give me first crack at the rights to your story."

"I'm sure something can be worked out." I can't help but smile hopefully as I say it, even though I know she's joking.

"You need to write down your email address for me so we can keep in touch."

"Yeah, I don't really have one."

"That's crazy."

"Well, I don't have a computer."

"That's kind of crazy, too."

"I have no income or possibility of income right now, so it's not exactly a priority."

"Oh, my God. That means you've never seen the websites about your dad?"

"No."

"Shit. I should have told you about them before. Just ... get an email address, and then I'll send you the web addresses. There are a bunch of them. It's so cool."

"What kind of websites are they?"

"They're mostly fan sites. Memories and stuff. But there's this one message board that swears your dad is still alive. That he's in LA and ghostwrites songs for the One-Named Indie Darling. That he lives in an apartment above his garage in Silver Lake."

"That's ... bizarre."

"Yeah, lots of stuff online is. But it's still very cool. I mean, there are no websites about my dad, good or bad. You should be proud."

We finish up, she pays the tab, and we stroll for a bit, pondering a bar. At the corner of Fourth Street, we turn with no real plan, and soon we're in the middle of a crowd on the sidewalk that spills out into the street, all gawking at a stoop on the south side.

A Sinatra impersonator in a black suit is swaying on the top step singing "Fly Me to the Moon" while a fiftysomething woman tap-dances on a piece of plywood on the sidewalk. What would be the downstairs garden apartment is a thrift store storefront, and it seems like they've provided some seating. Used couches and chairs line the sidewalk. Behind that the rest of the crowd stands, watching this spontaneous street cabaret.

"This is … amazing." Maggie's smile is wider than I've ever seen on her. Wider than when we jumped into the conveniently placed cab after the karaoke place. Wider than when I saw her on the street outside 7B. Wider than when I first explained what was going on with Finch and the cops in the glow of the jukebox in the back of International Bar.

I'm going to miss that smile.

I look around and realize it's not just her and it's not just me—it's everyone. Easily forty or fifty people all caught up in the moment. I don't know if I've ever been in a crowd this large where everyone was feeling simultaneous joy. Feeling so much happiness. Maggie and I lock eyes but stay silent. We both know we've stumbled on something special and unrepeatable. And yeah, special and unrepeatable happens all over New York. But this is ours. This is here.

On the street, homeless men act as traffic cops, protecting the crowd and guiding cars as they negotiate the people that are paying absolutely no attention to the passing vehicles. A Chinese food delivery guy rolls up on his bike, his handlebars weighed down by countless plastic bags. Unfazed by it all, he grabs one of his deliveries and crosses in front of Sinatra, seemingly acting like this is just another day on the job. The dude has to work, and he's focused on that task; some unexpected street party won't stop him. Sinatra leans in and asks him something off mic, and they talk for a brief moment before Sinatra goes into some improvised lyrics, still to the tune of "Fly Me to the Moon": "Oh, hey there, Mister Long—your fried rice and dumplings delivery is here." It's a little bit of a stretch, in terms of tempo and syllable matching–wise, but the crowd loves it. The delivery guy is buzzed in, and a few moments later, Mr. Long is in his window facing the street, eating his fried rice right out of the container and nodding along to the tunes. When the delivery guy exits the building, he's greeted by a unified cheer and applause, and his face reads like he's just noticed the crowd for the first time. He goes from surprised to triumphant and raises his arms Rocky-style as he heads back toward his bike and disappears into the night.

From behind us, the inevitable "Whoop! Whoop!" of a police cruiser announces its arrival on the scene as it slowly creeps its way across Fourth toward us. The smile drops from Maggie's face. "Oh, crap. Party's over." Everybody turns and the fear that this magic could suddenly end smothers us all. There's a long pause of dread, a hard silence as we all hold our breath and wait. Even Sinatra waits, but he never loses his smile, insisting on sending positivity their way, hoping the warmth will bounce back on him. And then it comes—the staticky click of a microphone coming alive, a tiny amount of feedback and then, through the speakers, "Hey ... play 'Summer Wind.'"

Sinatra doesn't miss a beat. "You got it." He knows exactly which karaoke track it is on his CD player, and he skips right to it as the crowd applauds, their smiles coming back strong. "This one is for our friends in the Ninth Precinct." And he goes right into it.

Maggie turns to me and smiles. "You wanna dance? We kinda have to dance, right?"

I smile at back at her. "Of course." Pretty soon we're swaying in the street, one of a few couples doing it, but soon more and more start to pair off and dance. Some are actual couples, some are friends and some are complete strangers that just happened to be standing next to each other.

We all dance under the streetlights of the East Village, lost in time and lost in each other.

And then it rains.

—

Maggie begs me to go back with her to the place where she's staying in Greenpoint, but it's not to hook up or anything exciting like that. She got me a good-bye gift and forgot to bring it out tonight. She's pissed at herself for forgetting to bring it, and she seems so desperate to give it to me, so I let curiosity add ninety minutes of subway commute onto my night. I kind of need to see what sort of gift Maggie thinks would be "perfect" for me.

We take a cab to Manhattan Avenue, close to the Greenpoint water-front. She moved out of her place a few days ago, and now she's crashing on the couch of some old SUNY Purchase friends. It's an overcrowded dump, but it's free and closer to LaGuardia Airport than her old place, close enough that it should knock fifteen bucks off her morning cab, which was definitely part of her plan.

She runs upstairs to get my gift as I kill time outside of her build-ing—she didn't want to annoy her roommates with a visitor, temporary or not. My foot gets stuck in something sticky, and when I look down, I can see that there's something gross caked all over the cement of the sidewalk. I squat down in the dark and realize it's all dried blood and feathers. They lead inside the building next to Maggie's friends' place. From behind the loosely closed wooden garage doors, I can hear the muffled, sad, repeated bleating of goats. That's when I finally see the sign above the doors—"Manhattan Avenue Halal Meats." It's a slaughter-house. Cartoon chickens, ducks and goats cover the signage. Hopefully nothing else bigger or bloodier is getting killed in there. I step back toward the doorway Maggie went through, into the light that spills out from the vestibule, and I check the bottom of my shoes for blood or anything worse.

She comes out, holding up a green work jacket and wearing a wide smile. "Here it is!" She hands it to me. It's one of those tough but light work jackets supers or janitors might wear, maybe oil truck delivery drivers.

"Thanks?"

"Look at the front!" She's bouncing on her toes with excitement. I turn the coat, and then I see it. Stitched in white cursive, just over the heart, it reads, "George." "I was selling some clothes at Domsey's today and was looking for something when I found it in the stacks. I couldn't *not* give it to you. To my Georgie."

"Thanks." It's both a better and a worse gift than I thought it would be.

"Whenever you wear it and somebody calls you George by mistake, you'll have to think of me. Now you can't forget me."

"I don't think I could ever forget you, Maggie."

We smile at each other, and I have that feeling again, the one that says, "Kiss her now or you never will," but what am I gonna do? Try to kiss her the night before she moves away to LA? End an amazing night by crossing a line that can't be uncrossed? Something that'll probably kill the friendship for good?

No. I decide to swallow the feeling down. I pull her in for a hug, and she hugs me back tightly. It's nice. She's a special one, and I don't want to risk losing her because I couldn't keep my glands in check for one night.

After a long squeeze, she holds me out at arm's length. "I'm gonna miss you."

"I'm gonna miss you, too."

She gives me a kiss on the cheek, and as she turns, I think I see some tears in her eyes. She opens the door to the vestibule and screams, "Get an email address, asshole!" as the door closes. Then she goes deeper into the hallway and up the stairs, and a few moments later, she's gone.

I smile and take a step toward Greenpoint Avenue. I don't have the scratch for another cab, so I'll have to hoof it to Williamsburg and the L and just hope I get home sometime before dawn.

As some point in the next step, I suddenly spin toward the building, like someone pushed me or twisted me, and I see a plume of dust as something chips away a chunk of brick in front of me.

Oh, shit.

I think somebody just shot me.

CHAPTER TWENTY-EIGHT

THE DOORS OF THE slaughterhouse seem like they could be from the original construction—sort of like those garage doors that Carroll Garden carriage houses have. They're wooden and gatelike, and they swing open in the middle, locked with a loose-fitting metal chain between the two sides. I manage to squeeze my body through them and get inside.

The smell inside is as bad as my shoulder stings, but I can't think about any of that right now. Outside, the unknown shadow that just shot me is crossing the street and will probably be inside with me very quickly. I start pressing against the exit wound on the front of my shoulder, trying to apply pressure, but I can't imagine I'm doing anything positive for the entry wound on my back. I picture every drop I stop from going out the front hole getting squished out the opposite way from the pressure.

I try to take a quick peek through the doors to the street. It's too dark to get a good read, but I know who shot me. Who else can it be? It has to be Rangers Jersey. He must have been following me tonight, waiting for me to be alone. When did he get out of the hospital? And why hasn't Wally figured out what to do with him yet? I look at my pager, and sure enough, Wally's number is there. It looks like he paged me somewhere between the *papadums* and the outdoor stoop cabaret. If I had called him, maybe he'd have given me a heads-up. Probably something along the lines of "You're probably fine, but watch your back, et cetera, et cetera, et cetera."

But it's too late for any of that now.

It's after hours inside, and I'm pretty sure I'm the only other person in the slaughterhouse. I take as quick a read of the dark room as I can. My best bet is slipping out a back entrance, but I'm not even sure if there is one. Maybe I can hide and then double back out the front and get to some help? I could buzz Maggie, but I don't even know which buzzer is for her friends' place, and I have no desire to drag her into this.

Ahead of me and deeper into the space, fifty or so goats are penned in tightly, most likely inhumanely. Behind them and to the side is an open door—it seems like it might be to an office? Maybe there's a phone. I shuffle around the goats in the pen, who bleat at me angrily, begging for their release.

Why not?

I find the gate and the simple sash cord looped over the post to keep it closed and lift it off, opening the gate. The goats immediately pour into the rest of the space, filling its void, expanding and crowding into the large room. Hopefully they make it harder for Rangers Jersey to see me when he gets inside. Somehow it seems like there are now more goats outside of the pen than there ever were inside of it.

Good. I could use the chaos.

Behind me, I can hear the clinking of the front garage door chain—it's either him trying to get in or the goats trying to get out. I'm not gonna chance it, so I get low and crawl on my hands and knees through the filth toward the small office.

The smell down here is not good. Blood, shit, piss, hay and mud. It's not pleasant.

I slide into the tiny office and find the phone cord in the wall jack and follow it up to the phone on the desk, quietly pulling it down and cradling it against my chest as I think about what to do.

Who do I call?

If I call the cops, this could turn worse for me and quick. Who knows who arrives? Who knows who Rangers Jersey can woo to his side? He flashes a badge and says a killer is inside, and bullets start flying before anybody even thinks about Miranda rights, let alone considers reading them to me.

I can call Wally, but what'll that do? I bet I'd be dead before he could even find his pants.

Frankie. Call Frankie.

He said to call him in times like this, and this definitely very much feels like a time like this, so I call him, but goddamn it if he doesn't pick up. I whisper a message with my hands cupped against the mouthpiece, telling him my approximate address. There can't be that many slaughterhouses on Manhattan Avenue near the waterfront in Greenpoint, right? I hope to fucking God there aren't. Just to be safe I also leave a message for Wally. It feels pointless, but who knows? He could make a call; he could get some other help.

I crawl closer to the open door and peek around. I can't really see anything beyond the bizarre, fuzzy outlines of goats moving—it sort of looks like that silhouette shot in *Close Encounters* when all the little kid aliens are walking down the ramp. Rangers Jersey has got to be inside the building by now. I can't stay in this tiny office. I need to either find my escape out the back or sneak around inside and then double back to the front exit.

I need to get out of here. There has to be a way out of here.

Deep breath. Deep breath.

I tell myself I can't panic, but who am I kidding? I'm fucking panicking.

I crawl farther into the darkness of the slaughterhouse. After about fifteen feet, the floor changes from cement to a flat, thin metal that buckles and clanks as my weight presses into it. It's aluminum or steel, and it's cold as fuck. A little farther on, and it turns into a slatted metal grate floor. I look up, and even in the dark, I can see the hooks hanging from the ceiling and the glistening metal knives against the wall. This must be the killing room. If this place is really halal, this is where the goats are bled out, right where my own blood is probably currently dripping.

I inch to the edge of the room and try to reach up to the wall—I need some sort of weapon, and one of those knives is probably the best I can hope for.

Shit!

I jerk back my hand—I must have cut myself on a blade. *Jesus, they're sharp as hell.* I worry for a moment about infection with tetanus or worse, and then I remember that I've already got an open wound from being shot in the shoulder, and I just crawled through twenty yards of wet goat shit. The cut on my hand is the least of my worries. I reach up again, more careful this time, and manage to grab one of the boning knives. As I pull it down from the wall, I knock another down next to it, and it crashes loudly onto a steel counter. The sound of metal clanging on metal is quickly followed by a spray of bullets sparking up the wall of knives.

I freeze and hope to God it fucking stops.

It does.

But Rangers Jersey is definitely inside.

Shit.

Shit, shit, shit.

I cower and crawl as fast as I can toward the back. There must be a back door, right? There has to be a rear exit. An alley or an air shaft leading to an adjoining building, something.

There better be, anyways. There better be a goddamn way out.

I hit a wall, and my fingers find the outline of the door within it. Thank fucking God. I reach up, but it's not the usual door handle. I expect there to be a metal bar to push or a handle or a knob, but this is more like an old-fashioned latch. While I'm squatting, I pull the metal latch toward me, and the door unlocks and opens. I immediately hear the hum. The buzz of refrigeration.

Shit.

This is not the exit.

But I have to keep going.

Behind me I hear Rangers Jersey as he curses and kicks his way through some misbehaving goats. He's close; he's pissed off and he's close. He'll find me soon enough if he keeps moving forward.

I enter the refrigerated room through the heavy, insulated door and try to close it as silently as possible. Once inside, I shiver as goose bumps rise on my flesh.

It's cold.

There's a dull blue glow from a small light on the refrigeration unit on the wall. I can just make out a couple dozen or so ovalish shadows in the room, slightly swaying. As my eyes adjust, I realize what they are—carcasses. Skinned and butchered goat carcasses, dramatically hanging from metal hooks that dangle from the ceiling. I'm sure it's a very functional setup, but right now it's creepy as hell.

I find the side walls and walk them, feeling for another door, a back exit, anything, but there's nothing.

Okay, maybe this was a horrible mistake. I thought maybe there might be a back loading dock or something for the frozen meat to get packed into trucks, but no.

I'm a fucking idiot.

I see Rangers Jersey pass by the small window of the door I just entered, and I push myself up against the back wall opposite it, trying to use the hanging carcasses as cover as I watch and wait. My movement has put them in motion, and they rock faintly on their chains. I get a glimpse of the window in the door each time they swing past my eyeline. It's still empty and I start to think maybe he didn't find the door; maybe he turned around and started looking for me somewhere else. But as the goat carcasses sway back again, they swing to reveal the silhouette of his head filling the window's square frame.

Fuck.

I hear the click of the latch being pulled, and my ears pop a little as the pressure of the room changes from the door getting pulled open. Even in this cold, my palm pours sweat around the handle of the boning knife in my right hand, so I quickly change it to my left, wipe the moisture onto the lapel of my dad's pea coat and then swap it back into my right.

Ahead of me, the door closes.

He's in now.

In the room with me.

I can hear him breathing.

What's my plan? Stab him? Am I really going to stab another living person? Kill him with my own hands? I don't think I can, even if he did kill Finch. Even if he wants to kill me. I try to slowly mirror him as he moves. He goes to his right, so I go to my right. There's no way he's not going to see me if I keep at this. The room can't be more than twenty feet by twenty feet.

Wait. What about under? Underneath the carcasses?

Quietly, calmly, I lower myself, squatting down. There's about two feet of clearance under all the skinned goats. I can belly crawl under them straight to the door. Rangers Jersey is working the walls, just as I did before, but his eyes are adjusting to the darkness, and pretty soon he'll be seeing as well as I can.

If I stay standing, he'll see me.

I lie on my stomach and feel the cold cement floor against my belly. It makes me shiver, but I can't react to it; I can't make a noise, or I'm fucked. I start to move slowly, but any pressure on my left arm makes the wounds in my shoulder ache, so I try to favor my right side.

Christ, I'm moving slow.

But I am moving. He's behind me now, against the back wall, but he's started to move forward, through the carcasses, pushing them aside.

He's gonna step right on me.

I roll to my left, onto my back, out of his path. I'm looking up, and he's looking down.

We lock eyes.

Goddamn it.

"There you are."

He extends his gun and aims, and all I can think to do is slice the boning knife across the back of his left ankle, across his Achilles. He screams and he shoots, but the pain fucks with his aim, and a frozen carcass above me gets the brunt of the bullets.

I ignore my own pain as I stand and run for the door, pushing it open and running through. He sees me and starts firing again, bullets chipping at the inside of the heavy, insulated refrigerator door as it shuts.

The goats that worked out so well for me before are now fucking with my escape path, but I manage to push through them.

The door to the street is closer.

Just twenty or so more feet ...

Bullets chip the garage doors ahead of me, and I cower, my hands up around my head, as Rangers Jersey fires from behind me, following my path.

Fuck, fuck, fuck.

I keep going, falling onto the locked chain and then squeezing under it, through the opening.

I fall to the sidewalk, stand and take a few gravity-motivated stumbles and then fall forward again, rolling into the gutter of Manhattan Avenue.

Behind me I hear the clink of chains as Rangers Jersey pushes through the garage doors.

Goddamn it, I need to find cover. I scramble on the street, frantically crawling behind a parked van, and then I hear the unmistakable sound of a skull cracking.

And then silence.

Slowly, I stand and peek out from behind the back of the van. Rangers Jersey is slumped over the chain of the door, stuck there between both sides, blood pouring out of a crack in his forehead and forming a bright pool on the sidewalk underneath him. It flows toward the street, mixing with the blood and feathers of the slaughterhouse.

Next to him stands Frankie, his metal steering wheel lock club in his hands. For a moment, he looks like Mike Piazza with his bat in his hands, in that brief post-swing moment when he allows himself to be impressed by his own strength before he begins to run the bases.

He looks over to me. "You all right?"

"Uh, no. I'm not actually. I sort of got shot."

"Oh. Cool."

—

Wally shows up shortly after. He quickly sends Frankie on his way and makes a call to set me up with a doctor who won't ask any questions about my bullet wounds. He says he'll deal with the slaughterhouse mess and that I don't need to know how it's gonna get sorted out. But he promises me that Frankie and I will be left out of it.

I pick up the jacket Maggie gave me off the sidewalk; I must have dropped it when I was shot. What a weird fucking ending to a sentence that is—"when I was shot." I think about maybe buzzing Maggie and filling her in. She'd get a kick out of all this. But Wally calls me a cab and sends me on my way.

I actually cash in my prescription this time and give in to the painkillers. Why not let it all go black for a little while?

I could use the rest.

CHAPTER TWENTY-NINE

I T'LL TAKE A BIT until I'm feeling 100 percent. My plan is to not do much besides sit on my couch for a few weeks, but I still need to go visit my great-aunt Ruby in Sunnyside, Queens. Once I feel the ability to be somewhat mobile, I call her up and make plans to head over. It seems like as good a sick-day activity as any.

My dad's pea coat is still getting cleaned—it's now on the second attempt to get all the blood and goat shit out of it—so I put on the George jacket and start the trek to Sunnyside. Ruby lives in the Phipps Garden Apartments in a rent-controlled place she inherited from her sister / my grandmother when she passed. It's a bunch of big apartment buildings built around a small courtyard, sort of like Stuyvesant Town in Manhattan but not as giant. It's a ten-minute walk from the 52nd Street–Lincoln Avenue stop of the 7 train and is sandwiched between Thirty-Ninth Avenue and the Long Island Railroad tracks. On spring days with the apartment windows open, you can hear the flanging sound of the tracks and the electricity as commuter trains roar by. It's distinctly different from the sound of the subway. More metallic, somehow. I've always loved it.

When I was kid, I would swipe a jar of maraschino cherries from Ruby's pantry and sneak up onto the roof to eat them and gawk at the various views. Bridges in the distance in almost every direction. Planes heading for JFK and LaGuardia. You used to be able to see the silvery steel Ronzoni pasta factory sign in Long Island City. When they shut that place down in '93, I used to daydream about stealing that sign—or maybe just the big O—but I could never come up with a plan or a willing accomplice; it would require a few, at least. The sign was on the building for a few months before they took it off and hauled it down south to the new factory. Or maybe they just took it to the dump. Either way, both the sign and the factory are gone now.

Back in the early eighties, when things in Sunnyside were a little rougher, I'd lean against the edge of the roof and watch the packs of feral dogs that used to roam the road by the train tracks. There was always parking on the road against the tracks, but it was treated as a last, desperate resort, to be used only when Fiftieth Street and Thirty-Ninth Avenue had no spots left. The dogs used to chase folks to and from their cars. From the roof it was hilarious. I'm guessing on ground level, it wasn't.

At the Phipps, Ruby buzzes me into building FF, and I start the climb up to the third floor. I can hear the opening of lock after lock as I climb—she must have at least six or seven of them. By the time I get to her landing, she's waiting, partially hiding behind the door in a stained terry-cloth robe.

"Hey, Ruby."

She hands me an Associated Supermarket paper grocery bag brimming with trash, wet through with egg yolks and coffee grounds. "For the incinerator."

The incinerator isn't an incinerator anymore. You can't burn garbage like you used to. You still dump your trash into it, but it leads to a dumpster or a garbage room or something. The shaft opening is just two feet away from her on the landing, but I guess she thought she was doing me a favor? When I would visit as a kid, I would beg to throw trash into the garbage shaft. The smaller and harder the better. If you had an apple even close to rotting, I tossed it down. A vaguely brown banana? Good-bye. I loved to hear it hit the walls and bounce around and then to hear that final thud of it getting absorbed into the larger pile. In my mind I always imagined them landing in the middle of the trash compactor scene in *Star Wars*. And I know that's an obvious reference, but when you're a kid, that's the kind of reference you make.

I grab the grocery bag from Ruby and open the door to the small shaft; the bag is too big for it, and I have to squish it down and stuff it in. Did trash bags used to be way smaller? What size trash bags were people using in the thirties when they built this place? I shake out my hands to get the wet goop off, but they stay mostly moist.

"Lock the door behind you. I'm eating my soup." Ruby turns and lets the heavy door start to close. I manage to reach out just in time to stop it from slamming into my face and step inside. All I can smell once I walk into the apartment is Lysol. Like … so much Lysol. I have no idea what it's covering up, but I assume the Lysol is preferable to whatever it's masking, so I'm thankful for it. I close the door and make the executive decision only to lock one dead bolt. I don't wanna feel entirely trapped in here.

The entry hallway has an oversized black-and-white photo of my dad as a kid in some sort of cute kids' interpretation of a military uniform. The photo looks rotted at the corners, and it's a bit off kilter in the frame. Above it, there's an even older photo of my grandfather when he was actually in the army. I guess you gotta be in uniform to earn a place on this wall. Short pants optional.

Ruby was serious about getting back to her soup. She's already at the tiny table in her kitchenette when I step in. By the time I sit down across from her, she's a few spoonfuls into her meal, messily slurping some very pale broth. I can't imagine it has any flavor beyond wet salt. She looks up at me. "Your face got fat."

"I'm sorry?"

"Your face. It got fat."

"Yeah, uh ... Okay." It takes all of thirty-five seconds to remember why I don't come out here more often.

"So, what's going with you? You still with that girl?"

"Um ... that girl? Who do you mean?"

"The one you brought by here before."

"Who did I bring by here?"

"I think her name was Liza or Liz, maybe?"

"Lisa? From college? Ruby, that was nine years ago."

"So, are you with her or what?"

"Uh, no. We broke up seven years ago. In 1991." She's earned two graduate degrees since then.

"She's an Oriental or something, right?"

Oh boy.

"Uh, no. But she's French. Maybe that's what you're remembering?"

"No, she's got those oriental eyes."

Jesus.

"Uh, well, no. She's French is the thing."

"She must have some oriental blood."

"I mean, maybe? But I don't think so."

"I dunno ..." She looks at me as if somehow she knows significantly more about this than I do. I can't believe I have to make an argument about this to convince her, but before I know it, I am.

"No, I'm pretty certain she's French. I mean, sure, she can be French *and* Asian, but I don't think that's the case here."

She puts her spoon down. "Jeez! You don't have to keep going on and on and on about it. I get it. You'd think I just broke a commandment or something." She's not done, though. "Why'd you two break up?"

"Why'd I break up? With Lisa? The girl from nine years ago?"

Get me out of here.

"Yeah," she says.

I think on it for a minute, and then I actually remember. "You know what? I do know why."

"Why?"

"She drove me nuts. She had this habit of never ever asking any questions; she would just make statement after statement after statement. Just constant statements. It didn't really create any opportunities for actual conversation."

"What do you mean?"

"Okay, so, say we're walking down the street and she sees shoes in the window. 'Those are nice shoes.' Okay, great, they're nice shoes. A red car drives by. 'Red's the best color for cars.' Is it? Does it even matter? I don't know. 'Wow, there's a lot of gum on the sidewalk.' What do you even say to that?"

"She's got a point, though. I've been noticing a lot of gum on the sidewalk lately." She leans in toward me. "I think it's them Arabs that have been moving into the neighborhood."

"It's not the Arabs, Ruby."

"Well, I don't think it's the Blacks. I don't think they even like gum. I always see them chewing those sticks."

I exhale and rub my eyes. *Why am I here again? What am I doing?*

Right. My dad. She has something of my dad's. Gotta get it and gotta get out.

"I liked her. The Oriental." Ruby is sincere about it. Both the warm sentiment and the racism. But then I remember, she did like Lisa but mostly because she smoked. When we said good-bye to her, Ruby hugged Lisa and slipped her two packs of Parliaments like she was secretly palming her some cash. "Don't worry; I got a carton in the freezer," Ruby whispered into Lisa's ear. We took the smokes to Blue and Gold Tavern and laughed about it while we got drunk and smoked more of them than we should have. I wonder what Lisa's doing nowadays.

Okay. Gotta refocus. There is a point to this journey to the Phipps.

"So, on the phone you said you had something of my dad's?" I say. "Something of his to give me?"

She ignores the question, or she doesn't hear me, but I'm going to bet it's the former. She knows once I get whatever it is she has, this visit is going to be over, and quick.

"What's up with that jacket?" she asks.

"What do you mean?"

"The name. Who's George?"

"Oh, uh ... I have no idea. It was a gift."

"Somebody gave you a gift, and they don't even know your name?"

"They do, but ... It's sort of an inside joke. Like, she was being cute, clever ... "

"Oh, right. I forgot how you and your friends like to do stuff like that. You're all so ... *creative*." She says the word *creative* with absolute, searing hate.

Get me the fuck out of here.

"So, my dad," I say. "The thing you have. What is it? What do you got for me, Ruby? Please, let's have it, okay? Now."

"Oh, right. I almost forgot." She struggles to stand and heads to the drawer below her toaster and opens it, is about to grab the thing and then turns back toward me. "Sometimes when your dad and his *mamacita* were on the outs, he would come and live here for a little bit. With my sister and me."

Mamacita.

They all called my mom that. All the women on my dad's side of the family. They'd say it, and they'd giggle and look at one another thinking there was no way anyone would be clever enough to get the racism of the nickname. It drove me crazy. If I called them out on it, they'd always say it was a term of endearment in her culture. *Her* culture. I'd remind them her culture is also my culture, and they'd scrunch their faces, unhappy at being reminded of the truth of my genetic makeup.

"When did my dad ever live here?" I say.

"It was a few times. Before you were born and after. She's a hotheaded *señorita*, that mother of yours. She kicked him out lots."

"She was married to an unfaithful drug addict, Ruby. I think she had a reason to be emotional."

"You know, I don't want to talk out of turn, but we always thought she was the one that introduced your dad to that stuff. Those Puerto Ricans are really into the heroin. It's sort of like Indians and the alcohol."

"Well, not that it should matter, but she's not Puerto Rican. She's Ecuadorian."

"Right, you're right. It doesn't matter. All those countries are the same—"

"Puerto Rico isn't a country, Ruby. It's part of the United States." *Jesus. I can't take it anymore.*

She gets the hint. "Anyways, I guess your dad made this for her, but he musta never actually gave it to her. I found it in an old box of his clothes. The clothes turned into a mouse nest a while back, but this still seems to be okay. I don't have a player for it, but I figured you might. One of them Walkmens or whatever."

She hands it to me.

Wow.

Goddamn it if this wasn't maybe worth both the trip and the generational racism.

"Thank you, Ruby."

—

When I get back home, I dig the double-As out of my Discman and put them into my old cassette Walkman. I take out Ruby's gift—it's an old mixtape from my dad to my mom. It didn't really have that much going on cover art design-wise, not like Maggie would have liked, but my dad did draw a big broken heart on it. In the corner he put the year—1980.

I was ten years old then.

He did title it, though: *Brooklyn Motto*. He wrote it in cursive on the spine. Side A is called "In unity . . ." and Side B ". . . There is Strength."

In Unity There Is Strength. I like that.

I put in the cassette, press Play and lie back on the couch. The first track is Roberto Jordan y su Grupo Amigo's "Ven a Darme Amor," their Spanish cover of Redbone's "Come and Get Your Love." It's a version I've heard my mother sing along with, a version I've heard her sing to herself. I can picture her over the sink washing dishes and singing it. I look at the other tracks on the jacket. They're all Spanish-language covers. All love songs.

I try to think like Maggie would with her mixtape hobby. Who gave this tape? Who'd they give it to? What did they want?

I know the answers pretty clearly, but I decide to let the songs tell me.

I'm just gonna lie here and listen and let it explain itself to me.

My mind wanders to Cookie and my mom. Wondering what they were like back then, imagining them arguing about my dad or about Cookie's girlfriends. Fights about one of those things most likely being fueled by the subtext of the other. I never asked my mom if she knew my dad was using heroin when she married him. She may have. It may have seemed different then. More casual. More of a side effect of their scene. I dunno. Maybe he told her. Maybe she figured it out. Maybe she changed her mind about how she felt about it. Investigating Katie's and Finch's deaths taught me that any truth can change if you've got enough power. That power can be political, financial, or maybe just the power of a good story. Sometimes it's all three. In the end Cookie didn't really know Katie. But she knew *a* Katie. Her Katie. My dad knew his version of my mom, and my mom knew her version of my dad. And I knew my version of them. I guess sometimes we only show one another what we want to show, and we only see in one another what we want to see.

Sometimes it works. Sometimes it doesn't.

Cookie seems satisfied with how Katie's case ended up—or I should say, how I told her it ended up. But it's gnawing at me. That first question Cookie asked me echoes inside my head—did I think Katie's death was connected to the Finch case? I didn't think so then, and I don't think so now, but that doesn't help any. I still want to know what really happened to her, who she really was. But wanting something doesn't bring it any closer. If anything, the desire just highlights the distance between where you are and where you want to be.

Things will never be as clean and as clear as I want them to be. I get that now. Some things are going to be unknown. Some things are going to have a gap.

Staring up at the ceiling, listening to the tape, I know I don't need this apartment to feel close to my dad anymore. I don't need his jacket; I don't even need this tape. They're all nice to have, but they're not necessary.

I can love what I thought he was and still be mad at who he revealed himself to be. I can hold on to old memories and still want to make new ones. My own.

Fascist Wally said if I wanted the gig, I could get Finch's old city contract with Fraud and Oversight. As much as I'd like to keep my distance from Wally, a contract like that would put me on my feet. I just need to incorporate first. If I hired an extra investigator or two, I'd have the freedom to take on other cases. Real cases.

Cookie would be a good hire. She seems interested and she's already shown she's got the skills. I could rabbi her through the process of getting the license. Maybe hire Frankie from time to time for some heavy lifting if I need it.

I need a good name for the agency when I incorporate. Something that means something.

I look at the mixtape again. I reread the title and smile.

Yeah, I should do it.

I should incorporate and open my own agency.

I should call my mom.

And I should get an email address so I can check in with Maggie.

I should sell this place.

I should move.

I should start this story.

For real this time.

Acknowledgements

Thank you to everyone who read and gave feedback on early drafts: Zach Barocas, John Barr, Ava Boyd, Matt Boyd, Pat Cassidy, Jim Flood, Katie Herman, David Horridge, Annie Johnson, Charlie LaRose, Alex Markman, Michael McDonnell, Cortney McFadden, Greg Richards, Phil Seiler, and Oksana Todorova.

A very special thanks to both Jonathan Bloom and Charlton Hoag, two old friends who have read and given feedback on almost everything I've written for more decades than I'd like to admit.

Thank you to my family, Annie and Charlie. To my brother Pete Johnson, my sister Nena Johnson, my father Joseph Johnson and my late mother, Elena Miranda Johnson.

Thank you to The New York Press and The Village Voice.

Thank you to the Angelica, Anthology Film Archives, the Beekman, Cinema Village, Film Forum, Kim's East and West, Lincoln Plaza Cinemas, MoMA Cinema. the Paris, the Pioneer Theater, St. Marks Cinema, Theatre 80 St. Marks, Village East Cinemas, Walter Reade Cinema, the Quad, and of course, the Ziegfeld.

Thank you to 7B, 9C, the Abbey, Bar Code, B&H Dairy, Blue and Gold, Brownies, Coney Island High, the Cooler, Dojo's, Donovan's Pub of Woodside, the Doray Tavern, the Ear Inn, El Faro, Great Jones, Great Lakes, Hanks Saloon, Holiday Cocktail Lounge, International Bar, Jimmy's Corner, the Knitting Factory, the L Cafe, Lakeside Lounge, Lucky Strike, Luna Lounge, Marion's, Mars Bar, Max Fish, Maxwell's, McGovern's Pub of Sunnyside, the Mercury Lounge, Molly's Shebeen, O'Connors, Odessa, The Pink Pony, Planet Thai, Rodeo Bar, the Scratcher, Shea Stadium (the baseball one), Siberia Bar, El Sombrero, Sophie's, Sunny's, Sweetwater, La Taza de Oro, Thread Waxing Space, Tonic, Tramps, Union Pool, Velselka's, and Yaffa Cafe.

About the author

Alex R. Johnson is a writer and filmmaker who lives and works in Brooklyn, NY.

His feature film TWO STEP premiered to critical acclaim at SXSW in 2014 and went on to become a New York Times Critic's Pick. His screenplay NORTHEAST KINGDOM was selected for the 2016 Black List, and his screenplay ANY ROUGH TIMES ARE NOW BEHIND YOU was selected by the Austin Film Society's Artist Intensive lab where he was mentored by late director Jonathan Demme. He also wrote the screenplay adaptation of Ernest Tidyman's novel, BIG BUCKS, for Pascal Pictures/Sony Entertainment.

Johnson's family hails from the Andes of Ecuador, where their 100-year-old dairy farm still operates.